The

Purple
Menace
and the
Tobacco
Prince

Wade Beauchamp

The Purple Menace and the Tobacco Prince

e-book ISBN-13: 979-8-9868862-8-2
Paperback ISBN-13: 979-8-9868862-9-9
Hardback ISBN 13: 979-8-9899942-0-5

Cover design by: Susan Roddey
Edited by: Lynn Picknett
Layout by: Jason Roach
Printed in the United States of America

Dedicated with love to my hometown of Winston-Salem, whose history and mysteries are far deeper than I knew.

Thank you, Smith and Libby for the inspiration

Acknowledgments

I owe an extraordinary debt of gratitude to my wife and daughter, my brother, dad, and friends, who have all listened patiently as I obsessed over the people and places in this story. Love to you all.

Thank you to Jason Roach, whose enthusiasm has made this book possible, and to Lynn Picknett, who made it eminently more readable.

I would like to acknowledge the research done by authors Patrick Reynolds and Tom Shachtman in their book *The Gilded Leaf: Triumph, Tragedy, and Tobacco: Three Generations of the R.J. Reynolds Family and Fortune*; Jon Bradshaw in his book *Dreams That Money Can Buy: The Tragic Life of Libby Holman*; the historians, librarians, and researchers with the North Carolina Room at the Forsyth County Public Library's Central Library.

Chapter 1

Baltimore, Maryland
Monday, April 7, 1930

The Bizzy Holt number had begun without Bizzy Holt. Fred Allen and Portia Foster's scene - *The Wild Party*'s tenth, if Wright had tallied the playbill's list correctly - was over and the audience was now in the hands of Max Salzer's orchestra, filling the Maryland Theater with sound. Bass and snake-charmer oboe pulsed and swirled, almost tangible tendrils of music insinuating over the crowd to climb and coil around the Maryland's Corinthian columns.

On stage, a room in a squalid Harlem tenement was depicted. Two walls flanked a dilapidated bed, under which a bottle of Gordon's gin was stashed. And across the rumpled sheets was slumped an unconscious pimp. Byron Fogg, the sweetback's portrayer, was somehow still haughty and debonair despite his drunken stupor.

Still no Bizzy. She would have to be invoked, it

seemed, conjured like a shedim. This was a ritual, Wright was realizing. The audience's anticipation was a silent incantation. The band were shamans, the priests through which Bizzy Holt might be summoned.

Salzer's baton bobbed and dashed in the air, writing in invisible cursive. The orchestra swayed like the plaster-relief reeds on the auditorium's entablatures. Rows of tuxedoed men effortlessly drew from their instruments a river of music, a deep current of rolling rhythm beneath eddies of brass and woodwind. The anticipation doubled, seconds becoming minutes; the song's opening bars stretched into stanzas. An effete Fogg momentarily surfaced from his debauched pimp character and incongruously checked his pocket watch, dispatching a ripple of murmured laughter across the audience. For the uninitiated, though - Wright Williams among them - an unspeakable dread began to dawn. Maybe something was wrong. What if she was not here? What if she was not coming? The musicians craned their necks and cast exaggerated glances toward the wings. They exchanged uncertain shrugs and barely concealed smiles, mirthful abettors in a cruelly anticipatory attempt to coax the singer into view.

Wright shut his eyes and breathed deeply, drawing into his chest the mixed scents of the old vaudeville house and its audience: the cherry wood of the seats, a neighbor's H. Upmann cigar, another's

Romeo y Julieta, Chanel No. 5 from all about him, the tannery oils and dyes from the leather of his newly-sewn riding boots, creaking with each impatient tap of his foot.

Wright opened his eyes to see a silhouette slide from the shadows and onto the stage. A spotlight swept through the proscenium until it found her. Tracked by the lone beam, Bizzy Holt strutted toward the tenement set, heels striking the wooden stage in perfect time with the orchestra's rhythm. Wright watched her walk, just like she wanted him to - like she wanted them all to - and for a moment he forgot all the flying-lesson warnings Mac McDonnell had given him about tunnel vision.

Bizzy's ill-fitting gingham smock was meant to impart a sense of shabbiness, congruous with its wearer's residence and profession, but she made it look fabulous. Every face in the audience followed her like a field of daisies tracking the sun. She ignored them all, head held high, the faintest smile curling her petulant lips as if she, too, were an amazed witness to her own sexuality.

As Bizzy Holt transited his front-row seat, Wright Williams could have sworn that, for the fleetest of moments, her slumber-eyed gaze met his. Her irises were twin cups of espresso on porcelain saucers, set on the round bronze table of her face, all framed by raven curls cascading about her temples. And then she was downstream, walking away toward her pimp, toward her Harlem flophouse. Wright's eyes dropped to Bizzy's hips. They swung perilously, like the autumn sickles on his father's tobacco farms. He futilely tried to focus on just one hip, to decipher its locomotion, but the centrifugal force of each swing would slingshot his sightline to the other one. Wright doggedly fixed his eyes on their geographic center, the very axis of her posterior, and watched that point trace, every two steps, a lemniscate of Bernoulli, like he had learned while studying Cartesian coordinates.

Holt arrived at Byron Fogg and circled the rumpled bed, surveying. She reminded Wright of his Savoia-Marchetti S.56 banking agilely around Pilot Mountain's knob back home. The orchestra looped to a crescendo and Miss Holt, hovering now above Fogg, began to sing.

I woke up this morning, quarter to four. Woke up this morning, moanin' and sore.

As lethal as her eyes, her hips were deadly. But Wright now understood that her weapon of choice was her voice.

I woke up this morning, knowing that my man don't love me no more.

That voice. When Wright's friend, Dwight Forbush Daub, *The Wild Party*'s producer and heir to the Forbush tractor fortune, had visited Winston-Salem last winter and invited Wright to Baltimore to see the touring company of his hit show, he had described Miss Holt's voice as heavenly. It was nothing of the sort. This was from someplace lower.

When Bizzy Holt sang, it was down in the husky purple depths of her register. Her voice was smoke and flicker, built to lament love's labors lost. Every line was a confession.

My sweet man, done up an' gone. My sweet man, left me all alone.

When Bizzy Holt sang, she wrang out vowels and elongated consonants, pulling and bending articles and prepositions until it sounded like a new, lewd language.

What have I gone and done, to make my sweet man run?

When Bizzy Holt sang, the Maryland Theater's lights seemed to dim and the flutter of folding fans dissipated and the sound of her voice sank into Wright's skull like absinthe into a sugar cube.

Oh, I need him so. Where can he be? Don't he know, he needs a woman like me?

Now Byron Fogg stirred, roused from his daze, and rose to dance, swivel-waisted, around the dingy bedroom. Holt's hooker handed over the night's earnings, withholding a few bills and slipping them behind the rolled top of her stocking, simultaneously surreptitious and pantomimed. Desirous of a more carnal tribute, the pimp descended upon Bizzy, clamping his hands over her shoulders, pulling her against his chest. Still singing, she protested with her gestures and expressions, all the while mapping an escape route with her eyes. She struggled but the pimp easily overpowered her, the most unconvincing acting of the night, Wright thought, given Fogg's slight frame. No matter, he knew. Bizzy had all the real power here. His arms might have been stronger, but his resolve was not. Bizzy Holt was a virgin sacrifice and King Kong rolled into one. Wright wondered if he was the only person in the auditorium who understood that.

Holt collapsed onto the ramshackle bed, sprawling across it, the ruffled hem of her dress lifting above her knees, exposing her stocking tops and the stashed cash pinned against her bare thigh. Her betrayal discovered, she pleaded with her implacable sweetback, imploring him to take pity. She sang *Come back to me, don't leave me moanin' and sore.*

Her body buckled, a cyclone of regret and yearning channeled into the song. Black ribbons of hair draped across her face, she clung to the bed's headboard as Fogg loomed over her. Wright could sense the entire audience behind him, pulses quickening in unison. They watched and listened, rapt. She was the center of their universe, for however long she desired to be. But for the tobacco farmer's son on the front row in his eighteenth summer, Bizzy Holt had made herself his goddess. She had become his mythology. His new religion.

My sweet man, come back and love me some more.

Fogg's hands crawled onto Holt's neck, encircling, contracting. The crowd behind Wright collectively did the same to their armrests. Bizzy unerringly sensed the audience approaching the precipice of their thrill and, with her dusky contralto, nudged them over it as her final breath was squeezed out of her. *Don't leave me moanin' and sore...*

Wright's world caromed on its axis, canting dizzyingly until he was shaken from the globe to plummet and tumble through the inky cosmos.

There were two large photographs of women Wright did not recognize framed and hanging on the wall in the backstage corridor of the Maryland Theater. In one photograph, a woman stood in the very dressing room Wright and Dwight Forbush Daub were now waiting outside - Daub patiently, Wright anxiously. A towel was wrapped around the woman's otherwise naked body, her hair wet and matted to her scalp. One eyelid was garnished with dramatically curled lashes, impossibly long, the other lid unadorned. Her face was contorted as she formed a lopsided *O* with her black lips. One claw-hand clutched at the towel, wrestling it into place while the other held a lipstick, meticulously delineating the Cupid's bow of her upper lip.

"Nellie," Mr. Daub said to Wright when he understood that his friend from North Carolina did not recognize her. "That's Nellie Burnside."

Next to that photograph was another, taken no more than half an hour later, Daub told Wright. There was Miss Burnside again, dressed now in a silk halter gown embellished with beaded rosettes and sparkling rhinestones. She stood, radiant on the Maryland's stage, arms outstretched, sleek waves tumbling onto alabaster shoulders, eyelashes and eyebrows immaculate and immutable.

"You best believe that shot," Daub nodded toward the dressing room photo, "would never have been hung if Old Man Kernan thought there was a ghost of a chance Nellie would ever haunt this hall again." Wright imagined a scene in which the vulpine woman from the photographs castigated the theater's owner over a seemingly innocuous glimpse behind the curtain. Daub went on to explain how, over the years, the image had been repeatedly lampooned by the theater's itinerant stars. Cartoon speech bubbles were affixed near Nellie's mouth, *Good to the last drop!* or *X marks the spot*. Various alternative instruments, Daub explained, were crudely sketched out and pasted over the lipstick. A cigarette, a tiny sword, even a penis. "You get the picture." But despite the defacements and chuckles, the images inspired the performers. "There's a thin line between reality and fantasy," Daub said. "We go to great lengths here to blur it."

A full five minutes after Daub had knocked on the dressing room door and announced himself and Mr. R. Wright Williams, Bizzy Holt replied from inside, finally, "Now."

Five minutes before that, before leading Wright through the labyrinth of backstage corridors, Daub had warned his friend to be unsurprised to see Miss Holt in the nude, her preferred state in her dressing room after the show. Daub told Wright, because of her propensity for casual nudity, to count on being but one of many hopeful visitors. He further cautioned Wright to not place his odds on being granted an audience with Miss Holt at better than fifty-fifty. Five minutes before that, in response to Wright cornering him and conveying to him the utter urgency of his introduction to Miss Holt, Daub had futilely explained that yes, he was *The Wild Party*'s producer, and yes, Miss Holt was technically in his employ, and yes, Wright was his guest, and he would see what he could do.

Wright figured Daub's forecast of nudity was hyperbole but took the threat of a small mob quite seriously. He expected to find Miss Holt, fully clothed, basking in the afterglow of the audience's adoration. Maybe there would be champagne. A steady procession of VIPs offering congratulations and accolades. Instead, he found her alone, standing before a lighted vanity mirror, violently scrubbing the lipstick from her plump mouth. Save for her heels and rolled stockings, she was indeed, as Daub had warned, naked.

The vanity's counter was studded with perfume bottles of diamond-cut crystal and prismatic etched glass, with plump atomizer bulbs, floral or turret-shaped stoppers, and embossed sterling silver covers. A wide, ivory-handled hairbrush sat in a clearing; scribbles of black hair knotted throughout its bristles. The room itself was a garden of long-stemmed roses, orchids, and Stargazer lilies that had been sent by admirers, set in vases wherever there was room, some on the floor. Their individual fragrances vied for supremacy, but the roses were victorious. The admirers themselves had been denied entry, Wright assumed. Only *he* had been granted an audience.

"Wright," Daub said, "I give you Bizzy Holt."

"R. Wright Williams," the young man murmured, tentatively taking a step forward and extending his hand for a shake, looking first down at a spray of orchids on the floor and then up at the ceiling. Anywhere but at Bizzy's bare body.

"Charmed."

Wright's furtive glance at Daub was met with an almost imperceptible shake of the producer's head. Wright withdrew to his original position just inside the door and desperately tried to think of something to do with his hands before finally stuffing them into his front pockets.

Daub said, "Wright here is the son of R.W. Williams. He's -"

"An aviator, Miss Holt." Wright straightened his back. He was suddenly aware of how rounded his words sounded as they rolled languidly out of his mouth, an almost foreign tongue compared to Bizzy and Daub's clipped, upright Midwestern cadence. He could not decide if he was proud or embarrassed.

Bizzy reached for a gold-plated case and withdrew from it a cigarette and a lift-arm lighter. She clicked the latter to life and held its flame to the former, orange light dancing across her face. She exhaled the thick smoke and Wright instantly recognized the aroma as belonging to one of his father's Taxi brand of cigarettes. In his later years, Richard Walton Williams had tested his youngest son's nose by having him discern between the brightleaf and burley tobaccos in his warehouses. Whether Bizzy was signaling to Wright that she knew exactly who his daddy was, or she simply needed a smoke, he could not be sure. But he knew what she was smoking, whether she did or not.

11

The Purple Menace and the Tobacco Prince

"An aviator." Bizzy tossed a red-smeared tissue onto the vanity and turned now to face her admirer, appraising Wright for the first time since he entered her dressing room. She inspected the riding boots and jodhpurs he had chosen to wear to the theater. "Did you fly here on a horse?"

"Actually, I was -"

"Tell me something, Mr. Williams. Why is there a drawing of a horse on a pack of Taxi cigarettes?"

Staring at the floor, Wright began what was clearly a well-worn reply. "My father got the idea for the name when he first visited London and saw the hansom cabs and all the people clamoring for them. He figured if people wanted a taxi so badly—"

"Front row," Bizzy interrupted and pointed at Wright, confirming his conviction that their eyes had met during the show. "It's alright. You can look at me."

He accepted the offer, but even with her permission he summoned the willpower to restrict his gaze to her face. Then, calling on a boldness he was not sure he possessed, he voiced the conclusion he had reached in Act II. "Miss, Holt, I believe I am in love."

"Christ, Williams!" Daub laughed.

"Oh, hush, you," Bizzy said. "Wright, dear, if you had not fallen in love tonight, Dwight wouldn't pay me. It's my job to make boys like you fall in love with me."

"It's true," Daub said. "Your voice is a kind of magic, my dear. And worth every cent."

"No, my voice is a goddamned soldier."

Wright visibly cringed at Bizzy's language. She took a long drag from her Taxi and posed, not as subtly as she thought, for him to get a good long look. Daub could see her bemusement when Wright steadfastly refused to look at anything other than her eyes.

She said, "*The Wild Party* is a battle, Dwight. Foggy, Fred and Portia, me, we're field generals." She took another draw on her cigarette, the ember glowing cherry red, making sure she had both men's attention before continuing. "We are waging a war against preachers and politicians and husbands and wives. A war against boredom. Enemies, all. Enemies whose vanquishing is so perpetually crucial that these shows get retooled and restaged every season."

Bizzy stepped close enough to Wright to squelch his fears that in her Baby Louis heels, she was taller than him. A nimbus of cigarette smoke whorled about her black hair. With a fortitude that seemed to amuse her, he held her gaze. "I turn twenty-six next month, Mr. Williams. I've got maybe four years left to fight this battle. If I'm lucky." Now she turned to Daub. "Ain't that right, Dwight?"

"Permanence is the illusion of every generation," Daub nodded. Wright was sure he had heard that

13

somewhere before but could not place it. Maybe it had been his daddy, although permanence would not have been the word he would have used. "Why, just a year ago, the National Silk Manufacturers Association named their new spring shade in this young lady's honor. A pale pastel, as I remember it, called Bizzy Blue."

Bizzy scoffed. "And that exact shade just got renamed for Helen Kane."

Wright saw an opportunity to contribute. "If you had told me on October 23rd last year that Wall Street was going to be castrated the next day, I would have called you crazy."

Daub replied, "And if *you* had told *me* on the night of the 24th that Bizzy and I would still be here, doing this, the very next week, let alone the next year, I would have called *you* crazy."

"Yet here we are," Bizzy said, "fighting stage to stage, with nothing less than the hearts and minds of the mink and ermine crowd at stake."

Daub checked his watch. He stepped to Wright and shook his friend's hand. Then, as he departed the dressing room, said, "Bizzy, behave."

She drew on her cigarette. "Dwight, if you really wanted to me to do that, you would have never hired me."

Daub closed the door behind him. Alone now,

Bizzy Holt and Wright Williams silently appraised one another. Her dark eyes roamed freely over him and he wondered what she saw. Was he handsome to her? Or, as his sisters had told him time and again, did his features seem fixed in the sulking expression of a spoiled child who had been denied some extravagance? Did Bizzy see the same paradox Wright saw in every photograph of himself? A man who was still a teenaged boy, worldly yet cloistered, emboldened by his station but also confined by it, yearning to step from the shadow of his father's fortune but here only by the grace of it.

Wright, too, beheld a contradiction. Before him stood something both enchanting and obscene. With her angelic voice she sang of earthly desires. Dirty and divine.

The two held each other's gaze. Wright was confident, but it was born from what he had been bequeathed. Bizzy's confidence, he could see, was something she had won for herself. What brief tug-of-war there had been between their wills, she had won easily, and Wright reflexively averted his eyes.

Bizzy poked the cigarette into her mouth and turned to walk away, meticulously placing each heel and toe on an invisible tightrope. Smoke trailed in her wake like the tail of a comet. Wright breathed, filling his skull with the comingled scents of this woman: the Turkish and Virginia blend his father had carefully chosen, the Shalimar—if he knew his perfumes as well as he did his tobacco—on her throat, and the sweat the Klieg lights had produced during the show.

Bizzy detoured behind a hinged Oriental dressing screen and Wright feared she might cover herself with a robe. She immediately emerged, still nude, and her eyes met his once again in the mirror. Determined to overcome his resolve, she swiveled her derrière like the Lindy Loop at Luna Park. Then, finally, Wright surrendered and looked at her body. And, for the briefest of moments, he thought he felt his infuriatingly recalcitrant erection stirring in his jodhpurs.

Bizzy watched the poor boy blink his eyes shut. When he reopened them, he could not bring himself to look at either her face or her body, instead focusing on her shoes, their black patent leather agleam, toes shaped like bullets. Slender straps were buckled across her insteps and the heels angled steeply into the floorboards like a pair of sharpened chisels.

"You like them," she said. It was a statement of fact, not a question. All Wright could do was nod in agreement. She sauntered in a lazy circle now, letting him look, hips rocking to and fro. He felt as if the entire dressing room was revolving like a Victrola turntable as she walked. The vanity's trellis of incandescent bulbs lit

Bizzy's olive skin and made her legs seem to glow from within, framed by her snug silk stockings and the shimmering satin of her shoes. "But do you know why you like them?"

In that moment, Wright did not care why he liked her shoes. He did not even realize that fact until Bizzy told him so.

She said, "The biological purpose of life is to reproduce, right? The perpetuation of the species. To send your genes into the next generation." Wright was only hearing every other word, too busy trying to make sense of how he had gotten here, alone with this woman in her dressing room as she paraded naked before him. "The easiest way for you to do that is to knock up as many women as possible. The easiest way for me to do it is to rear as many children as possible, preferably with the help of a fabulously wealthy man. Or men."

Wright, no longer even trying to resist, watched her shamelessly now. This was a performance, he understood. He was the audience. She was acting. Her embezzling prostitute had been more believable. He did not care.

"A man will lust after a woman," Bizzy said. Wright nodded in distracted agreement. "And, yes, sometimes we will lust after you men. But not in quite the same way you do us, and not with the same pathetic, predictable regularity. Most women, I think, are less driven by lust than the desire to feel lusted after. Am I making sense?"

She was not, Wright thought, but it did not matter.

"Good shoes make a woman feel lusted after. We like to moan and wail about them, about how uncomfortable they are, but clearly the desire to feel desirable trumps aching arches. And just like in the animal kingdom, being desirable to the opposite sex equates to a better selection of mates."

Reminded of her sore feet, Bizzy sat on the velvet-upholstered stool at her vanity. She extended her long legs, scissored them, and crossed her ankles before resting the heels on the floor with a click. All this, Wright knew, was for his benefit.

"Anatomically speaking, women walk differently from men. It's not a choice, we're simply built differently. A man's walk is more about velocity, a longer stride, and more head and upper body movement. With women, it's all about the hips." With that, Bizzy sprang to her feet again to demonstrate. "A little bit of heel exaggerates those differences, accentuating the more feminine aspects of how we move. In mechanical terms, they amplify pelvic rotation, vertical motion of the hips, shorter strides. In other words, high heels make a woman walk more like a *woman*. And maybe it increases our appeal to you cavemen."

"Some might argue it makes it harder for you to run away."

Bizzy laughed at that. "Some might." Tired again, she flopped back down. She reached for her cigarette case, retrieved another Taxi, and then offered the open case to Wright. He stepped toward the naked woman on the velvet stool, but only as close as need be to pluck a cigarette from its gold case. He nodded in thanks and produced his own lighter.

Bizzy said, "R. Wright Williams, why are you here?" Wright opened his mouth to recite the speech he had composed in his head in the corridor outside her dressing room. She spoke before he could. "I don't mean here to see the show. I mean *here*."

Wright regarded the cigarette between his fingers and then tucked it into the corner of his mouth. "The Puritans banned it, you know?" he said, twin streams of white smoke jetting from his nostrils. "'Tobacco's an Indian weed,'" they said. "As if anything could be more American." He took another drag. "I suppose it's ironic, but I went sixteen years before my first cigarette. Buck Moore—that's my best friend—he started when he was ten. When he finally talked me into trying it, he rolled my first one for me. I didn't even know how to hold it." Wright laughed at the memory. "The smoke

19

filled my head, made my eyes water, nostrils on fire. I had barely inhaled." Now Bizzy laughed, too. "I was more worried about how I looked doing it, not whether I was doing it right. Was I making the tip glow as brightly as Buck's? Did the smoke roll out of my mouth like it was supposed to? Buck took the cigarette from me and showed me how to do it."

Wright drew deeply on his cigarette, shoulders lifting as he inhaled. "When he handed it back to me, I did my best to imitate him. Now the smoke filled my chest. My throat felt like a chimney, heat radiating out of it. I was certain my lungs had been punctured. The floor rushed up at me; my head spun. And I had two immediate and opposing thoughts: Something was wrong—and something was right. I took another drag." Bizzy laughed again. Wright said, "I've never felt it again. Not like I did that first time." He looked at her. "Not until tonight."

She watched him for a moment until she was sure he had finished his soliloquy. She sighed. "I know who you are, Mr. Williams. I knew before Dwight told me. I know how old you are. And how young you are. How rich you are. And how married you are."

Suddenly, Wright could not get his voice to work. Even if he could have, he had no idea what he would have used it for. As Dwight had led him backstage, he imagined himself Odysseus, Bizzy the siren. The mast he was lashed to was back home in Winston-Salem, no doubt asleep at this hour. How Bizzy had known about Anne, Wright had no idea.

Bizzy returned to her reflection at the vanity and went back to removing her makeup. "I'm not what you want," she said and then proceeded to enumerate the reasons why. The nomadic nature of her profession, the trains, the crowds, the cities. Those were the things she said. But what Wright heard was how misplaced she saw him in her urbane world. How soft his hands looked to her, spared the tobacco factory weathering his father had made sure his older brother's hands had received. How crisp and clean his boots were, despite their intended function. How easily she had rendered him mute and brooding with only the slightest of rebukes.

Wright vowed, then and there, to invert every one of the opinions he imagined Bizzy had of him before they met again. He would begin immediately by excusing himself from her company before she did it for him. He opened the dressing room door, revealing two dozen freshly minted devotees in the corridor, awaiting their turn at bat. "Miss Holt, thank you for the opportunity to introduce myself. Congratulations on your performance tonight."

In the mirror Bizzy watched Wright exit. "Good night, aviator."

Chapter 2

Boca Morada, Florida
Sunday, April 20, 1930

Wright curled his knuckles to knock on the front door. And, like his previous three attempts, withdrew and retreated to the sandy driveway that meandered through the oaks to pace and circle as he let his courage rebuild. Hands in pockets, he wove between the Cord Phaetons and Auburn Boattail Speedsters and Cadillac V-16s and Duesenberg Model Js haphazardly parked among the trees. Their sweeping clamshell fenders and streamlined grilles were glittered throughout the woods like chrome and enamel Easter eggs. Cherokee Red, Cepheus Green, Venetian Yellow, Cynosure Blue.

Even out here amidst a legion of trilling treefrogs and thrumming hummingbird wings, Wright could hear the laughter of the automobiles' owners wafting from the bungalow, punctuated intermittently by the siren song that had lured him inexorably to the Sunshine State from the Tarheel one: Bizzy's Holt's voice.

This time, though, as Wright wandered the woods, his reservoir of resolve refused to refill. He eyed his Savoia-Marchetti S.56 amphibian aeroplane through the crouching trees, glinting in the Florida sunrise, gently bobbing by the dock in the bay. It was close enough that he could hear the water lapping at its hull. In five minutes, he could have the radial engine purring and the plane pointing into the wind, skimming the choppy waves as it took flight back to North Carolina.

It had been fourteen days since he had first seen her, first heard her. In the hours since, he had thought of little else. In the Maryland Theater's dressing room, Bizzy had reminded Wright that he was married, but what he left unsaid was that Anne Vogler Williams had been living in her father's mansion since New Year's Day. Their daughter had been sent to live with her grandparents. "The richest baby in the world," the press called her. But now she had neither parent in her life.

On his predawn flight this morning, Wright had practically skimmed Joe Vogler's rooftop, hoping to startle his estranged wife awake with the roar of the Savoia's engine at wide-open throttle. He also wanted to verify what he had suspected from the ground on his only other visit: his father-in-law's house was smaller than Peace Haven, and Vogler's nearby textile mills paled in comparison to the veritable city-state that was R.W. Williams Tobacco Company.

Satisfied, Wright had pointed his aeroplane south at a hundred and ten miles per hour, the mill village of Vogler Station on his right, in the darkness along with the rest of the sky as far as he could see. On his left was the sunrise, splitting the world into halves, luminous sky above and shadow realm below. Memories of Anne fell starboard; the pregnancy, the shotgun wedding, the fight at the Robert E. Lee Hotel, dinner plates crashing onto the streetcar tracks below. On the port side, thoughts of Bizzy had risen with the dawn.

The bungalow door opened, the song and laughter that had been previously muted spilling outdoors at unfiltered volume. Bizzy's full-throated rendition of "Knocking on My Door" sliced into the morning, a ray cleaving the fog. Wright spun to see a dapper figure emerge in a herringbone suit and a necktie impeccably knotted around the collar of a crisp white shirt. They winced and recoiled from the sun, seemingly caught off guard by its presence. Squinting, they donned a pair of green-lensed sunglasses and began to survey the ad hoc parking lot.

Wright instinctively crouched behind the louvered hood of a Buick Marquette Roadster. He peered across its prow, shielding himself with it hood ornament, a lithe chrome woman, a silver scarf billowing behind her like a pennant, sparkling in the sun. The searcher's gaze swept across the cars like the beam of a lighthouse until it was aimed at Wright. Slowly, he stood.

"Are you coming in?" It was a woman's voice. "Or are you just shopping?"

Drawn as much by his curiosity as his detection, Wright walked toward his discoverer. Her strawberry blonde hair was slicked straight back, the continuance of a line that started with her slender nose and carried through her porcelain forehead. Young, beautiful. As Wright approached, he saw that she was barefoot.

"She knows you're out here. We all do. We've been watching you for half an hour."

The suited woman ushered Wright into the bungalow. Pulling the sunglasses from her face, she guided him around the outskirts of the sitting room, circumnavigating the cluster of revelers. They all faced the middle of the room, tidally locked planets orbiting their star. There, at their center, Bizzy rose like Winged Victory, a coffee table for her plinth.

Unlike the last time, Wright was in her presence, she was dressed, if barely. She wore a jade green silk Chinese pajama top, unbuttoned to her navel, embroidered with a kaleidoscope of swallowtail

26

butterflies. The only other article of clothing apparent was a pair of thigh-high lisle stockings, black, almost opaque, but not quite.

Bizzy sang to two dozen guests, roughly half of whom were awake. The others were draped across armchairs and petit-point-tapestried settees, comatose. A troposphere of cigarette smoke, perfume, and the scent of juniper berry juice hung just above Bizzy's blur of unruly black hair, stirred occasionally by a humid hibiscus breeze sauntering through the open hurricane shutters. Crepuscular rays of Sunday morning sunlight streamed through the haze in wide shafts. A brace of aloof Afghan Hounds pranced through.

Passing by an end table studded with cut-glass tumblers containing varying hues and depths of liquid, Wright's guide plucked one for herself as readily as if it had been offered it by a cocktail tray-bearing butler. Wright watched her swirl the clear anonymous fluid, releasing its aroma, which she sniffed, identified, and approved of before taking a sip.

Wright began to realize this was not a party that had commenced at dawn but rather one that had refused to end then. Even without the benefit of knowing any attendees, he could easily separate them into those who had been asked to come and those who had been brought along. The invitees were focused on Bizzy, men and women alike, bewitched by her singing.

Their companions watched them watching her. The conscious ones, at least.

Wright's conductor found an unoccupied corner of the sitting room and the pair turned and stationed themselves so that the remainder of the guests were within their purview. "Bizzy insists I attach some names to faces for you. Who do you know here?"

"Beyond Bizzy, not a soul."

The woman took a swig. "Not that you know Bizzy." Before Wright could mount a defense of his presence here, she gestured with her glass at a slender, swaying woman in a silver dress. "Kay Swift." He nodded, feigning recognition of the name but not fooling his attendant. "'Can't We Be Friends?'"

"Why, of course, I would hope we - "

"It's a song. 'Can't We Be Friends?' She wrote it. Kay Swift."

Wright nodded again, still pretending.

Now his chaperone's raised glass pointed to the balding man Kay Swift was using to steady herself. "James Walburg. The husband. A banker." Another swallow of bathtub gin or moonshine or whatever sloshed in her purloined glass. "Last summer, when *The Wild Party* was at the Music Box, Kay and James used to ferry Bizzy and me up to their place in North Greenwich where we would…" She cleared her throat. "Spend weekends."

Wade Beauchamp

The woman scanned the crowd. She pointed at a tanned man in a silk polka-dot dressing gown. A long, elegant cigarette was balanced between his index and middle fingers. "Noël Coward." Again, she waited for the light of recognition to flicker in Wright's eyes. When it did not, she said, "Playwright. Composer, actor, singer. Quintessential Brit. *Easy Virtue. Bitter Sweet.*"

"Are those titles of plays or descriptions of the man?"

"Mr. Williams, he's arguably the most successful playwright on either side of the Atlantic. He made fifty thousand pounds last year." Still, he seemed oblivious. "Surely, even in North Carolina -"

"*Someday I'll find you,*" Wright began, not quite singing, but more than simply speaking. "*Moonlight behind you. True to the dream I am dreaming as I draw near you.*"

Now the woman, singing in earnest, responded, "*You'll smile a little smile for a little while. We shall stand, hand in hand.*"

The two smirked knowingly at one another. Wright said, "Yes, even in pastoral North Carolina we love Noël Coward."

"Well, the only person here who loves Noël more than Bizzy is Noel." Now she was pointing at someone different. "That's Beatrice Lillie. 'Funniest

Woman in the World.' Actress of Noël Coward plays, singer of Cole Porter songs. And the wife of Sir Robert Peel, Fifth Baronet, who, cross my heart, was a used car salesman when Bea married him, which should give you some idea of how important a *Fifth Baronet* is." She laughed. "Sir Bob is also a gambler of considerable enthusiasm and misfortune. On their honeymoon in Monte Carlo, he lost all of Bea's money. But she made more."

With a gulp, the woman emptied her glass. "There's Tamara Geva, you'd like her: Russian dancer, Kirov School of Ballet in Leningrad. And there's Lillian Lorraine. Ziegfeld Girl, of course. Still has the thighs to prove it." Wright had stopped listening to her, but still, she talked. "There's Marilyn Miller, another one of Ziegfeld's discoveries. She got engaged to Michael Farmer last month, but everybody knows he's fucking Gloria Swanson. Too bad *she*'s not here. Crawford's not here, either. Josephine Baker was here last night but should be back in Paris by now. And thank *God* Nellie is in London."

Wright's senses were now fixed solely on Bizzy. He heard only her voice, dripping thick and slow like honey. He saw only the bee-stung pout that was making that sound. On his fingertips, he felt the imagined texture of her stockings.

He became dimly aware that the woman next to

him had finally fallen silent. He realized he had been staring at Bizzy's legs and turned to see his companion watching him, not quite smiling, but not disapproving, either. "I like the stockings, too," she said. "Onyx, if I know Bizzy. And I do." *Better than you*, was left unspoken.

"Onyx?" Wright asked obligingly, understanding that he was meant to.

"Onyx Hosiery is a sponsor of the *The Wild Party*, so she feels beholden. She won't be wearing them for much longer, though." Before Wright could fully visualize Bizzy peeling off her stockings in front of the entire congregation, the woman added, "I keep telling her in another two years she will be wearing my uncle's pointex." She paused now, waiting for Wright's next question.

Heretofore relegated to only asking this woman to clarify herself, Wright now found his opening. He may not have known show business, but he knew American business and he had heard that word: *pointex*. And he knew that *Forbes Magazine* had listed the synthetic fabric's inventor, Allard Powder & Chemical, only seven spots below R.W. Williams Tobacco Company in 1929. "Your Uncle Pierre."

The curled corner of her mouth told Wright he had guessed correctly. He resented giving her the satisfaction of seeing him acknowledge her as a fellow child of the kind of wealth even the Broadway cognoscenti here could not fathom. But he relished robbing her of being able to surprise him. She extended her hand for Wright to shake. "Lucy Allard Conrad."

The tobacco scion and the chemical heiress watched Bizzy Holt sing.

"Brooks Atkinson," Louis said, "the *Times* critic, called her 'the Dark Purple Menace' and 'Broadway's preeminent torch singer.'"

"'Sloe-eyed houri'," Wright added. "I believe Howard Stahl coined that one."

The pair regarded one another for a moment, each having just tacitly confessed to monitoring Bizzy's press. Lucy nudged Wright's elbow. "Come on."

With him in tow, Lucy moved into the crowd. She wove her way through drinkers, dancers, and sleepers. On a love seat that he and his guide floated past, Wright saw a familiar face. Bizzy's *Wild Party* pimp, Byron Fogg, sat in a velvet smoking jacket, sandwiched between a pair of young, nattily dressed Black men.

As they passed by, Lucy leaned to Wright's ear and said, "That's Ramona and Kimono. Or at least that's what Foggy calls them. His *valets*, he says. He fires and rehires them both almost weekly." Lucy looked around her. "It's a safe bet Gertrud isn't here, or Foggy wouldn't be getting so cozy."

"His wife?" Wright asked.

"Mother."

Next, they walked behind a man straddling the saddle of a three-legged folding stool. He was hunched over a large drawing pad, a vine charcoal stick between his thumb and forefinger. His head angled up at Bizzy, who was still singing on her pedestal in the center of the room, then down at his paper, then back up, rhythmically, almost in time with the song. Wright paused at the man's shoulder, forcing Lucy to retrace her steps. Together they discreetly watched the artist's hand, his charcoal frantically scratching at the paper like a polygraph needle. His eyes roamed over Bizzy's body and then sent the signal to his wrist to delineate the shape of her legs, her shoulders. On his paper, formed from a frenetic snarl of lines and curls, was Bizzy Holt.

"Casimer Cislo," Lucy whispered directly into Wright's ear in yet another seemingly senseless confluence of syllables. His pinched brow told Lucy that he was back to needing clarification for everything she said. She pulled Wright a step away, just out of earshot. "The chrome hood ornament on that Buick you were hiding behind?" Wright nodded, admittedly. "It's called the Flying Goddess. He designed it."

Wright glanced at Cislo's face as if he might recognize him.

"Legend had it that Casimer intended the

Goddess to be a tribute to Isadora Duncan. Surely you know her."

He shook his head.

Lucy sighed. Then, gauging her proximity to Cislo, she took yet another step back, beckoning Wright to come with her. Lowering her voice further still, she said, "Isadora was a bohemian dancer. Scandalous. Bisexual, atheist, communist. She would have fit in well here. Three years ago in Nice, Miss Duncan -"

"France."

"Yes, Mr. Williams, Nice is in France." She stared at him for a beat. "May I?"

He nodded.

"Miss Duncan was a passenger in a car owned by one Benoît Falchetto, a French-Italian mechanic. Isadora was wearing one of the long, flowing scarves she was fond of, this one hand-painted by Russian artist Roman Chatov." There was a glint in Lucy's eye as she added, "It was a gift from her lover, Mary Desti. Desti, in addition to being Isadora's lover, was also a lover of Aleister Crowley. But that's a story for another morning."

Wright saw Cislo's head tilt, just slightly, as his wrist stopped moving. Lucy saw it, too, and the pair took yet another step away from the eavesdropping artist. "Mary Desti was there that night in Nice and suggested to Isadora that she wear a cape in Falchetto's open-air automobile on that chilly night, but Isadora would only wear the scarf. As Benoît sped off with Duncan by his side, Isadora's parting words were, *'Je vais à l'amour!'*"

Wright thought and then translated, "'I am off to love.'"

Lucy nodded, visibly impressed. "Isadora's silk scarf became entangled in the spoked wheels of Falchetto's car, instantly snapping her neck. According to dispatches from Nice, Isadora was all but decapitated."

Wright and Lucy stood in somber silence for a moment. He then checked again on the progress of Cislo's sketch while Lucy returned her attention to Bizzy. Then, just loud enough for Wright to hear over the song, she said, "That voice is Bizzy's scarf. And Broadway is going to be the goddamned wheel."

Wright pretended not to hear, stepping close to Cislo again and focusing on the drawing, which, like Bizzy's performance, was now in its final throes. Both song and sketch were explosions of kinetic, chaotic whorls, coiling and curling all around, gleefully defying the constraints of paper and verse. Cislo's tangle of linework and Holt's final run of coos and murmurs crescendoed simultaneously. Casimer's frenetic markings coalesced into an image of the singer as her voice evaporated in a series of quavering aftershocks that left her guests in hushed awe.

Wright peered over Cislo's shoulder. At close range, the drawing was an almost indecipherable thatch of knotted lines and alluvial fans of dots. From only one step away, though, the unmistakable form of Bizzy manifested on the paper. The artist had magnified her proportions, amplifying what appealed to him. The lisle stockings sheathed impossibly long legs, her hips were jutting cliffs, every curve and swell exaggerated by the illustrator's feverish linework. Not how she looked in reality, but how she existed in his mind. He had rendered Bizzy as an electric, pulsating force. It was the same way Wright saw her.

As a finishing touch, the artist licked his thumb and used it to smudge the charcoal swirls around Bizzy's face into a blurred, fuzzy head of hair.

Byron Fogg rose sprightly from his cozy nest between Ramona and Kimono and stepped to the coffee table Bizzy was standing on. Ramona and Kimono also rose and followed Fogg, flanking and attending to him as he, in turn, steadied her as she descended from her perch. Fogg pressed his lips to the back of Bizzy's hand and then fell to the wayside as she was absorbed by the accumulation of her guests. Wright wondered if she had been singing since the night before.

Bizzy slipped through the compressed crowd

with ease, a shark parting a school of menhaden. She was showered with praise, most of it genuine, some of it tinged with barely concealed envy. She arrived at Lucy and, with Wright watching—with *everyone* watching—the two kissed each other's mouths.

"Wonderful," Lucy beamed.

"Thank you, dear." Bizzy returned Lucy's smile and they both turned to Wright. He thought Lucy's demeanor was that of an English Pointer who had retrieved the quail Bizzy shot. "My aviator." Wright inhaled, careful not to let Bizzy see how deeply, and identified each ingredient of her nectarous scent: gin and cigarettes, Shalimar and sweat. She had been drinking and smoking and singing for a half-rotation of the Earth, Wright figured.

Lucy said, "I found this one skulking amongst the Caddies and Cords."

He bowed. "Miss Holt."

"Do I want to know how you found me on Easter morning?"

"Dwight."

"Dwight." Bizzy pursed her lips and nodded. Wright convinced himself it was a look of admiration for his doggedness. Lucy's expression of contempt, however, was unmistakable.

"May I fix you a drink?" Bizzy asked.

Lucy said, "That's my liquor."

"Fine. May Miss Conrad fix you a drink?"

"You do it," Lucy said, reaching inside her suit jacket and producing a single Lucky Strike. She tucked one between Bizzy's lips. From the front pocket of her trousers, she produced a lighter. "Sorry about the brand. They beat the hell out of your daddy's, though."

"Luckies are second place for a reason," Wright said.

Bizzy pulled the Lucky Strike from her lips and tipped it into Lucy's mouth. "He's right, you know." Then, turning to Wright, "You got one of your old man's smokes on you?"

He pulled a pack of Taxis from his pocket, tapped one out, and offered it to Bizzy. He could feel Lucy glaring at him as he struck a match and lit the cigarette in Bizzy's mouth.

Bizzy sighed a cloud and said, "Now, about that drink."

Wright followed her into the bungalow's kitchen. Only once did she check over her shoulder to see if Lucy would join them. He refused to look but deduced from the resigned shrug of Bizzy's shoulders that it would be just the two of them.

On the drainboard of the sink stood a skyline of bottles of various heights and hues: Gordon's, Four Roses, Kübler, Jameson, Belmont, Green River, Jack Daniels. An array of finger bowls held olives, maraschino cherries, lemon slices, rosemary sprigs, cinnamon sticks, mint leaves. Scattered throughout were jiggers, strainers, and muddlers. The basin held stacked pyramids of glasses, flutes, goblets, and snifters. "Lucy won't tell me where she gets it all," Bizzy said. "Her father's stockpile if I had to guess. Marrying into the Allard family has its advantages." She watched Wright as he inspected the colorful labels. "What's the matter, never seen liquor before?"

"Not in storebought bottles. The Volstead Act went into effect when I was nine."

"I keep forgetting you're a baby. So, what'll you have, baby?"

Wright shook his head. "Ladies first. I insist." He stepped to the sink.

"Make mine a -"

Wright held up a politely silencing finger. He studied Bizzy for a moment, smiling slyly, the first time she had seen him do so and reached for a glass. As she watched, Wright poured two parts Four Roses, one part sweet vermouth, a dash of bitters, and then turned to eye her again. She tried to make her expression as enigmatic as the Mona Lisa, Wright could see. She was impressed that he had guessed her drink but did not dare show it.

Wright skewered a pair of brandied cherries with a pick, balanced them on the rim of the tumbler, and handed Bizzy her drink.

She smiled and nodded. "Thank you, sir."

"You seem like a Manhattan kind of girl."

"There *are* no other drinks," Bizzy said, doing her best Joan Crawford. Or maybe it was Mae West, Wright was uncertain.

Bizzy took a sip and let out a little moan. She licked her lips and regarded the drink in her hand. "It's not Lucy's Manhattan, but it ain't bad." She took another sip before setting it down on the kitchen table and saying, "My turn."

Wright tamped down his excitement, ready to play the game from the other side and see if she could guess his cocktail, but more than that, thrilled at the thought of Bizzy Holt thinking about him for more than a few seconds. She looked at him for a moment, then a moment longer. Making up her mind, she selected a tumbler from the sink, plunked a sugar cube into it, and then wet it down with a splash of club soda and Angostura bitters. Reaching for the muddler, she crushed the sugar as she rotated the glass, lining it with sugar grains and bitters. From the icebox, she fetched a jagged cube and dropped it into the tumbler with a clatter.

She turned again to Wright, who was watching expectantly. "Now," she said, searching his face. She tapped at her chin. "What is Wright Williams' spirit of choice?" She turned back to the sink and danced her fingertips across the caps before landing on the Four Roses. For a moment he considered pointing out to her that he was a civilized man and drank rye, but then decided a civilized man would keep his mouth shut. As if reading his mind, Bizzy looked at him once more, eyes narrowing, deducing, and then skipped her hand over to the Old Forester. Wright tried to affix some deeper meaning to her choice but could not.

Bizzy wrapped her fingers around the bottle's neck and decanted it into the glass with a satisfied nod. She garnished it with one of the orange twists Wright was certain Miss Conrad had prepared, and then turned to present him with his drink.

"Wright Williams' Old Fashioned," she smiled.

"Yes, he is." He took the glass, took a sip, and smacked his lips.

"It's a classic," Bizzy told him. "Masculine. Never out of fashion." Wright wanted to believe she stopped just shy of adding, "Like you." Instead, she said, "What a person drinks says a lot about them, I think," which he thought was almost as good.

"And what does a Manhattan say about Bizzy Holt?"

She let out a little laugh. "You tell me."

Wright took another sip of his Old Fashioned. "Except for the vermouth instead of sugar, you're not that much different from me."

Bizzy plucked the cocktail pick from her glass and used her teeth to drag a cherry into her mouth. "I think," she said, sucking the brandy syrup, "I think maybe I'm more like Manhattan itself than the cocktail they named after it. From the outside, looking in, it's clean and shiny. From across the river, it's all skyscrapers and architecture." Her eyes became slits. "It's not until you cross the bridge that you see how dirty it really is."

Wright coughed, the whiskey's flammable vapors singeing his nostrils and making his eyes water.

"You should come," she said next. "To Manhattan. To see me."

He coughed again. "I've seen you." With the back of his wrist, Wright wiped away a tear before Bizzy could see it.

"You've seen me in Baltimore. You haven't seen me on Broadway." From the sitting room, the sound of jaunty, tinkling piano playing emanated. "That would be Noël," Bizzy said. She cocked her head and listened. "'Forbidden Fruit.' And that means we're almost done here. First song he ever wrote; last song he plays at our parties. Dance with me." She placed her half-empty Manhattan on the kitchen table and offered her hand to Wright.

He laughed. "I can't."

"Can't or won't?" Bizzy pulled Wright by his wrist toward the sitting room and its guests, all of whom not passed out were rising to their feet and pairing off with partners. She tugged at him, singing Noël's lyrics now. *"Every peach, that's out of reach, looks so delightful."* She flashed a wide smile. *"And every guy, that spies it high, thinks it exciteful."*

"Can't," Wright repeated.

Bizzy sang, *"And if he can. get it in hand, he'll find the taste alrightful."*

Focused on Wright, Bizzy backed into Lucy, who had made sure to position herself directly in their path. Bizzy turned to identify her obstacle. Upon seeing the young barefoot woman in the suit and tie, she dropped Wright's hands and said to Lucy, "You, then."

Bizzy slipped a hand into Lucy's open palm. To Wright, she said, "Lucy here is a rare bird. Isn't that right?" Lucy smiled, looking only at her. With her other hand, Bizzy stroked Lucy's slicked-back strawberry waves. "You see, Wright, the gene for Lucy's red hair is recessive. Not just to brunette hair, but to true blonde, too. Two parents, both carrying the gene for red hair, still only have a..." Bizzy looked to Lucy for confirmation, who held up first her index finger and then all four of them. "A one-in-four chance," Bizzy continued, "of conceiving a redheaded child."

Wright knew all this - he had learned it at R.W.

Williams High School - and wanted desperately to let both women know he knew. But he found the restraint to simply listen and nod appreciatively.

"Have you ever danced with a rarity?" Lucy asked Bizzy. Wright watched as Bizzy let Lucy lead her into the sitting room. They found a clearing in the crowd where Bizzy spun on the stockinged balls of her feet and swathed herself in Lucy's arms. As the two began to dance to Noël Coward's piano, Wright could see Lucy whisper something to Bizzy. Whatever she said made Bizzy laugh, deeply, the sound of it ringing melodiously above the din of the party.

Watching Bizzy dance, Wright felt an unfamiliar fluttering in his stomach. He thought for a moment it was jealousy but assured himself it was not.

"Don't worry," a voice said at Wright's side. He turned to see Byron Fogg standing next to him, cinching the belt of his smoking jacket, shadowed, as always by an attentive Ramona and Kimono. "She's Lucy Allard Conrad *Jennings*, wife of one John Lord Jennings, Allard Chemical executive. Lucy likes to omit that minor detail from her autobiography. She's harmless, darling."

"I'm not worried," Wright replied, hoping it sounded more truthful to Fogg than it did to himself. He went back to watching Bizzy and could feel Fogg, in turn, watching him, gauging his reaction to seeing the reason he flew in the dark from Winston-Salem to Florida ignoring him in favor of someone else.

"She's quite beautiful," Fogg said. Wright nodded. "Lucy, I mean," Together, Wright and Fogg watched as Bizzy rose on her toes, lifted her arms above her head and dropped them around Lucy's shoulders, moving with her. "Bizzy is not beautiful." Before Wright could find the words to defend Miss Holt's honor, Fogg added, "Bizzy is sexual."

Fogg seemed to wait for Wright to reply; Wright waited for Fogg to continue. Finally, Fogg said, "There are many beautiful women here tonight. But beautiful and sexual are two different things." Wright watched Fogg, trying to decide if he agreed with him or not. "Sexuality is ten percent looks, ninety percent attitude, Mr. Williams."

"I like that," Wright concluded.

"Feel free to appropriate it. With proper attribution, of course." And with that, Byron Fogg took his leave, Ramona and Kimono following in his wake.

Alone now for the first time since he stepped into the bungalow, Wright unabashedly focused his attention on Bizzy. He could see the women's mouths moving but their voices were lost in the cacophony of conversation, laughter, and music. Bizzy said something that made Lucy laugh, or rather give the exaggerated performance of a laugh, tucking a loose ribbon of her rare strawberry hair behind her ear, looking down at her bare feet and losing her equilibrium momentarily, grasping for Bizzy's arms to balance herself, fingertips fluttering along the crest of her breasts.

He watched as Lucy moved her hands to Bizzy's sides and then let them slide down onto her waist, palming the green silk of her pajama top, gathering it, pulling it taut across the small of her back. Lucy nuzzled Bizzy's slender neck, whose head lolled to give her better access. Wright could see Lucy breathing in the scent.

If he had convinced himself he wasn't envious of Lucy a moment ago, now he could not deny it. He wanted to do what she was doing, and so much more. He wanted to smell Bizzy, smell her throat, her hair, behind her earlobe, the crook of her elbow, the cleft of her breasts, the arch of her foot. He imagined the scents trapped in the dense weave of her lisle stockings.

Wright could feel his heart hammering at his sternum. He was slowly becoming cognizant of a dull aching in his pants and realized, incredulously, that his erection, intermittent since puberty, was straining against his fly. Bizzy floated in Lucy's arms, rising balletically on her toes. Now the crowd closed around them, blocking Wright's view. With the heel of his palm, he angled down the lever of his erection, subduing it as best he could, scanning the crowd, making sure no one was watching.

Wright searched for Bizzy again, unable to locate her at first, but then the bodies surrounding her and Lucy parted and allowed him an unobstructed view. Bizzy's arms waved above her head. And then they were obscured again, reappearing only seconds later, her hands now swirling down to light on Lucy's shoulders, fingertips tracing twin paths down her lapels. They moved through the crowd: the crowd spiraled around them, blocking them from Wright's sight again. They emerged moments later, Lucy's hands having migrated in the interim, now onto Bizzy's swaying hips. Again, other dancers hid the women from Wright. This time when they reappeared, Lucy's hands had moved back up to Bizzy's waist, as if she knew they had been somewhere they should not have been in public.

They spun through the room, disappearing and reappearing through transient gaps between bodies like a blinking image in a zoetrope. Bizzy smiling and squinting at Lucy. Lucy's chest pressing onto Bizzy's, starched Egyptian cotton sliding across mulberry silk. Bands of white, naked thigh blinking out from under green hem and above black stocking.

Finally, Noël Coward brought "Forbidden Fruit" to a close. Wright triangulated Bizzy's path among the exodus of dancers and moved to intercept her. Nimbly outflanking Lucy, he blocked Bizzy's way. Her eyes on Lucy as she exited the de facto dance floor, she almost collided with him.

"Oh." She was out of breath and coated with a dew of perspiration. "You're still here."

Not allowing himself time to weigh the consequences, Wright said. "Fly with me." He caught Bizzy stealing a furtive glance at his tented trousers and expertly concealing a smile. Lucy watched her, too, smirking as she awaited the impending rebuffing of Wright's invitation. Lucy's expression melted from anticipation to confusion and then into consternation as she realized Bizzy's rejection of him was not forthcoming.

"Biz, no."

Bizzy was not listening. In her eyes, Wright and Lucy could both see she was deciding whether a pajama top was appropriate flying apparel. "Those things aren't safe, Biz. Three weeks ago, two men were killed demonstrating a flying boat for the French Navy."

She was right, Wright knew. How she knew about the tri-motored Latécoère 340, he was unsure. The same way she knew about eye color genetics and pointex polymers, he surmised. She was the granddaughter of a scientist and engineer, after all.

Bizzy looked at Wright, and then to Lucy. And then back to Wright. "Give me five minutes."

48

He spun on his heel and slipped through the crowd like a knife, across the sitting room, and out the front door. He trotted down the sandy drive, between rows of candy-colored coupes and cabriolets, determined to get the Savoia-Marchetti's engine fired and warmed up before Lucy could talk Bizzy out of it. Riding boots clomping against the boards, Wright sprinted onto the floating dock, panting as he climbed into the aeroplane's cockpit. He reached for his leather helmet and goggles—the only pair he had brought—then realized a gentleman would let the lady wear them.

Wright cinched the webbed harness across his lap, closed the latch-and-link buckle, and then clamped both hands onto the control stick to keep them from shaking. As he sat in the gently bobbing aeroplane, he watched where the dock's boardwalk disappeared into the woods and waited.

Five minutes was an eternity. Relying on the timing exercises Mac had taught him, Wright counted off every second in his head. The first five minutes came and went. Then another, the only visitor to his plane a low-flying snowy egret. Just as he began to accept that Bizzy had played the cruelest of tricks on him, and she and Lucy and Fogg and Coward and all the rest were in the bungalow laughing, she appeared at the top of the gangway.

She was wearing pants now, the silk pair that

matched her pajama top, and she had on a pair of black pumps, not the ones from Baltimore, these were taller. She was quite drunk, Wright could see, to a degree that had not registered with him in the bungalow. She made her way toward the plane slowly, watching the boards, planning her every step, sometimes setting a toe down and then drawing it back to place it elsewhere, avoiding the gaps in the planks that would have snared a heel and sent her headfirst into the bay. In her caution, gone was the feminine grace she had so aptly displayed strutting onto the stage in Baltimore to sing "Moanin' and Sore," absent was the swing those shoes were meant to give her. The heels clattered in staccato clicks on the planks. She walked stiff-legged, a silken marionette. Still, Wright Williams had never seen anything as alluring as the sight of Bizzy Holt walking toward him and his aeroplane that morning.

She finally finished her trek and climbed gingerly into the passenger's seat next to Wright, her cocktail of scents following her in. His erection had long since retreated but Bizzy's closeness now and the way she smelled did all they could to resummon it. Any other man, he knew—with the possible exception of Byron Fogg—would be contending with more than just the Savoia's joystick in their laps right then.

Wright handed Bizzy the helmet, watching as she fastened the strap under her chin, errant tufts of raven frizz jutting from behind wool trim. Next, she situated the brass-framed googles across the bridge of her nose, the glass flashing in the sun, still low in the sky on this Easter morning.

Eyeing something in the cockpit's floor, Bizzy pointed and asked, "Are we expecting pirates?"

Wright looked and saw the small semi-automatic pistol he kept in a leather holster tucked next to the pilot's seat. With a subtle swell of pride, he said, "Mauser, Model 1914. .32 Caliber."

She nodded. "And what's it for?"

Now Wright's pride deflated, punctured. He shrugged. "Mostly I use it to blackmail my brother and sisters into giving me what I want."

"By threatening to shoot them?"

"No," he laughed. "No, of course not."

"Who, then?"

Wright simply smiled at her and asked, "Ready?"

Realizing the subject had been changed, she replied, "Aye, aye, sir."

"That's the Navy."

"Are we not in a boat?"

"For now."

Wright pressed the starter and the Savoia-Marchetti's big Kinner B-5, centered in the top wing just above their heads, coughed and grumbled to life. He nudged the throttle forward, letting the radial

51

engine warm up until it was purring. The sweet scent of spent gasoline mingled with the smell of the brackish bay water. Wright reached out of the cockpit and whip-snapped the dock line loose from its cleat. The plane drifted free. When the bow was aimed toward open water, he cracked the throttle, slightly at first, giving the big engine just a sip of fuel. Then, when it was ready for more, he opened the throttle wide, letting the B-5 gorge itself on gasoline, its roar reverberating across the water, scattering an alarmed bevy of sanderlings that had been combing the nearby beach.

The Savoia eased forward, an aeroplane portraying a boat. Gathering speed, the water rushed beneath the hull until its whoosh rivaled the bellowing engine. They built momentum, their bodies pressed into their seats. Bizzy gasped as the fuselage rose from its reclined position, rising off the hull's step. Gaining knots, they bounded across the bay's choppy waves, the cool spray from their bow wake showering their faces.

The rush of the water faded to a whisper, then to nothing, overtaken by the wind buffeting the cockpit as the plane rose into the air. Higher they climbed, the horizon receding beneath the outstretched silver wings. Bizzy stretched her neck, looking all around. Wright banked sharply, eliciting another gasp from his passenger, and soared over the beach, giving her a chance to see her bungalow from above. It looked no bigger than a dollhouse nestled between the branches. Wright pointed the plane skyward, ascending until the forest canopy was a thick green carpet and the lakes were shards of broken mirror strewn about.

They flew south, following the coastline, tracing the ribbon of sand that divided land from Atlantic. The air rushed into the open cockpit hot and thick and damp, making Bizzy's hair whip and lash about her face. She was everything Anne Vogler was not: wild, free, and dangerous. Wright could not keep his eyes off her.

"Do you know about target fixation?" he asked. Bizzy leaned toward him and pointed to her ear. Wright all but shouted so she could hear him over the engine and wind. "Target fixation!" Bizzy shook her head. "It's when a pilot becomes so focused on a target that they actually increase their risk of colliding with it." Now she nodded. "You fixate so intently on something that you steer in the direction of your gaze," Wright said. "It happens when you become too focused on one thing. Mac told me—"

"Mac?"

"McDonnell. My instructor at the Curtiss Flying School. Mac says target fixation is caused by lots of things. It can be something distracting, like a flock of birds. Or something dangerous, like a storm. It doesn't even have to be an object. It could be something exciting, too." Wright and Bizzy looked at one another for a moment. "Like trying to arrive at a destination in a certain amount of time," he finally said. "That's what Mac calls an 'anticipated success.'"

Wright saw Bizzy raise an eyebrow behind her goggles.

He eased the stick to the port side and banked east, leaving the land behind, soaring out over the glassy ocean in a clear sky, the only clouds a distant bank of towering cumulonimbi peering over the horizon. A thousand feet below, they could see their shadow, a dot skimming across the swells. They flew for miles until the entire world was only a plate of turquoise below and a dome of azure above. They could have been the only two souls in the world.

Bizzy leaned to Wright and said something, her mouth moving but her voice lost in the hurricane. He shook his head. She leaned closer still, shouting now. "Faster!"

Wright eased the throttle lever forward, a riot of sound filling the cockpit: the roaring wind, whistling through the wing struts; the pulsation of the propeller; the engine, droning reliably, broadcasting its note through the atmosphere.

"Faster!" Bizzy shouted again and laughed.

Wright wiped his watering eyes and opened the throttle further still. Tipping the stick forward, he sent the plane into a steep dive. She squealed and reached for him, clinging to his shoulder. The shimmering water of the bay rushed toward them, the Savoia's shadow growing from a pinpoint on the surface to a giant, looming blackbird.

"Wright!" Bizzy screamed, squeezing his arm so tightly it hurt. At the last moment, he yanked back on the control stick and leveled the plane's course just yards above the waves. She let out a hoarse yell, eyes wide, smile wider.

Wright jammed the throttle open, the engine giving a banshee howl. The wind swatted their heads like a boxer. A steel floor pan, a phonebook's thickness of seat cushion, and a pair of silk pajama pants were the only things separating Bizzy's backside from the whitecaps blurring beneath like a belt sander at a hundred miles per hour. Wright looked at her. In her eyes he saw the same flash of thrill he felt in his heart.

Bizzy, shouting directly into his ear, said, "You know, the first blowjob I ever gave was in an aeroplane."

Wright's heart now leapt into his throat. Entirely sure he had heard her incorrectly, he shouted back, "What?"

"Of course, that plane couldn't pull a sick whore off the piss pot. This one's fast."

"What kind?" Wright asked, immediately

ashamed of being more curious about the aeroplane than what had happened in it.

"How many kinds of blowjobs are there?"

Even with the wind slapping his face, Wright could feel the blood rushing to his cheeks. "Plane. What kind of aeroplane."

Bizzy shrugged. "No idea. Pan Am. Cincinnati to New York. You do know what a blowjob is, don't you, Mr. Williams?" She mimicked the act, holding a phantom shaft in her hand and poking her tongue against the inside of her cheek. "I had never heard it called that before until I read it in a naughty book."

Now it felt as if flames were leaping from Wright's face.

"He was a producer, of course," Bizzy said. "The man on the plane. I remember his name, but I won't repeat it. Marion—my sister—we were on our first big trip without Mother. This producer, he saw me reading the playbill for a show at the Selwyn Theater. He told me he could get me an audition if I would just do a little favor for him. There couldn't have been more than a dozen passengers. And the back row was empty. He said we could go talk about my audition back there in private."

Wright pictured the spartan interior of a Ford Trimotor; he knew Pan American Airways' founder, Juan Trippe, was partial to the Tin Goose.

"He said all the right things," Bizzy went on. The volume of her voice sometimes dropped below that of the wind and engine, causing gaps in the story, but the gist remained intact. "Telling me how pretty I was. I was eighteen, you realize. Never been anywhere. And I already knew I wasn't pretty. That was always Marion. But he didn't pay any mind to Marion, and I loved that."

Wright smiled and nodded, remembering how it felt on the rare occasion one of his father's associates showed more interest in him than his older brother.

"I asked him if there would be any singing and the old bastard took my hand and stuck it right down his pants. Right down the front of his pants. And he was hard. And it felt huge. I had never even seen one before, much less held one. I had no idea what to do so I just held it, you know? Like I was holding his hand or something." A burst of laughter escaped Bizzy, louder than the plane's engine. "He reached into his pants and started to jack himself but using my hand." Again, she pantomimed the action, this time using the Savoia's control stick as a prop.

"Marion wouldn't even look back at me, furious that she wasn't the one. He unbuttoned his pants and let it stick out through his fly. It was even harder than before. And it looked like it hurt. Hell, maybe it did. Then he clamped his hand on the back of my head and pushed me down."

Bizzy fell silent and stared overboard at the ocean rushing by underneath as if accessing the memory. Then she said, "I could feel him watching me, and I liked that. I wanted him to see what I looked like doing it. I wanted Marion to see, too."

Wright simply flew the plane and listened, transfixed, like a boy listening to a ghost story around an Appalachian campfire.

"He was telling me not to stop, telling me how good I was, how beautiful I was. But I didn't care if he thought I was beautiful or not. Only that he thought I was good. I remember he called me 'Baby' a lot. I knew it was because he couldn't remember my name."

A crosswind crashed into the fuselage, rocking the entire plane and startling Wright so badly he almost sprang from the cockpit. Shaken from his trance, he pulled the Savoia into a lazy arc and aimed it back toward land. The coast was a flat line seen through a constellation of splattered insects on the windscreen.

Bizzy said, "I remember he asked me if I liked it. And I told him I did. I knew that's what he wanted to hear. But I didn't like it half as much as I liked the look on his face when I told him I did." She said nothing else for a few minutes as if letting everything she had told Wright sink in.

Finally, Wright said, "Did you get the part?"

"I didn't even get the audition."

He told Bizzy to fasten her lap belt and then he angled the silver Savoia down toward the bay. The plane fluttered lower until they heard the sound of the hull cleaving the surface and sluicing water to each side. The mist showered their faces. Wright taxied until they were within a hundred yards of the dock and then cut the power to the engine. Bizzy watched as the propeller slowed and snapped to a halt. He explained that it was a visual phenomenon called the stroboscopic effect that had made the prop appear to spin in reverse for a moment as its rotational speed decreased. Bizzy nodded and tried to formulate a response that would make him believe she cared, but she could not. Instead, she said, "Now we're in a boat again."

Wright looked at her, lounging in the passenger's seat, jade silk legs stretched out before her, ankles crossed. The black pumps glinted in the shadows of the floor; the heels pointed in stick-'em-up parallel like twin barrels from a pair of pistols.

The Savoia drifted leisurely toward the dock. Hypnotized by Bizzy, he ignored the rudder pedals that would have steered them.

"Wright," she said, eyes darting between the approaching dock and her bewitched pilot. Still he gazed, blinking. "Wright, the dock. *Wright.*"

The plane floated quietly past the berth, he never

once taking his eyes off Bizzy to find the rope coiled next to his seat. They overshot the pier, missing its corner by scant feet. With a muffled crunch, the hull scraped the sandy bottom of the bay until the plane was beached, rocking gently as each wave lapped at it. Bizzy pulled the goggles away from her face and lifted them onto the leather helmet.

They sat in silence, staring at one another, listening to the popping and hissing of the engine as it cooled.

At the same time, they lunged for one another, their open mouths crushing together, and for the first time in two years Wright was kissing someone other than Anne Vogler. He could taste the sweet spice of vermouth and whiskey on Bizzy's breath.

They separated and gasped for air. Panting, he said, "Everyone at the party was looking at you."

"Well, it's my party."

"Especially Lucy."

"Lucy's harmless."

"So I've heard." Wright cradled Bizzy's face in his hands and kissed her again, lips sealing hungrily over hers.

"Did you like watching me dance with her?"

Wright's shallow breathing answered for him.

A smile crept across her face. "I could tell." She glanced into his lap, looking for the proof she had seen in the bungalow. "Show me."

Wright laced his arms around Bizzy's waist and pulled her body off the seat, pulling it against his own. She kissed him, almost angrily, tugging at his lower lip with her incisors when she pulled away, grinning. Her smile unleashed torrents of dopamine into his bloodstream. She reached for his wrist and drew his hand to her face, her eyes alight. Staring at him, Bizzy guided Wright's middle finger into her mouth and sucked, snaking her tongue around it.

With a wet pop, she pulled it free. Her eyebrows raised when their eyes met, red lips curling into a devilish smile. "Do you like it?" Before he could answer, she closed her mouth over his finger and sucked again, this time moaning as her eyelids fluttered shut. Wright knew it was all a show she was putting on. But he did love a good show.

Bizzy let her free hand venture between Wright's thighs, cupping the pouch between them. And then her smile faded. "Where'd it go?"

He sighed, his shoulders slumping. "Its presence is occasional, I'm afraid."

"And what was the occasion in the bungalow?"

"I was at a remove."

Bizzy thought for a moment. "But now I'm... *here*."

Wright nodded. "Now you're here."

Now she nodded, too. "I think I understand." He watched her for a moment. It was not the first time a woman had said that to him, but it was the first time he had believed it.

"I want you to marry me."

Bizzy stared at Wright, blinking, for a long moment. Then she let out a laugh like a ribbon of caps yanked through a pop gun. "Mr. Williams, I'm already married." He felt as if a block of ice had just been dropped into his stomach. "To the theater."

Now he breathed again. "Divorce it and marry me."

"If I'm not mistaken, you've already entered into one such contract."

"Yes, still valid and binding," Wright nodded. "For now. You sound like Buck."

"I've known you for two weeks."

"Marry me."

"You're too young."

"For what?"

"I'm too old."

"You're in your prime. Ask anyone at the party."

Bizzy sighed, smiled, and watched him for a few seconds. "I do believe that you and I make a nice pair, Wright. I like to perform, and you like to watch."

He saw Lucy standing on the beach at the top of the boardwalk. Her arms were crossed tightly across her jacket and tie, one bare foot tapping. Bizzy turned to see her, too.

She rose to her feet in the cockpit, bent, and slipped off her shoes. Wright watched her clamber onto the lower wing, steadying herself against a strut as she rolled up the cuffs of her pajama pants. She stepped into the ankle-deep water and climbed the slope to the beach. High heels dangling from her fingers, still wearing Wright's leather helmet, she began trudging through the soft sand toward Lucy.

After a few shifting steps, she turned back to him. "How far can your boat fly?"

"Around the world. That's the idea, at least."

Bizzy resumed her walk. She called back over her shoulder, "You should fly it back home to your wife."

Chapter 3

Paris, France
Saturday, July 12, 1930

A steady rain was falling, turning Rue Blanche into a sheet of Lucy's Uncle Pierre's cellophane, smeared with the reflections of a thousand red and cyan neon signs and the headlamps of Peugeots, Renaults, and Citroëns. Wright clutched the lapels of his linen suit jacket and trotted across the cobblestone to the brass and glass door that was the main entrance to Chez Florence.

Wright checked his wristwatch; it was after midnight. He dodged the rivulets of water streaming off the awning and joined the river of people slipping into the womb of the nightclub through its sunken doorway. He dropped thirty francs in *le physio*'s palm, announcing in English for the man to keep the change, and then stepped into a nether realm of glow, shadow, and throbbing, languid rhythm. The terraced floor seemed to undulate under a groin-vaulted ceiling supported by bulging columns. It was impossible to discern the boundaries of the space through the veil of tobacco and marijuana haze that shrouded what were either mirrored walls or arched passageways to antechambers, Wright could not be sure.

Everywhere he looked, he saw round tables, no wider in diameter than a barrel hoop, cramped with seated patrons. Each had four, six, eight occupants, ringlets of smoke rising from the cigarette in every other hand. White linen tablecloths were cluttered with amber, green, and clear bottles, and glass ashtrays bristled like pincushions with extinguished butts. Every face was angled toward the center of the room where, in a small clearing at the axis of the tables' array, a petite, brown-skinned woman in a glittering sequined gown stood and sang into a ring-and-spring microphone, backed by a three-piece band. Wright did not recognize the song.

He moved discreetly, hugging the mirrored wall to avoid distracting the crowd from the singer, surveying the room for his quarry. He neared the chanteuse and her combo, close enough to feel the double bass thumping in his chest and hear the rasp of the wire brushes on the drumhead. On the far side of the room, Wright saw one table behaving unlike the others. Its patrons were obscured by a tight circle of people standing around them, looking inward instead of at the singer. On a hunch, he changed course and redirected himself toward the busy table, cutting directly across the floor, no longer caring whose view he interrupted. Halfway there, a momentary gap opened and Wright caught a glimpse into the circle, confirming his suspicions. At the center of that isolated audience, holding court, sat Bizzy.

Wright insinuated himself into that same gap and watched as he waited for her to notice him. A mink stole was draped across her otherwise bare shoulders, the animal's taxidermized snout nestled in her cleavage. She was wearing a lavender off-the-shoulder satin gown under the fur and her hair was being begrudgingly tamed by a jewel-encrusted comb that sparkled among the dark looms. The encircling admirers were speaking en masse, imploring Bizzy to take the stage and sing, proffering napkins as they demanded autographs. One man asked her to press a lipstick kiss onto a Moët et Chandon label he had peeled from its bottle. Bizzy politely but adamantly refused the requests to sing as she went about signing her name on everything shoved toward her.

Wright took stock of the entourage flanking Bizzy. On her right, of course, sat Lucy Allard Conrad in a tuxedo and monocle, its gold chain threaded through her lapel's buttonhole. Her strawberry hair was precisely parted on one side, as shiny and hard as a beetle's shell. Clenched between her teeth was an opera-length tortoiseshell cigarette holder, a Lucky

The Purple Menace and the Tobacco Prince

Strike tucked into its tip. On Bizzy's left was Byron Fogg in his de rigueur smoking jacket. Noticeably absent were Ramona and Kimono, replaced at Fogg's side by a rotund, wide-faced woman whom Wright could only assume was the mother Lucy had mentioned in Florida. And on the other side of Lucy, Noël Coward sat in a white dinner jacket with a red boutonnière, craning his neck in a vain attempt to see Chez Florence's singer through the wall of people. Eager to complete the bungalow reunion, Wright took half a step forward and cleared his throat.

"Ah," Fogg said dryly. "If it isn't Wright Williams, the flying circus."

Wright nodded at him, unsure if he had just been complimented or insulted. Lucy's reaction was decidedly less ambiguous, her face contorted in disapproval at Wright's presence. But his focus was solely on Bizzy, ready to examine her response upon noticing him. If she was happy to see him, what the others thought was of no consequence.

For the duration of his transatlantic cruise, Wright had imagined two competing and equally plausible scenarios. In his waking hours, he imagined Bizzy's eyes brightening and smile widening, flinging her arms open to welcome him. In his nightmares, he saw something more akin to Lucy's expression, telling him that in the half-season since Florida, the chemical heiress had poisoned Bizzy's feelings toward him, assuming there had been any to begin with.

When she finally saw him, neither his hopes nor fears were realized. "Wright?" Her face did not light up, he had to admit to himself. But it was already aglow and alive, was it not, as she chatted with her adoring fans? And his appearance at her table did nothing to dampen that mood, he told himself. The fact that she did not leap from behind the table into his arms did not mean she was not happy to see him.

"Scooch," she said to Fogg, brushing at him with her hands until he explained to his mother—accompanied by performative annoyance from both—that they were to relocate one seat over to make room for Wright next to Bizzy. He shuffled around the table and took the now-empty slot next to her. The instant he was seated, Bizzy held his face in her hands and kissed him on the cheek, branding him with a perfect pair of burgundy lips. "Do I want to know how you found me this time?"

Wright opened his mouth to explain with pride that R.W. Williams Tobacco Company retained more than a few private detectives. Before he could say a word, however, Bizzy turned back to the congregation clamoring for her signature.

Fogg, unable to resist an opportunity to commiserate, touched Wright on the sleeve and said,

"Don't take it personally. She does it to all of us."

"It's how you know you're in with her," Gertrud leaned across her son's chest to add. "If she expects you to wait while she signs autographs."

Lucy leaned up and said, "So, Wright, how is Anne?"

"You would have to ask her; we haven't spoken since Christmas. How is John? Your first wedding anniversary is next week if I'm not mistaken."

Before Lucy could verbalize the daggers in her eyes, Fogg adroitly steered the conversation back to Bizzy. "She'll swear to you she loathes this aspect of the job. Mother, do you remember Fifth Avenue?"

Gertrud scoffed. "Of course."

To Wright, Fogg said, "We were strolling down Fifth Avenue with Bizzy, Mother and me. I had been approached once or twice for autographs and handshakes, but no one had recognized Bizzy. She was wearing her beloved overcoat—the one that looks like it was made from the pelts of several rabbits with rabies—and a ratty old beret. After the third or fourth incident, she suddenly turned to me and said, 'Would you like to see the Purple Menace now?'" Fogg straightened himself in his chair, expertly impersonating Bizzy. "A subtle lifting of her shoulders. An alluring elongation of her back. A coy tilting of her head and a suggestive swinging of her hips." Wright could picture it vividly. "*Et voilà*! Immediately she was mobbed. She needn't change into a sequined evening gown or start singing. And her trademark fuzzy black hair remained hidden under her beret. But this woman knew how to create a full-blown scene with only the slightest adjustments in posture."

"And attitude," Gertrud added.

Mid-signature, Bizzy said, "I can hear every word you're saying."

"We know, dear," Fogg replied. "That's why we say them."

Lucy said, "You remember Sime Silverman in *Variety*, the week after *The Wild Party* opened."

Bizzy handed a personalized napkin back to its owner, thanking them, and then, to Lucy, said, "No one remembers Sime Silverman."

Fogg, changing his voice from his usual erudite, effete timbre to a mockingly lower-class growl, "'She's not an actress, heaven knows.'"

Lucy drew on her Lucky Strike and blew a silver veil of smoke that momentarily obscured her face. "What Mr. Silverman was unable to understand is that Bizzy's use of her..." Lucy appraised her décolletage. "Physical attributes, to express aspects of a character is as much of an acting skill as the ability to convincingly deliver dialogue."

"Hear, hear," Fogg said, with a rap of his

knuckles on the tabletop.

Wright was quietly watching each speaker in turn, unable to contribute to the conversation. But if he felt any impulse to discuss something he was more familiar with—aviation, perhaps—it was negated by his interest in hearing anything anyone had to say about Bizzy.

"Chicot was kinder." Gertrud quoted him, "'Here is the sultriest stage star since Louise Brooks. She has more intelligence than Etting. She out-lures Lombard and out-serpentines Stanwyck. She makes any other glamour girl you care to name look housewifely.'"

Fogg added, "He called her 'the Hips That Rule Broadway.'"

"They remind me of the taffy-pulling machine at Moretti's," Noël chimed in, causing the entire group except Wright to erupt in laughter.

Bizzy signed a parking ticket for the last lingering fan. "I'll let you all in on a little secret," she said. "I cut a quarter inch off the right heel of every pair of shoes I own. You don't think my fanny wiggles like that by itself, do you?"

Before the table could debate the veracity of Bizzy's claim, the singer in the center of the room thanked the audience for their latest round of applause, making Wright suddenly aware of the fact that neither he nor anyone at his table had been participants in it.

"Miss Holt," the vocalist said into the microphone, "if it's quite alright with you, I would like to perform my next number."

The entirety of the nightclub's crowd turned to look at Bizzy. She calmly lit a cigarette, eyeing Chez Florence's headliner through the swirling smoke. "By all means. You may have them back now."

Muted laughter rippled throughout the club, accompanied by a stray call to, "Let Bizzy sing!"

"Yes, Bizzy," the singer said. "Let's have it." She took a step backward and gestured invitingly at the microphone.

Bizzy smiled and shook her head. "No, I have pilfered enough of your spotlight for one night. Please, Florence, continue." Now the crowd laughed louder.

Unwilling to spar further, the singer turned to her band and angrily counted off the next song.

Bizzy took a drag on her cigarette and said to Wright, "Florence Emery Jones, if you don't know." The look on his face told her that he, in fact, did not. "The reigning queen of Montmartre after midnight, they call her."

"As in Chez Florence?" Wright asked.

Bizzy nodded. "Louis Mitchell's name is on the deed, but the name of the club should tell you who really runs the place."

Eager to change the subject, Noël, in his clipped,

staccato diction, said, "Paris is the... *sexiest* town on Earth, don't you think?"

Lucy answered first. "Burnside might disagree."

"What does Nellie know?" Bizzy said. She cleared her throat and began speaking in an exaggerated Alabamian accent. "Sex? *Ah'm* bored with sex. What is it, after all?"

Lucy laughed, pulled her cigarette holder from her lips, and did her own impression. "If you go down on a woman, you get a crick in your neck. If you go down on a man, you get lockjaw, *dahling*."

Now Fogg added his own Nellie Burnside caricature to the chorus. "And fuckin' just gives me claustro*phobia*!"

Again, the whole table, save for Wright, released a burst of laughter, loud enough to draw a glare from Florence Jones. Chastened, the group dutifully listened to Mrs. Jones for half a song until Fogg said, "For someone who professes to despise it so, sex certainly is Nellie's favorite subject."

Noël said, "The lady doth protest too much, methinks."

"You know, Bizzy," Fogg said, "Nellie and I once tried to estimate how many men you have gotten off on Broadway just by walking across the stage every night."

"Byron!" Gertrud gasped, slapping the back of

her son's hand.

"Yes, stop it, Foggy," Lucy added. "You're embarrassing poor Mr. Williams."

"Well, let's see," Wright said. *The Wild Party* opened on Broadway in April of '29 and ran until February of this year. That's about forty weeks. Eight shows a week; three hundred and twenty shows."

"Three hundred and twenty-one, to be exact," Bizzy said.

Wright continued. "The Music Box theater holds, what, a thousand people?"

"A thousand and twenty-five," Fogg nodded. "Minus thirty or so for the orchestra."

"We'll call it an even thousand. Assuming the shows were sellouts—"

"They were," Bizzy and Fogg said simultaneously.

"Three hundred and twenty thousand people saw *The Wild Party* on Broadway, roughly. Let's say half the audience were men, that's…" Wright closed one eye and looked at the ceiling, doing the math.

"A hundred and sixty thousand men," Lucy said, invested in the calculations now as well.

Wright said, "You figure, conservatively, half of the men in the audience every night either saw Bizzy in their heads later that night while they were fucking their wives, or they saw Bizzy in their heads later that night while they were doing it for themselves. That's eighty thousand men."

Fogg was nodding in agreement. "Nellie guessed fifty thousand."

Lucy was smiling at Bizzy. "That's a lot of psyches to set up shop in."

"That's how many people live in Winston-Salem," Wright said. "You could make my whole town come."

For the first time, something Wright said was the cause of their laughter. And, for the first time since he sat down, he smiled. Then he saw Bizzy do something he thought her incapable of: blush.

A waitress appeared at tableside. Lucy showed the girl her empty champagne flute; Noël ordered a Jack Rose. Before anyone else could place an order, the waitress interrupted. "I'm so sorry, but Mr. Mitchell has asked me to inform you that your tab has been closed and you are being invited to leave."

Every eye at the table turned to Florence Jones, who had the slightest smirk on her face as she sang.

Fogg, the master of haughty indignance, spoke first. "Good." He stood from his seat, offering his arm to Gertrud. "We have grown bored with the evening's entertainment anyhow. We simply thought it impolite to exit mid-performance. Please extend our gratitude to Mr. Mitchell for providing the opportunity to seek out higher talent elsewhere."

Wright stood and pulled a money clip from his front pocket. He peeled from it a crisp hundred-dollar bill and offered it to the waitress.

She shook her head. "Mr. Mitchell insists."

"For Mrs. Jones, then." Wright placed the bill on the table.

Now they all stood, heads held high as they filed past the waitress. Led by Bizzy, the line wound around the table and directly across the clearing that Florence and the band were using as their stage.

Outside Chez Florence, the group huddled together under the awning, enclosed on three sides by curtains of rain.

"Mother and I are off to Bricktop's," Fogg announced. "Perhaps the hospitality there will be more forthcoming. Anyone else?"

Noël raised his hand.

"I think Miss Conrad and I shall retire," Bizzy said.

"Yes, goodnight, Mr. Williams," Lucy said immediately.

Bizzy shot Lucy a chastening glance and then said, "Wright, do you have a place to stay?"

Out of the corner of his eye, Wright witnessed a brief but violent altercation between Bizzy and Lucy's feet, Lucy kicking Bizzy's ankle, Bizzy responding in kind, then a ceasefire.

"I do, thank you," Wright replied with a slight bow.

"He does," Lucy said.

"Where?" Bizzy asked.

Wright named the first Parisian hotel he could think of. "The Ritz."

Bizzy eyed him for a moment. Fogg, Gertrud, and Noël interjected to bid the others farewell with promises to reconvene tomorrow and do it all over again and then disappeared into the downpour. Bizzy turned her attention to the weather. "A taxi should be along."

"Nonsense, I'll drive you." Wright immediately dashed into the rain, stopping in the middle of Rue Blanche to beckon the women. "Come on!" With resigned shrugs, Bizzy and Lucy ran after Wright, bounding over puddles and uselessly trying to shield their hair with their hands. They trailed him as he sprinted toward a chrome and yellow Rolls Royce Phantom II parked across the street. In the neon glow, it looked like a bed of spring jonquils sprouting from the sidewalk.

Bizzy shouted after him. "Did you drive here from North Carolina?"

The three dove headfirst into the car and slammed the doors behind them. Wright was behind the wheel, Bizzy and Lucy were sliding onto a tuck-and-roll upholstered backseat deeper than most sofas. He wiped the rain from his face, dried his hands on his trousers, and pressed the Phantom's starter. The four-hundred-sixty-eight-cubic-inch engine snarled to life, and they shoved off.

"Maison Souquet," Bizzy said.

"That's a hotel," Lucy added.

Wright heard Bizzy hiss, "Stop!" under her breath at Lucy.

"Ten Rue de Bruxelles?" Wright asked.

"Well?" Bizzy said to Lucy. "Is that the address?"

Quietly, Lucy said, "I believe so, yes."

Wright guided the Rolls down the narrow, curving corridor of Rue Blanche and then turned left on Rue la Bruyère, a cobblestone riverbed at the bottom of a Haussmann-style canyon. The avenue widened and he revved his way through the gearbox, letting the Stromberg carburetor breathe deeply. Perched on the Phantom's prow, seemingly half a mile away, a chrome lady leaned into the wind, pointing the way.

Wright adjusted the rear-view mirror until he could see Bizzy and Lucy in the blue shadows of the backseat, intermittent bands of light sweeping across their faces. They drove under streetlamps and neon.

The Purple Menace and the Tobacco Prince

The colors of the city at night—hydrogen red and mercury blue, warm ambers from the strata of lighted windows above—streaked across the automobile's bonnet like rainbow-hued comets. The windshield wipers thumped like a heartbeat.

"How'd you get 'Bizzy'?" Wright asked, then laughed at the way the question sounded aloud.

She laughed, too. "Marion, my sister. She couldn't say 'Elizabeth' when I was born. Mother wanted Marion to call me Bitsy, but it came out 'Bizzy,' and it stuck." Wright could see her smile at the memory. Bizzy said, "So, what's *her* name?"

"Who?"

"The car, of course. All good cars have names."

He found himself at a loss for words.

Bizzy scooted to the edge of the seat and rested her elbows on the partition that divided chauffeur from passengers. She peered over, surveying the Rolls' ornate dash and Birdseye maple trim. "Let's think. She's beautiful if a little brash."

"Big," Lucy added. "Big fenders. Curvy."

"Loud," Bizzy said. "Deep voice."

"Elizabeth," Wright said.

"Elizabeth," Lucy echoed, Bizzy being once again the only thing she and Wright could agree upon.

Bizzy smiled and sank back into the seat. She reclined, kicked her shoes onto the carpet, and raised her legs into the air like a dreadnought's main guns. She propped her ankles on the partition sill, crossed them, found that uncomfortable, and then uncrossed them. Wright looked at them over his shoulder. Bizzy's legs were in black net stockings, the woven diamonds just large enough to slip fingers through, he estimated.

"You're in their hometown, you know?" Bizzy said, her eyes meeting Wright's in the mirror. "Fishnets. Yes, sir. They were made famous by the dancers and actresses and prostitutes who populate *la Ville Lumière* at night, particularly the liberated ladies of the infamous Moulin Rouge."

Wright glanced at Lucy just in time to see her eyes roll. She said, "It was the Paris Opera Ballet."

"Whose story is better?" Bizzy asked. When Lucy refused to answer, she continued, "Yes, Miss Conrad is correct in that it was the ballerinas of *le Ballet de l'Opéra national de Paris* who were the first to swap their opaque tights for fishnets. But it was the artists and intellectuals who frequented the Moulin Rouge who exported their enthusiasm for the look. Turn here. Next left."

Wright swung the Rolls onto Rue Pierre Fontaine and gunned the big motor, climbing up into the Montmartre district. When his eyes returned to the rearview mirror, he could see Lucy's hand gliding up Bizzy's leg, fingertips tracing the stockings' zigzag pattern over the swell of her knee and then disappearing under the hiked lavender hem of her gown.

"Turn here," Bizzy said. "Next left. Rue de Douai. Victorian fashions had kept women's legs hidden so, naturally, stockings became fetishized in Victorian society. You always want what you can't have." In his head, Wright heard her singing Noël Coward lyrics again. *Every peach, that's out of reach, looks so delightful...*

He turned the car left. Bizzy was watching him, eyebrows raising when her eyes met the reflection of his. She gathered the skirt of her gown in her hands and bunched it around her hips, raising it like a curtain. Looping her thumbs through openings in the fishnets' weave, Bizzy wiggled and shimmied, rolling them down to her calves. She cranked down the Phantom's rear window, wind and rain crashing through the opening, and swung her feet out into the night. Wright watched as she used her heels to push the fishnets down until they clung to only her toes, whipping like pennants from the masts of a tall ship. Suddenly they vanished, caught by the wind, gone into the night.

Laughing, Bizzy pulled her wet, bare legs back into the cab of the Rolls and spread them wide before her. In the mirror, Wright watched Lucy's hand slip into the dark, deep vee of Bizzy's lap, who closed her eyes and let her head loll back against the seat, rain spraying onto her face through the open window. Wright glanced at Rue de Douai, making sure the Rolls was not drawing a bead on a pedestrian or bollard, and then immediately looked back at the mirror to see Lucy hinging her wrist, rocking her hand back and forth between Bizzy's thighs.

Between sighs, Bizzy said, "My first pair of fishnets were a gift from Polly."

Wright, unsure if he was still a part of the conversation, tentatively asked, "Should I know her?"

A sigh slipped from her mouth and then she explained, "Polly Adler. She was my… employer, while I was at Columbia."

Lucy said, "Polly was your pimp."

Without acknowledging or, Wright noted, refuting Lucy's addendum, Bizzy said, "Polly's fishnets helped me get my first theater job." Her voice was becoming unreliable, breaths becoming gasps.

"Of course they did," Lucy said.

Bizzy exhaled and said, "Silk stockings aren't ideal for a… wide range of motion… on stage."

Wright took another snap glance out the windshield and then returned to the rearview mirror. He could see the dexterous movements of Lucy's hand, knuckles churning now. The cabin of the Rolls Royce was filling with octaves of Bizzy's moans and the inebriating scent of her vagina.

As Wright watched, Lucy removed her cigarette holder and picked out the still-lit Lucky Strike. She flicked it through the window in a shower of orange sparks. Next, Lucy removed her monocle and tucked it and the cigarette holder inside her jacket. Then, with the slow reverence of someone bowing before an altar, she dropped from view.

Wright could see Bizzy, settling into the seat, sliding down, draping one arm across the seatback, the other over Lucy. Frantically, he repositioned the mirror and sat up straighter in the driver's seat, straining to see in the darkness, breathing when he could remember to. Over the growl of the Phantom's engine, he could hear Bizzy practically purring.

Wright glanced quickly at the street ahead and then back at the mirror. He peered into the backseat and could barely make out the dark shape of Lucy's body, curled onto the bench next to Bizzy, her head weaving in her lap. Bizzy's gaze locked with Wright's, and he stared at her helplessly, unable to turn away, her eyes white slits, mouth hung open, rain trickling down her face like tears. Wright suddenly felt that she had expected this, that she knew from the moment they met that he would be simply an audience for her shows. He wanted to hate Bizzy for her arrogance, but all he could see was the confidence of someone who was not afraid to enjoy their life, and he was envious.

Wright could hear Bizzy babbling, her voice ragged as she begged Lucy not to stop. He could hear Lucy's breathing, heavy and labored while Bizzy's urgings grew more insistent. She gasped—a sharp, stuttering hiss—and he saw in the mirror her fingers threading through Lucy's brittle shell of hair. Then the noises from the back settled into silence, except for Bizzy's panting. Lucy rose, smiling at Wright's reflection with narrowed eyes, tucking a stray strand of hair behind her ear. In the headlights of an oncoming automobile, he could see her mouth, glistening wet, her chin red and raw from the abrasion.

Bizzy sat up and began to close the window, struggling to complete a full revolution of the handle without stopping to catch her breath. "Here," she said hoarsely. "On the left."

Wright steered the Rolls to the curb and stopped in front of Maison Souquet. No one moved or spoke for minutes until finally Bizzy produced a cigarette from somewhere and lit it. "It used to be a brothel. And then a school for girls." She tilted her head back and blew a plume of smoke against the headliner. "I suppose those are the same thing, though."

Wright could hear Bizzy and Lucy whispering, the words mostly washed out by the rain drumming against the Rolls' roof. The conversation had the push and pull of a negotiation, Wright thought. Eventually, Lucy pressed her hair to her scalp and ejected herself into the rain. He watched her dash to the entrance of the hotel, leaping a narrow stream that was coursing down the sidewalk before disappearing inside.

Before Maison Souquet's door closed, Wright had sprung from behind the steering wheel and was clambering over the partition into the rear compartment. He dropped onto the backseat beside Bizzy, the leather splattered with rain. He could hear the soaked carpet squish beneath his feet.

For a moment, they watched each other with what Wright thought was curiosity, gauging one another's reactions to what just happened. Bizzy's hair was matted to her head, her face damp. The drenched mink stole hung heavily around her bare shoulders, its snout dripping steadily into her cleavage.

"Marry me," Wright blurted.

"Did you come all the way to Paris to ask me that?"

"Marry me."

"No."

"Why not?"

Bizzy laughed. "All the reasons I gave you in Florida, plus a couple of new French ones."

They listened to the rain for a few minutes. she used the heel of her palm to clear a circle in the condensation on the Phantom's window and peered through it at the hotel. "You know, they say the old gal is haunted."

"I can sympathize."

"Do you have ghosts, Mr. Williams?"

"It's been three months and five days since I first saw you. Every day since you're the first thing I think of when I wake up and the last thing before falling asleep. Every hour of every day something triggers the thought of you. Whenever I hear someone singing. When I hear the crackle of a phonograph needle dropping into the groove of a record. When I see a curtain rise." Wright shook his head. "You're everywhere, all the time. I think about you whenever I hear applause. When I hear an aeroplane overhead. Every morning in the paper, every evening on the radio, when there's a mention of Baltimore. Or Florida. Or Manhattan. When I'm at home, in my mind I'm giving you a tour of the place. When I speak with my brother or sisters, I'm not hearing a word they say because I'm silently rehearsing how I would introduce you to them. Whenever I see someone fumble with something— their utensil at dinner, a cigarette lighter—I remember how I struggled with the aeroplane's controls, taking off from the bay after our Florida flight, my hands suddenly trembling, all the excitement and fear and adrenaline that I had suppressed while we were in the air flooding through me."

"Wright…"

"The smell of a cigarette being lit. The sound of the lighter. Sometimes simply looking at the sky will do it. The smell of orchids. When I see a woman in heels. When I see a woman wearing stockings. When I see someone dancing. Anytime anyone calls me 'Mr. Williams.'"

Bizzy watched him for a few seconds, making sure he was finished. "You're sweet, Wright. Really. That's another reason I won't marry you."

He could no longer look at her, watching instead the tributaries of rain snaking down the window.

"Oh, don't pout, Wright."

"Should I go home?"

"Because I won't marry you?" Bizzy laughed.

"That's where the Mauser is."

"Stop." She took his hand and waited for him to look at her again, studying his eyes until she was convinced that he was not serious. "That's not funny."

"I know."

They said nothing for a minute, then Bizzy said, "You know, I visited North Carolina once when I was a girl. One summer, Daddy loaded up Mother, Marion, and me into his brand-new Ford—we were the first house on the block to have one—and drove us down to see the Blue Ridge Mountains. We stayed in a log cabin. When the sun went down, the air would just glitter with fireflies. Father used his pocketknife to punch air holes in the lid of a Mason jar and that first night Sissy and I caught so many they made our bedroom glow."

Wright was smiling at a similar memory with Walt, Mary, and Nancy.

"Mother made us promise to turn them loose the next morning," Bizzy said.

"But the next morning they were all dead."

She nodded. She watched Wright for a moment and then said, "I'm in Paris with half a dozen friends. I signed thirty autographs tonight. I've got a warm, dry room at Maison Souquet. There's champagne up there, Wright. Yet here I sit, cold and wet, in the back of your car, talking to you. Don't put me in your jar."

He stared at her and then finally nodded.

She leaned to him and gave him a matching lipstick kiss on his other cheek. "Goodnight, Mr. Williams." She patted the wet upholstery. "And goodnight to you, Elizabeth." She opened the Phantom's door and dashed through the deluge toward the golden glow of the hotel's entry.

Wright stepped out of the car and stood in the rain for a moment before reinserting himself behind the steering wheel. He drove toward the Ritz despite his doubts there were any vacancies on Bastille Day weekend.

Chapter 4

New York City
Friday, November 7, 1930

"I call this move the Sportster," Wright whispered. He and Buck Moore watched from the front row as Bizzy rounded the microphone stand and charged downstage toward the audience. "After the Gee Bee Model X racer. Fast and dangerous."

Buck was gazing at Bizzy and nodding, slowly. Now she was stalking the full length of the Selwyn Theater's footlights from stage left to right. Her posterior swung like a hypnotist's pendulum, entrancing Wright and Buck equally. Back and forth the halves of it pitched beneath the dress, locked in a dance of gravity, like the tides. Wright leaned to his friend. "This move I call the Fokker," he said softly. "After the T-2, the first plane to fly nonstop coast to coast in '23."

"*Shh!*" a woman in the second hissed. Like all the other times, Wright ignored her.

By his second straight week of attending *Three's*

a Crowd, he had given each of Bizzy's moves a different name in his head. Now in his third week, Wright had flown Buck to New York City to join him. When the curtain rose on Bizzy's first number of the night, "Something to Remember You By," there she was, poised and ready in a white silk halter dress, he had tilted his head toward Buck and said, "I call this pose the Kitty Hawk, where it all began." That comment had elicited the first *shoosh* of the evening.

Now Bizzy stood at centerstage alone, hands on hips, singing the opening lines to "Body and Soul." Her voice was a stone skipping nimbly across the glass-smooth swells of Max Salzer's orchestral lake, plunging into its blue abyss at the end of each verse. Then, just when it had seemingly sunk, she would fill her lungs and that voice became a depth charge, bursting above the surface and exploding in arcs and spirals that drenched the audience.

For this song, Bizzy had changed into a silver sheath of a gown, her olive shoulders bare. If the intermission scuttlebutt that Wright had overhead in the lobby on opening night was correct, no one had ever seen a strapless gown before. He certainly had not. "I call this the Vega," he whispered to Buck. "After the Lockheed that Amelia Earhart flew to become the first woman to cross the Atlantic solo."

"*Shh!*"

Wright made himself take his eyes off Bizzy long enough to glance at his friend. Buck was spellbound by the woman in the spotlight, just as Wright knew he would be. Since they were boys, Buck had always been so impressed by the things he showed off to him. The swimming pool at Peace Haven, the Rolls Royce, the Savoia-Marchetti, the Mauser semi-automatic, the skyscraper with his daddy's name on it that loomed over Winston-Salem.

Since touching down at Floyd Bennett Field, Buck had marveled, perpetually slack-jawed, at the arched Gothic towers of the Brooklyn Bridge; the exposed steel jutting from the summit of the Empire State Building, almost finished now, blonde Indiana limestone sheathing three-fourths of its height; the Italian Renaissance interior of the Selwyn Theater, with its Pavonazzo and Green Alps marbles, gold-leaf ornamentation, scrolled modillions, and imposing murals. But none of it had enchanted Buck like Bizzy Holt. Wright could almost see the ivy vines of her voice crawling toward his friend, climbing his legs, scaling his arms, twining around his head, curling into his ears.

Bizzy sang, *All you need do is ask, I'll surrender to you.* Her hips seemed to move of their own volition, swiveling and pivoting ceaselessly. One hand glided down onto the chrome-plated microphone stand, the other cupped the microphone's ring, drawing the diaphragm to her open mouth. *I'm yours for the taking, body and soul.* She stood, resplendent, shining like an idol, every inch of her gown catching the light and mirroring it back across the Selwyn's thousand seats in a fan of silver rays.

"I call this one the *Spirit of St. Louis*," Wright said to Buck, picturing Lindbergh's custom-built monoplane and the jeweled pattern inscribed on its aluminum engine cowling. "That's my favorite."

"*Shh!*"

"Admiral Balbo sent me." Wright's breath condensed into a fog that hung in the night air.

The square window cut into the wooden door banged shut in Wright's face. He gave Buck, shivering and clenched at his side, a reassuring nod. The rattle of a trio of locks—a barrel bolt, a deadbolt, and finally a chain lock—being released followed. Finally, the door creaked open.

The air inside Tony's was a swirling eddy of sound and smell: the clack and clatter of billiard balls, smoke and sweat, tinkling piano, bubbling laughter, clinking glasses, oregano and pungent garlic. Throughout the low-ceilinged cigar box of a speakeasy, champagne corks popped, permissive women squealed and pretended to resist, and an utter disregard for the outside world floated like laughing gas. Each time a cloche-hatted or Eton-cropped woman ordered a Gin Rickey, or fedoraed men raised their glasses to toast, Wright heard in their voices the blissful ignorance of the upper crust. The real world was nothing more than an intermittent nuisance for them, to the extent that they acknowledged it all. On the exceedingly rare occasion that reality clashed with their lifestyle, reality was where the fault lay.

As they made their way to the bar, Wright listed for Buck the reasons he loved Tony's. He loved the food—the best Italian in Manhattan. He loved the porcelain coffee cups Tony served his liquor in. He loved it when Tony stood on his head and sang Puccini. He loved knowing it was *the* Tony's, not to be confused with any of the other Tony's in New York City. He loved knowing that the Algonquin Round Table made Tony's their second home. He loved the frequent sightings of Peter Arno or Lucy Parker or Robert Benchley or Heywood Broun or Wolcott Gibbs. More than all of that, Wright loved seeing Bizzy in her element.

What he did not tell Buck were the reasons he hated it. He hated not knowing who would be in Bizzy's entourage night to night. He hated not knowing if Byron Fogg would be there, because he hated not being able to tell if Fogg was making fun of him or not. He hated that he had gone to the wrong Tony's after the opening night of *Three's a Crowd*. He hated knowing Lucy would be there, every night, and that she always got there before he did. He hated that Lucy had to tell him who the Algonquin Round Table was. And who Arno and Parker and Benchley and Broun and Gibbs were.

"Exhibitionists all," Wright remembered Bizzy explaining to him on his first night at Tony's. "Yours truly among them." Then, with a wink, she said, "And there's nothing an exhibitionist loves more than a voyeur."

Wright and Buck pushed their way to the bar. Lucy was already there and Wright introduced her to Buck, carefully watching the exchange of cordialities that followed. Wright was proud of his friend for betraying no hint of the preparatory slander he had filled Buck's head with on the cab ride from the Selwyn to Tony's. Just as Wright and Lucy were facing the inevitability of being forced to make small talk themselves, their attention was diverted to the door, which had opened barely long enough to let in a cold gale and a shapely silhouette backlit by a streetlamp. Every head in Tony's turned to watch the woman slip out of an ankle-length fur and drape it over the doorman's forearm. All eyes on her, Bizzy twisted like a sidewinder through gaps in the crowd, high heels clicking against the parquet until she had wedged herself between Wright and Lucy. The bartender had a Manhattan mixed and waiting on her.

"Goddamn, what a dress," Lucy said.

Wright watched as Bizzy and Lucy traded kisses on the cheek. Lucy took half a step back and lifted both of Bizzy's arms away from her body to look at what she was wearing. Wright and Buck took the opportunity to do the same. She had left her *Spirit of St. Louis* gown in her dressing room at the Selwyn Theater and arrived at Tony's in an ivory silk crepe sheath. It was long and sleek, sleeveless. The angled seamwork and texture of the material looked vaguely Egyptian to Wright's untrained eye. It clung tightly to Bizzy's hips, and from those curves the dress draped in a column straight to the floor.

"Goddamn," Lucy repeated, dropping Bizzy's arms and letting her palms slap against her thighs. Standing next to one another, Bizzy in her ivory gown and Lucy in her crisp tuxedo, Wright thought they resembled a wedding cake topper come to life.

"So, Mr. Moore, Wright tells me you two here have been inseparable since grammar school," Bizzy said.

"Just Buck, please." He took a sip from his coffee cup, grimaced and shuddered, then nodded. "Yes, ma'am. He's my oldest buddy."

"Buck, yes. And what do you do down in

Winston-Salem?"

"Anyone he can," Wright answered. "He'd screw a snake if you held its head."

Buck elbowed his friend in the ribs. "Well, Miss Holt, at the present I'm Mr. Williams' private secretary."

"Just Bizzy, please." She smiled.

Wright said, "He was a doffer at Chatham Mills for eighteen cents an hour before I came to his rescue. That's what happens when you can't graduate from high school."

Another shot to the ribs, this one sharp enough to make Wright groan. "I don't think I've ever seen *your* diploma, Wright? Which is funny, considering your daddy's name is on the school."

Lucy said, "Mr. Moore, are you even old enough to have graduated high school?"

"No, ma'am, not yet. But I've abandoned the pursuit in favor of others."

"How old are you, Buck?" Bizzy asked.

"I'll be eighteen next month, Miss Holt. *Bizzy*."

"And a doffer, you say?"

"Yes, ma'am. You see, in textile manufacturing, there is a…"

Buck's sentence trickled away as he realized Bizzy was listening to the piano and not him. "'April in Paris,'" she said. Wright saw a flickering glance between

Bizzy and Lucy at the mention of the City of Lights. "Vernon Duke composed it on that very upright."

Wright could tell from his friend's blank stare that Buck was no more familiar with the song or its writer than he was.

Mainly to Bizzy, but wanting Wright and Buck to hear, Lucy said, "You know, Burnside gave him head while he wrote it, on her knees under the keys. And the back room," she nodded toward the darkened corridor behind the bar, "is where Mae Dix says her second abortion was conceived."

"I haven't heard this one," Bizzy said.

"New Year's Eve, '28. Half a dozen partiers crammed into the galvanized livestock trough Tony mixes his gin in."

Wright and Buck both took suspicious glances at the alcohol in their cups.

Lucy continued. "Kiki Roberts fucked 'Legs' Diamond right there in the tub in front of everyone."

"Legs is a bootlegger," Bizzy clarified, for Wright's benefit, he knew. "Kiki was a Ziegfeld girl, of course, before she was Legs' moll."

"I thought you said Mae Dix?" Buck asked Lucy.

"I did. Come Valentine's Day and Mae missed her period, she swore up and down it was because she had been in the trough with Legs Diamond's jizz after he schtupped Kiki. Which would have been

99

impossible."

"Why?" Buck asked.

"The alcohol would have sterilized it," Lucy replied matter-of-factly. "But Legs Diamond didn't know that and ended up paying for Mae's procedure. And Tony, being the cheap bastard he is, sure as hell wasn't going to waste a whole tub of gin. For weeks, us regulars brought our own hooch while the newcomers got served the Knock-up Gin, we called it."

Wright watched his friend, knowing Lucy was counting on Buck to react as he himself typically did before he had become accustomed to her sordid anecdotes. He knew Lucy wanted to see Buck blush, laugh nervously, and then awkwardly bow out of the conversation when his attempts to change the subject only backfired. Instead, Buck took a swig from his coffee cup and said to Wright, "You remember Bessie Nifong?"

Wright let out a huff and nodded.

Buck said, "We knew a girl who got pregnant from swimming in the pool at Wright's house. Fourth of July party."

Bizzy and Lucy eyed one another with a mix of suspicion and amusement. Wright gave Buck an almost imperceptible shake of his head. It was either unseen or disregarded.

Buck said, "Hell, Wright paid her to keep her

mouth shut about where it happened."

Bizzy and Lucy both looked to Wright for confirmation.

"Winston-Salem isn't New York City," he offered. "People would have talked."

"She was either lying or stupid," Lucy said. "Or both. You can't get pregnant from swimming."

Buck said, "Tell that to Bessie Nifong."

"Even if there had been semen in the water, it would have had to escape the pool's pump and filter," Lucy countered.

"The pool at Peace Haven is fed by artesian wells," Wright said with pride. "There's no pump." He glanced at Bizzy, hoping to see some sign that she was intrigued by his family's estate. He saw none.

Lucy went on. "Bear in mind that sperm doesn't survive very long outside the body and that chlorine kills it on contact."

"No chlorine," Wright said. "Plants filter the water. Hyacinth. Waterlilies. Mary begged Mother for an indoor—"

Lucy cleared her throat and said, "Even if the water was warm," Bizzy said, "it's only going to live a few minutes outside of the body. Even less if the water isn't heated."

Wright shook his head. "It's not."

Buck nodded. "Hell no, it ain't. That water is

colder than a witch's tit coming out of that spring." He glanced down at his crotch. "Just ask Little Bucky."

Lucy said, "I'll have to take your word for it. But, for the sake of the argument, let's say the sperm miraculously survived in the cold water and were blessed with extraordinarily long life. And that this amazingly hearty dollop of semen just happened to make its way between poor Bessie's legs." Bizzy laughed at that. "At this point, it would still have to get past her bathing suit."

"She wasn't wearing one," Buck added. Wright nodded.

Lucy continued. "Still, the chance of the sperm making it into her... *her*, would have been slim to none."

Wright almost laughed now, too. He watched Buck, who was visibly dejected at the hypothetical failure of Bessie Nifong to have gotten impregnated by the swimming pool.

Lucy almost seemed to take pity on Buck. "Fine. Let's say some of it made it inside. And despite the time passing and the cold water, those anonymous sperm cells were still alive and kicking. And we'll further assume that Bessie was in the fertile period of her cycle. Even then, what are the chances that this droplet successfully navigated her fallopian tubes and fertilized an egg?"

Wright was realizing he had paid very little attention in biology class, which helped explain the absent diploma Buck had pointed out. Finally, Buck said, "So, you're saying it's possible?" Wright could see that Bizzy was uncertain if Buck was joking or not. Lucy chuckled and massaged her temples.

Bizzy stepped to a rack of billiard cues on the wall. "On the subject of pool..." She perused the selection and chose her stick. She used it to point first at Lucy, who waved off the invitation. She aimed the pool stick next at Wright, eyebrows raised. As he took a step forward, Buck took three, accepting the challenge. He swiped the cue from Bizzy's hand and said, "Let's see what you got."

Wright eased back against the bar and stood next to Lucy, wordlessly sharing with her their only connection. Together, they watched as Bizzy and Buck circled the pool table, sizing one another up. Bizzy racked the balls and positioned herself to break them. Buck made sure he was standing behind her as she bent at the waist to line up her shot, elbow sawing back and forth. With a crack, the balls scattered, ricocheting off the rails in all directions.

Bizzy stumbled, teetered on a heel, and spun like a top into Buck's arms, catching herself with an open palm against his chest. She looked down at the toes of her pumps, peeking out from the silk hem of her dress.

"These things are impossible to play in."

Lucy coughed.

Buck steadied Bizzy's wrists as she righted herself. She had sunk the six and turned back to the table to scout her next shot. Wright watched as she slowly orbited the table, ignoring the obvious shot to pick a trickier one that afforded her the opportunity to bend over in front of Buck again. With an ungainly stroke, she banged the three off the rail and sent it careening into the center of the table.

"She did that on purpose," Lucy said under her breath. Wright knew she was right.

Buck lined up his first shot, setting the nine in his sights like a sniper and dispatching it into the corner pocket with ease. "That was some dress in the show," he said as he rounded the table on the hunt for his next shot.

"Did you like it? I do hope it causes a scandal. Do you know the *Portrait of Madame X*?"

Wright could hear Lucy sigh beside him. Buck shook his head.

"It's a painting," Bizzy said. "John Singer Sargent. His model was Virginie Amélie Avegno Gautreau, an American expatriate who remade herself as a Parisienne socialite, notorious for her infidelities. She posed for Sargent in a black satin dress with jeweled straps. One strap had fallen down her shoulder, exposing Madame Gautreau's pale collarbone for all the world to see. Well, the art world, at least."

Bizzy was quiet while Buck set up his next shot. The instant he sank the eleven, she said, "When the painting was unveiled at the Paris Salon in 1884, her dress so offended French sensibilities that it sparked a firestorm of outrage. One critic wrote in *Le Figaro* that if you were to stand before the painting in the Salon, you would hear every curse word in the French language." Bizzy laughed and then muted herself long enough to watch Buck sink the thirteen. "Gautreau's own mother begged Sargent to take the portrait down, but the most he would do was change its title in a tardy attempt to protect Virginie's anonymity. The scandal was such that she eventually retired from French society."

Bizzy stood behind her pool cue, not unlike the pose she struck behind the microphone stand on the Selwyn's stage and looked on as Buck finally missed.

"That's what I want," she said, stepping to the table. "That's what I hope my dress does." Bizzy angled her shoulders toward her next shot but then stood again. "You see, the Paris critics would not have known this, but Madame Gautreau's dress couldn't have fallen down, even if she and Sargent had wanted it to. Her shoulder straps were purely ornamental; the bodice was constructed over a whalebone foundation. That's how we did my gown tonight. We put grosgrain under the bust with darts and three stays." Bizzy was pointing to her ribcage. "One in the center, two on the sides. Then we softened plastic over a gas flame and molded it around the top of the dress. No matter how I moved, that dress wasn't going anywhere."

Wright could see on Buck's face that he had stopped listening a few shots ago. Bizzy saw the same thing and reverted to her previous method of holding the young man's attention. She bent over the pool table and aligned her cue.

"Here, let me show you," Buck said. "You'll never make the shot that way." He moved in behind her, cupping her waist with one hand and squeezing the other over her shoulder, carefully correcting her posture. "Stance is key." He repositioned her, straightening her back. "Roll your shoulders back." Bizzy did as she was told. "Good. Now, don't be afraid of your hips. Stick them out. Spread your legs a little. A little more. There you go. That distributes your body weight evenly." Buck stepped back to appraise her. "Looks good."

"Jesus," Lucy said just loud enough for Wright to hear. "Why the hell did you bring him?"

Bizzy took her shot, firing the four across the felt and into a side pocket.

Wright said, "I can't remember." He slapped a

hundred-dollar bill on the bar, gathered his peacoat, and without a glance back, stepped out into the November night.

He cinched the wool collar around his neck and followed the narrow alleyway, sidestepping overturned trashcans and their attendant rats and fetid effluence. He paused by a fire escape, listened for footsteps behind him and, when he heard none, clamped his hand around the turgid column of his penis. Like trying to throw the switch on a breaker, Wright pushed his erection down, knowing the discomfort would hasten its abatement, mashing it against the inside of his thigh, strangling it.

Once his hardness had subsided enough to be inconspicuous, Wright traversed the remainder of the alley and emerged onto the sidewalk of West 49th Street. Although he was only eight blocks away from the Selwyn Theater, he felt as if he were in a different city altogether. The boisterous herd in their Russian sables and top hats, bathing in the golden incandescent glow of 42nd Street, were not here. In their place, Wright saw only one couple, lingering on the opposing sidewalk, arm in arm just outside the yellow halo of a lone streetlamp. He realized the pair had been en route to Tony's until they spotted a stranger at the mouth of the alley. Now they milled about in the shadows, waiting until the coast was clear.

The Purple Menace and the Tobacco Prince

Wright obliged, walking west toward Sixth Avenue, hands in his pockets. Over his shoulder he could hear the couple, whispering and futilely trying to stifle giggles as they trotted across the street and into the dark slit between buildings. He was halfway to the intersection when he heard steps again behind him, only one set this time, heels clicking against gritty concrete.

"Wright, wait."

He turned to see Bizzy trailing him, wrapped again in her fox fur coat. Wright paused. When she reached him, they watched one another for a few silent seconds. Finally, Bizzy said, "It was for you." She seemed to be waiting for a reply of some understanding, but it did not come. Wright wanted to be indignant but his envy, so intrinsically entwined with his arousal, had evaporated in conjunction with his erection. "Don't tell me you're jealous." Bizzy smiled, waiting for him to return it. When he refused, she slipped her wrist into the crook of his elbow and said, "Come on, let's walk."

They headed south on Sixth, a wide way dotted with creamy lamplight. The iron beams and crisscross trusses of the Sixth Avenue El loomed over the street and sidewalks, which were slightly more populated with pedestrians and motor vehicles than 49th but still mostly empty after midnight. Bizzy's footsteps were a sharp, metronomic report echoing between the stone and

108

glass façades. The skyline of Lower Manhattan loomed in the distance, a jeweled tiara against the velvet-black night. In the midground, straining to reach the waxing crescent moon, rose the black silhouette of the unlit Empire State Building, dominating the skyline even unfinished, its uppermost reaches indicated by the twinkling of dozens of welding torches working around the clock.

"How's the Savoia coming along?" Bizzy asked. "When will it be ready for the trip?"

She knew exactly how Wright's upgrades to the plane were progressing. For months he had kept her apprised of his plans, in great detail, every day when he telephoned. She knew about the short-wave radio, the new receiver, and transmitter, the one-hundred-fifty-gallon tank that would let the plane fly a thousand miles before needing to refuel. He had told her about L.H. "Slick" Carpenter, yet another boyhood friend who had spent afternoons playing with Wright, Walt, Bowman Smith Jr., and other children whose parents had grown prosperous from tobacco. Slick was now a reporter for the *Winston-Salem Journal* and had agreed to ghostwrite the story of a solo flight around the world Wright intended to make in the seaplane next summer. Slick would syndicate it through a national press agency and keep half of whatever he sold the tale for. Bizzy knew that he trusted Slick to make the account of the circumnavigation and its pilot vivid and dashing. Other than Walt, only she knew that Slick would be writing about stops in Cairo, Constantinople, Burma, French Indo-China, and—most intriguing of all to Wright—Hong Kong. And Wright knew that Bizzy did not need to hear all of that again, but he also knew her query was an attempt to resuscitate his spirits, so he told her again anyhow.

There was more to it than just lifting his flagging mood, though, he suspected. He sensed that she saw him differently when he spoke so passionately about what he could, and would, do in an aeroplane. He hoped that when he talked of grand exploits in faraway ports of call and aviation records waiting to be heroically broken, he sounded like a gallant adventurer to her.

Bizzy said, "I can't leave my apartment without a girlfriend on my arm, but you can fly across the ocean by yourself."

"I don't like to open my mouth when there are more than three people at a table. You walk onstage every night and bask in the undivided attention of a thousand watchers. You're braver than me."

"Eye of the beholder, I suppose."

They walked arm in arm, taking turns reading aloud to each other the slogans and quotes on the spotlit billboards lining either side of Sixth Avenue on second stories and atop roofs.

Bizzy was looking at a Red Rock Cola sign, a squinting Babe Ruth brandishing his Louisville Slugger. "'It's the finest cola I ever tasted,'" she said, doing her best impression of the Bambino.

Wright eyed a Camay advertisement featuring a bedroom-eyed Carole Lombard. He affected a lilting, high-pitched voice and cooed, "This secret will help you win romance. For all types of skin...dry...oily...in-between.'"

"Goddamn talkies," Bizzy snarled. She nudged Wright and pointed to a brightly lit Louise Brooks. "'Winx eyelash beautifier. It's waterproof, even while you swim. And when you cry - if cry you must - do not fear, for Winx is tearproof too. Seventy-five cents.'"

Now Wright tried to impersonate the debonair gentleman dancing with Irene Dunne on an Ivory Soap sign but ended up sounding more like a Brooklyn gangster. "'Nothing doin', fellas. She's *my goil* for the evening.'"

Bizzy giggled and looked up at Amelia Earhart in her leather flying helmet and read the text beneath her. "Lucky Strikes were the cigarettes carried on the 'Friendship' when she crossed the Atlantic. Don't rasp your throat with harsh irritants. Reach for a Lucky instead. It's toasted."

"'Toasted,'" Wright scoffed. He scanned the

advertisements for a friendly face. Perched on a parapet like a Wall Street jumper, he saw a familiar grinning man, clutching his lapels, a lit cigarette in his mouth. Proudly, he proclaimed, "'I'd run a city block for a Taxi.'"

"Of course you would," Bizzy said.

Wright made sure to recite the small print. "R.W. Williams Tobacco Company, Winston-Salem, North Carolina." Then he spotted an even more familiar face. "Hey," he smiled up at a twenty-foot-tall Bizzy Holt, coyly watching Sixth Avenue over an alluringly bare shoulder, her painted pout at its most coquettish. Her glossy black waves were the size of Atlantic breakers.

"Oh, lord." She hid her face behind her hands.

Like a radio announcer, Wright began to recite the text on the billboard. "'With a throaty cry of frustration, Bizzy Holt weaves a spell of beauty all-powerful." He cleared his throat and began to imitate her deep, smoky voice. "'The most important charm of all is certainly a beautiful skin. By using Lux Toilet Soap, I can keep my skin delicately smooth and soft as a baby's.'" Bizzy punched him in the arm, hard enough to make him grimace. He chuckled and then returned to his former authoritative voice. "'Bizzy Holt, now starring in *Three's a Crowd*, is one of the countless famous stars who use Lux Toilet Soap. Lux Toilet Soap, ten cents.'"

Now they both laughed, ricocheting off one another's shoulders, stumbling down the sidewalk. When the laughs faded to smiles, she said, "I'm sorry about the pool game. With Buck. I thought you would like it."

Wright watched the sidewalk in front of him. A cold wind swirled dry leaves around his ankles. "I did."

"But at the same time, you didn't." She was right, and Wright opened his mouth to try to explain it, but he did not know how. He wanted to tell her it felt like both poles of a magnet at the same time, simultaneously attracting and repelling, but he could not think of a better word for *repel.* "It's alright, I get it," Bizzy said. "Got a smoke?"

Wright pulled the pack from inside his peacoat and then dug his lighter out of his trouser pocket. He cupped a hand around the flame, shielding it from the wind, and held it to the cigarette's tip. Bizzy's cheeks hollowed as she puffed it to life. Smoke as thick as cotton batting streamed from her mouth as she said, "Thanks. Buck and Lucy are both Lucky Strike men."

"You'd think Buck would smoke Taxis. He does it just to get my goat. Whenever he's at Peace Haven, he takes his Luckies and puts them in a Taxi pack. If my brother knew, he would never let him in the house."

"Well, I like him."

"Everybody likes Buck."

113

The Purple Menace and the Tobacco Prince

"Sometimes I wonder what that's like. Then I remind myself that I don't care."

"Your friends don't like me."

"They don't like anyone, Wright," Bizzy said. "Least of all themselves. But keep picking up tabs and they'll come around."

He smiled. "You're the only person I know other than Buck who tells me the truth."

"Yeah, it's funny, ain't it? All my friends stopped telling me the truth as soon as I started making a little money."

A yellow pair of headlights scintillated in the distance. The oncoming taxicab lit Wright and Bizzy like a spotlight as it grumbled past in a whoosh, bouncing over manhole covers and potholes. A wall of frigid wind hit them and flung open her fox coat, revealing the tight white satin sheath beneath, glowing in the light.

"I left Buck my car in my will," Wright shook his head, laughing at how the words sounded aloud.

"You plan on dying soon?"

"I wrote it in school, the will. And a suicide note. It was a joke, mainly. To get attention, you know."

"No, I don't know." Bizzy seemed ready to chastise him but then realized the hypocrisy of her admonishing him for wanting attention.

Wright went on. "My college girl turned me

down, so I wrote: *Goodbye forever. Give my love to Mary, Nancy, Walt. Goodbye, cruel world.* It was a joke, mainly."

"Mainly."

"Mainly. I left my money to Walt. My good looks I left to Mary. 'She needed it', I said. I left my car to Buck." Wright let out another laugh.

"I don't think it's funny." They walked, staring up at the Empire State Building, a dark obelisk blocking an entire slice of the starry sky now. "What is it you want, Wright?" Bizzy said suddenly. "Do you even know?"

"I want you."

"Yet you're most excited by me when I'm with someone else."

He could only shrug.

"Tell me something," Bizzy said. "Why do you like it?"

"You said you understood."

"I do. I want to see if you do. You'll tell me it's because of your…" Bizzy cleared her throat. "*Occasionality*. But I don't think that's it. At least not all of it."

Wright said nothing.

"I'm the last person to judge, believe me. I'm just curious. Is it some kind of possession thing? Maybe you want to be the guy who takes me home at the end of the night? You want to be the one I choose? But I have to make a choice. Is that it?"

It sounded right, but he did not say so.

"And this passion play would, of course, require incessant restaging and reinterpretation when the high wore off. Or maybe it's a kind of masochism. Dr. Woodworth, my psychology professor at Columbia, told us about it. He said the masochist derives pleasure from being humiliated. He said it can be a form of escape at times of guilt or insecurity. Perhaps you feel some guilt at how easy your life has been."

"You think my life is easy?"

"You don't?"

Wright looked straight ahead and did not answer.

"Or maybe you just want to be the kind of man who could turn a whore into a housewife. But she has to be a whore first. And then she would have to be a wife. And I'm neither of those things, Wright Williams."

He tried his damnedest to decide which of those two things he wanted more, but he could not.

Bizzy took a pull on her cigarette and then let out a little laugh. "It's like wanting your cake and eating it, too, but backwards. You want your cake, but you want someone else to eat it. Maybe you just like feeling jealous. You wouldn't be the first."

Wright laughed at that, too. "It's not jealousy.

Not really. It's this other thing I feel, like a... I don't have a name for it. It's the thing I feel when any normal man would be jealous. It's a funhouse reflection of jealousy. Reversed, inverted. It's an ache, but the kind you like, you know? Like when you can't stop tonguing an empty tooth socket."

"Or scratching poison oak."

"Until the blisters burst and bleed, yes. I was a child the first time I felt it. I liked watching Buck play with my Christmas toys. It wasn't generosity. It was the opposite. I needed validation that what was mine, what I had, others wanted. I knew that when Buck had gone home, the toys would be mine again and Buck would wish they were his. I would let him drive my car. First car he had ever ridden in, let alone operated. I let him drive it just so he would have to watch me drive off in it. I wanted him to know what he was missing."

"But to miss it, he had to have to taste."

"It's terrible, I know."

Bizzy did not tell him otherwise.

They walked without speaking for a block, then she said, "Speaking of missing things, I left an unfinished Manhattan back at Tony's."

Elbows locked together, they turned and began the walk back.

Chapter 5

New York City
Monday, November 10, 1930

Wright marched purposefully across the plush green carpet of the Ambassador Hotel's lobby, weaving through a maze of ferns, ashtray stands, and wingback chairs, a flat package wrapped in brown butcher paper tucked under his arm. Wide, tilted shafts of midday sun beamed through the haze like flying buttresses. An operator in a drummer boy hat and double-breasted uniform that perfectly matched the burgundy crushed velvet upholstery on the lobby furniture smiled at Wright as he approached the bank of elevators. The young man stepped aside and ushered him inside his mahogany-paneled car.

The operator closed the scissor gate. "Floor, sir?"

"You tell me," Wright replied.

"Beg 'pardon, sir?"

119

"Bizzy Holt's floor."

The two regarded each other for a moment before the operator said, "Sir, even if I knew your…"

"Miss Holt." Wright switched his package to his other arm and reached into his trouser pocket.

"Yes, your Miss Holt. Hotel policy prevents me from—"

"Perhaps the 22nd and 24th President of the United States might persuade you to reconsider?" Wright produced a twenty-dollar bill and displayed the green-gray portrait of Grover Cleveland to the elevator operator.

"Ah, Mr. President, welcome to the Ambassador." The operator plucked the twenty from Wright's fingers and shifted the control lever, the elevator ascending with a rumble.

The pair rode in silence until the arrow on the indicator dial above the door crawled past *ten*. The operator eased the elevator to a halt, slid the brass gate aside, and opened the door. With a sweep of his open palm, he gestured Wright into the eleventh-floor corridor.

Wright stepped out of the car but quickly turned back to the operator. "Which room?"

"I'm certain I have no idea which room is yours, sir," the boy began to pull the outer door closed.

"Wait." Wright again reached into his pocket,

once more withdrawing a twenty.

The elevator operator pulled on the door again. "I'm sorry, Mr. President, no vacancies."

"Wait!" He fished in his trouser pocket again, this time pulling out a fifty-dollar bill and offering it to the boy.

The boy took the bill from Wright's hand and examined it. "General Grant, good to see you, sir." He folded the fifty and slipped it into his jacket. Then the operator resumed pulling the elevator door shut.

"Which room?" Wright was practically pleading.

"I have no idea what you're talking about, sir. But wasn't it old Ulysses who signed the law that made Thanksgiving a federal holiday?"

Wright tried futilely to solve the puzzle. "Just tell me, please."

"And I do believe Thanksgiving falls on the 27th this year." With a thud, the elevator door bumped shut, followed by the jangle of the scissor gate closing behind it, and finally, the rumble as the car began its descent.

Wright stood alone in the hallway, adjusted the package under his arm, looked left and then right. He still had no answer for the operator's cryptic clue, assuming it was a clue at all. After a mental coin flip, he began to tentatively walk to his left. The first door he passed bore the numbers *eleven nineteen*. Then came *eleven twenty-one*. Confidently now, Wright strode down the wide corridor, scanning each door. *Eleven twenty-three, eleven twenty-five.* Then, *eleven twenty-seven.*

"Eleven twenty-seven."

Wright stopped and faced the door. He stood there in his jodhpurs and riding boots, the same ones, he realized, he had so proudly worn for the first time to the Maryland Theater nine months ago. Now, though, the leather was careworn and creased by hundreds of hours and thousands of miles behind the Savoia-Marchetti's stick.

He had spent the weekend alone, leaving Buck to his own bucolic devices in the Big Apple. For two days, Wright had roamed Manhattan, avoiding the speakeasy and the Selwyn and anywhere else he might see Bizzy, hoping the time to himself might temper his heart the way the hours in the aeroplane had weathered his boots. He was not ashamed of his unnamed feeling - he relished it too much - but he was embarrassed by how unready he was for it at Tony's. He vowed not to lose the reins again.

Maybe Bizzy would notice, he thought as he stood in the hotel hallway. Maybe she would see his new resolve. Maybe she would see a man and not the petulant, rapacious boy who would demand she stop seeing Lucy and who had sulked and emptily threatened to put the Mauser to his temple when she refused.

Wright stiffened his back, striking a pose that

matched how he felt, and knocked on the door. As he waited, he rehearsed in his head the explanation he would offer room eleven twenty-seven's occupants if the elevator operator had simply been talking about Thanksgiving after all. *I beg your pardon; I was under the impression this was Miss Holt's room. I don't suppose you could point me in the right direction...*

The door swung open. Bizzy was in a thick terrycloth bathrobe, its belt hanging untied at each of her hips, a vertical alley of bare skin visible between the cotton plackets. "Wright?" She sleepily rubbed her eyes with her knuckles. He discreetly checked his wristwatch to make sure it was, in fact, the afternoon. "How'd you..." Bizzy tousled her lopsided frizz and shook her head. "Never mind."

She stepped aside just enough so that Wright could slide past her into the room. The windows would have overlooked sunny East 51st Street if he had his bearings, but the drapes were drawn tight. The room was in a sort of forced gloaming, the only light coming from the open bathroom door.

"For you." Wright held the package out toward Bizzy, smiling.

"Well," she raised an eyebrow and sat on the edge of the bed, situating the gift in her lap and tugging at one end of the twine bow. She folded back the butcher paper wrapping and lifted from inside it an

123

ornate, gilded picture frame. She held it up, examined it for a moment, and then let out a loud laugh that seemed to wake her fully in a way that Wright's unannounced arrival had not.

A hissing that he had not noticed until its absence, stopped. Bizzy watched the open door to the bathroom and within seconds Lucy filled its frame, her naked body dripping water from her elbows onto the carpet as she wrapped a towel into a snug turban around her head. Without acknowledging Wright's presence, Lucy nodded toward the frame in Bizzy's hands. "What's that?"

Still chuckling, Bizzy rotated it and displayed its contents for Lucy. Wright, too, took a moment to admire it again. Over the course of his wandering weekend, he had drifted from one sidewalk newsstand to the next, rifling through issues of *Collier's*, *Harper's*, and *Life* until he found the two pages he was looking for. Back at his own hotel room, wielding his pocketknife with a surgeon's precision, Wright removed the sheets from the magazines, trimmed and reshaped them, and then, with a glue bottle and brush, spliced them together on a piece of pasteboard. From a Taxi cigarette advertisement and one for Lux Soap, he had created an image of a crosshatched and fedora-wearing man, a cigarette clenched in his grinning teeth as he gazed at a sultry, bare-shouldered Bizzy, the mismatched typeface proclaiming *I'd run a city block for - Bizzy Holt.*

Lucy scoffed. "The highlight of your career, I'm sure. Doubtless, you dreamed of this moment since you were a girl."

Bizzy turned the frame to look at it again. "I think it's sweet. Thank you, Wright."

He beamed.

Bizzy said to Lucy, "And what did you want to be as a girl, I wonder, if not adored?"

Another scoff. "Not the wish of a farmer's son, I can tell you that much."

Lucy's barbs had no effect on Wright's smile. "What, then?" he asked her.

She regarded him for the first time since she stepped out of the shower. Her complete nakedness was less of a distraction for him than the sliver of skin Wright could glimpse through Bizzy's parted robe, but he was still vigilant to keep his eyes fixed on hers.

"Magic," Lucy said, "I wanted to be magic." She turned and walked to the dresser, lit a Lucky Strike, and then sat on a tapestried armchair by the window. Wright imagined an upholstered scene of a petticoated Rococo woman swinging in the Gardens of Versailles, being soaked now by the wetness of Lucy's bare derriere.

"The Astounding Léger," Lucy said, punctuating

the name with a flourish of her hand, trailed by cigarette smoke. "It was my fourteenth birthday. The Nixon Theater, Philadelphia. He was standing alone in the beam of a spotlight in the center of the stage, rolling up the sleeves of his tuxedo jacket to show us that nothing was there, but we were all focused on his lovely assistant. Or at least I was." Lucy crossed her lithe legs and puffed on her Lucky. "Léger's top hat sat discarded on the stage just outside the circle of light." Wright could see it clearly in his mind. "Behind him were two gurneys, the kind they use in the hospital, each one outfitted with various restraining devices. Big leather belts and buckles, manacles, locks. Léger's forehead shone with sweat as he went about his work, checking the gurneys, tugging at the belts. His assistant posed patiently, a curvy hip cocked, smiling, waiting for her cue."

Lucy uncrossed her legs and leaned forward, elbows on her knees. "She was blonde. Pink corset, pink knickers, feather bustle with these fabulous silk tassels. I'd never seen anything like her."

Lucy leaned back again and took a long pull from her cigarette. Smoke spilling from her lips with each syllable, she said, "Léger readied himself at center stage, sized up the audience for a moment, then looked up. Above him, suspended from the theater's rafters by metal arms and braids of chain and electrical cables, hung a circular saw blade the size of a dinner table. The spotlight panned up to show it to the crowd and we issued a collective gasp."

Bizzy and Wright were fully entranced now. Lucy stood from the chair and began pacing at the foot of the bed, the beads of water on her skin glinting in the low light. In the voice of the Astounding Léger, she said, "*And now, ladies and gentlemen, for my final trick.* Léger glanced up at the giant saw. Nervous chuckles percolated through the audience before a wave of anticipatory applause washed over us. *Thank you, ladies and gentlemen, but it is not I who deserves your accolades, for this particular magic is not my doing. It is the power of this accursed blade!'* Lucy shot a finger upward in an imitation of Léger. Wright instinctively followed it, finding only the hotel room's ceiling there. "*This hexed blade, a boon from the devils who aid this damned art!* Léger stalked across the stage. *Ladies and gentlemen, the blade above me has taken the arms of twenty-three men and the lives of thirteen. It was only after that thirteenth death—a freak accident that severed a cabinetmaker's spinal cord so cleanly and swiftly that his legs remained standing upright after the blade had divided him in half—only then did his widow divest herself of the saw the mill workers had named… the Devil's Teeth.*" Wright had to actively resist breaking into applause. Bizzy laughed and clapped her hands at Lucy's performance.

"Léger and the blonde exchanged knowing

glances and barely concealed smirks. The audience had fallen deathly silent. Léger began to reposition the gurneys, arranging them parallel to one another lengthwise, side-by-side." Lucy moved about the room, pantomiming the magician's actions. "He finished with the gurneys and looked to his assistant, extending his hand." She held out her own hand. "*If you please.* The blonde walked to Léger and he escorted her, arm in arm, to the gurneys." Lucy crooked her elbow and walked with the imaginary woman across the room. "She climbed onto a gurney and lay down. Léger began latching and locking the bulky shackles to her wrists and ankles. She made a show of testing the restraints as Léger draped a thick leather belt over her waist, cinching it tight and buckling it. Then, Léger himself mounted the other gurney, lying on it with his head at his assistant's feet."

Lucy took the last drag from her cigarette and stabbed the butt into a glass ashtray. "Léger looked up at the saw and then, with a metallic whir, the blade began to slowly spin, gathering speed until the teeth were a blur." She made a buzzing noise in her throat. Bizzy giggled. "He gestured for the saw blade to descend as the blonde began to struggle against the shackles, her eyes widening as she helplessly watched the saw blade lower toward her. Murmurs rippled through the audience. I remember Mother leaning over and whispering something to Father, and he quietly assuring her it was all fake. But I knew better."

Lucy bowed her head and unwrapped her towel turban, tossing it in a wet clump to the floor by the bathroom door. She ran her palms across her strawberry blonde hair, smoothing it to her scalp. Then she said, *"Ladies and gentlemen, please don't be alarmed. I assure you this is completely safe!* The saw blade descended, closer, closer. The blonde seemed to be succumbing to panic, wrestling uselessly against her restraints. The spinning blade dropped within reach and Léger reached up and took hold of a handle on the saw's armature. As the blade lowered still, he began to work it back and forth like a giant pendulum above both his body and his assistant's." With exaggerated movements, Lucy swung a pretend saw back and forth over the bed. *"Perfectly safe!"*

Bizzy had stopped laughing, simply listening now, rapt.

"The blade lowered the last few inches and began to disappear first into the wide leather belt around the blonde's waist and then into Léger's cummerbund. Neither seemed to be in pain but his assistant was overwhelmed with fear. He arced the blade back and forth with a big sawing motion until it finally emerged on the underside of the gurneys. He pulled the blade back through and free, then gestured for it to rise back into the rafters. The blonde was still scared and panting, but clearly relieved to have made it through the ordeal intact."

Wright could hear Bizzy release the breath she had been holding.

Lucy said, "With exaggerated difficulty, Léger began to struggle to sit up, clawing at his assistant's gurney. I rose in my seat to see until Mother shoved me back down. Then, suddenly, the gurneys and their passengers separated, pushed apart by the magician into four halves." Wright heard Bizzy gasp. "On each of the gurney sections lay half a body, legs twitching on lower halves, eyes wide with bewilderment on upper halves. The crowd shrieked in shock, hands flying to gaping mouths." Lucy held her hands up and became the magician again for a moment. *"Please, ladies and gentlemen! Remain calm!* Léger strained to reach the other gurney halves, barely within his grasp, pushing and pulling them, rearranging them, spinning them on their casters like a shell game until they finally came back together. Only now, the assistant's legs were paired with the magician's upper body and vice versa. Léger eyed each gurney, making precise adjustments here and there, making sure the alignments were correct. Then, with a loud clap and a wave of his hands…" Lucy did the same, the sharp report making Bizzy flinch. "…he sprang to his feet. With seasoned panache, he began to unbind his assistant, first undoing the shackles, then the belt. When he was finished, he stepped away and the woman started to tentatively move, sitting up, examining her reconstructed body. Carefully, she dismounted her gurney and stood next to Léger for the audience to see."

Lucy was quiet for a few seconds, remembering, smiling. "The crowd erupted, riotous applause. Even Mother. The assistant stood in her pink corset but now with Léger's tuxedo tails attached and wearing black trousers. The magician was still in his black jacket and bow tie but now had on pink knickers with a feather bustle, showing off the pair of shapely legs he was standing on. They both seemed stunned, exchanging bewildered glances with one another between gazing dumbfounded at their swapped lower bodies. Léger bent and retrieved his top hat, dusted it off, and gently tapped it onto the blonde's head." She chuckled. "We jumped to our feet. Standing ovation. The Astounding Léger beamed with pride. The blonde joined him, smiling widely now, dropping the ruse. They took a bow and the curtain fell."

Lucy returned to the tapestried chair and flopped into it, crossing her legs, and reaching for another Lucky Strike. After she had blown a billowing cloud toward the ceiling, she said, "That's when I knew. That's what I wanted to be. Magic. Mystery. I decided that night. I wanted to be that blonde. And I wanted to be the magician, too. Both of them in one. And I didn't want anyone to know how I had done it. That's what I wanted to be."

Wright and Bizzy watched Lucy for a moment. He realized that Lucy had become exactly what she had set out to be.

She looked at Wright and said, "And you? What did the Tobacco Prince want to be when he grew up?"

Utterly unprepared for Lucy's interest in his own backstory, he stammered. "Well, I suppose the truth is that I wanted to be anything but a prince." His answer sounded woefully inadequate in the wake of Lucy's yarn. She and Bizzy both watched Wright and waited for him to offer something more. He thought for a moment and then said, "My first aeroplane was a Jenny. That's what they call the Curtiss JN biplane. I bought it used from an old barnstormer named Roscoe Turner who had flown to Peace Haven when I was twelve. I begged Uncle Gray for the five thousand dollars Turner was asking. Gray said no, but when my brother Walt said he would loan me the money himself, our uncle gave in."

Wright found an armchair of his own and sat. "The Jenny smoked a little, used too much oil, and rattled like a hardware store in an earthquake. But I loved it. Out on the lawn, I mimicked my older brother, gazing down the plane's knife-edged wings and box of a fuselage with stars in my eyes. Uncle Gray was circling it, tugging on the struts, pushing against the ailerons, crouching to inspect the landing gear. He pulled me aside, away from the plane, out of earshot of Turner, who was waiting patiently for his five grand. Gray, as gently as he could, said to me, 'Son, I know you think this is what you want, but this plane…'" Wright smiled at the memory. "I could see it coming a mile away. Uncle Gray didn't understand; the same way he couldn't understand what was so thrilling about a Hudson Super Six or a Chris-Craft runabout. To him, they were just vehicles. Simple transportation, nothing more. As he tried to talk me out of it, I was staring at the plane. Even in her ragged condition, the Jenny was gorgeous."

Bizzy was resting her chin on her hand. Even Lucy was listening intently. Wright said, "Uncle Gray told me the plane was trouble. I could tell how hard he was trying not to crush my dream. He said we had no idea how much money it would take to get it safe and reliable; Roscoe had barely limped the thing to Winston. They were fair points. But my mind had been made up the moment Mr. Turner couldn't get the Jenny started again and announced right there on the lawn that the plane was for sale and he was throwing in the towel. I spent the next five minutes defending my intention of buying the Jenny with the fervor of a Founding Father espousing life and liberty." Bizzy laughed. "Finally Uncle Gray clapped his big hand over my shoulder and nodded." Wright saw Lucy smile.

"Before Roscoe Turner had departed Peace Haven, Walt was giving me the talk." Wright deepened his voice. *"There's nothing friendly about an aeroplane like this. All the refinement of a baseball bat."* Wright laughed at that. *"A plane like this is built for one thing: going fast.* It wasn't true, of course. And Walt knew it. The Jenny could barely do seventy. But he wanted me to respect it. And I could hear him trying to mask the enthusiasm in his voice. *This is an unforgiving machine, Wright.* I could see a smile creasing his lips. Walt watched the clouds as he talked to me about the thing I had just purchased as if he were warning me against marrying a loose woman he knew would break my heart, a woman he knew was no good, but a woman he knew his little brother was powerless to resist. And he did know. He had answered that same siren song years earlier, been smashed on those same rocks despite Gray's wishes. It had been an Avro 504 for Walt, left over from the Great War. Still had the Foster-mounted Lewis gun on it."

Wright caught the women glancing and shrugging at one another. He went on. *"These things are dangerous, Wright. Take her for granted, just once, and she'll kill you. If you want to just take off and fly, and never have to worry about adjusting your valves or setting the float level in your carburetor, this ain't the aeroplane for you. If you don't want to learn all that stuff, if you're scared of busting your knuckles, then let's go chase down Old Man Turner and get your money back."*

Wright stood and moved to the window, pulling aside the drapery and squinting out at the sunlight. "I assured Walt I was ready. I promised him I could handle it. *It's going to be loud*, he said. *It'll make all your clothes smell like gasoline. You'll sweat to death in the summer and freeze in the winter.* But I couldn't stop smiling. And I'll never forget Walt looking at me with that exact same grin." Bizzy smiled, too.

"We went to work right away. It didn't take us long to get her running again. Running well, though, would be months away. The OX-5 V-8 initially refused to confine its combustion to the internal side. It leaked oil like a sieve and smoked like a freight train. Brand new, that engine put out seventy-five horsepower, but that had been a decade and who knew how many hours of operation ago. On our first few trial runs of the motor, anything that could break, burn, or burst did so with the regularity of the 'Anvil Chorus.'" Bizzy nodded appreciatively at the reference. "On the late nights, we would fire up the woodstove in the workshop, put on a pot of Maxwell House, and play Walt's Carter Family records." Wright noticed the mention of A.P., Sara, and Maybelle Carter did not spark the same recognition

Verdi had.

"Sometimes we worked as a team, ganging up a stubborn rocker arm, Walt with a socket wrench, me with the Channellocks. Other times we worked solo, one of us hunched over a cylinder head, the other doubled up under the dash. For three months, Walt and I practically lived in the workshop. After a couple of weeks, I stopped trying to get my fingernails clean. My denim coveralls slowly turned Havoline black. Miss Pluma—one of our housekeepers—complained constantly about the laundry. Uncle Gray came down to check on us every few days. Never once did he say I told you so. Night after night we worked, a couple of mad scientists in a greasy lab. We replaced the Bosch magneto with a Berling. We scrapped the old Schebler carburetor in favor of a heavy-breathing Duplex Zenith. New valve springs and piston rings. All new wiring and hoses."

"Was there anything left of the original?" Bizzy said with a chuckle. "Was it still the same plane when you two were done?"

"Of course."

"Even if you had completely rebuilt it?" Lucy asked. "With all new parts?"

Wright nodded. "The idea of the aeroplane, its purpose, is unchangeable. Wood and canvas rot. The metal will rust. Glass breaks. And it's all replaced. A plane isn't just wings and a propeller. It's more than that." It made perfect sense to him, just as it had when Walt explained it to him in the shop all those years ago. "And when those barn doors finally opened, and that OX-5 fired up and the windows shook, and Miss Pluma peered through the Venetian blinds, it was the same aeroplane that taxied out. But I was different. These were different:" Wright tapped first at his temple, then pointed at his heart, and finally held up his hands for the women to see. "I was more than just my daddy's money. I was someone who could do something. And that's what I wanted to be."

Wright could not be certain, but he thought he saw a measure of respect in Lucy's expression. After a moment, he and Lucy turned, almost in unison, to Bizzy, wordlessly demanding her origin story next.

She laughed, understanding that it was now her turn. "Alright. My father, Alfred Holtz, and his younger brother, Russell, were the principals of a firm of investment bankers in Cincinnati, trading in bonds and securities. Holtz & Company." Wright eyed Lucy, looking for signs that she had heard this story before, but saw none. "They had seats on the New York and Chicago stock exchanges. Chicago Board of Trade, too. Father was the company's founder and its chief executive. He was proud. We all were."

Bizzy carefully placed her framed Taxi/Lux

advertisement on the nightstand, positioned so they all could see it, and reclined onto the bank of pillows piled against the bed's headrest. "Uncle Russell was the firm's frontman, with his silver tongue and rakish good looks. Father and Russell wanted to become millionaires and, according to family lore, their shared dream was almost within their grasp when I was a child. Soon, though, whispers began to swirl through Cincinnati's financial circles that Holtz & Company were in dire straits. Father vehemently denied the rumors, but within weeks the firm declared bankruptcy. It was the largest failure in Cincinnati's history. Investor losses were almost a million dollars. Father did his best to shield the family from the reality, but I will never forget the sound of his voice, despondent, desperate, confessing to Mother one night that the loose change in his pocket was all we had left in the world."

Now Wright was certain, given Lucy's slack jaw, this was the first time she had heard this tale. Bizzy said, "Russell told Father that he would go to Louisville to raise the funds necessary to keep the firm's doors open. Only days later, officials from the Georgetown Power Company came marching through those very doors in search of a hundred-fifty thousand dollars in bonds that, without my father's knowledge, Russell had borrowed from them. My uncle was never seen again. We heard stories that he had fled to Mexico. Father seemed to believe Russell would have tried Honduras. There were rumors of suicide—never confirmed. It was the talk of the town that summer. Despite my father's innocence, he was vilified and publicly castigated with the same furor his brother was."

Bizzy reached behind her and repositioned the pillows. "I used to daydream about him, my uncle. In my mind he was 'Uncle Honduras' and I saw him as some kind of knight-errant, a heroic outlaw, like Robin Hood. I pictured him happily redistributing his ill-gotten gains to poor villagers in Central America, his plan all along." Bizzy laughed at her childhood naïveté. "The newspapers call us *The Doomed House of Holtz*. Father found the occasional job as an attorney for insurance companies, but it never lasted. He had no choice but to sell our big house in Chestnut Hills and move into my Uncle Thomas's apartment, too small already for his own family. Father saw himself as a Stoic—capital *S*—a devotee of Emerson and Epictetus, and believed that this, too, would pass. And it did, eventually."

Still not comfortable and unable to make the pillows comply, Bizzy bounded from the bed, cinching her robe's belt around her waist. "Mother did not share Father's optimism, however. She was mortified at her new situation. For her, being poor was an abomination. Before the bankruptcy, my mother had been a drinker.

The Purple Menace and the Tobacco Prince

I never saw her drunk, mind you. Never heard her slur a single word. Never once saw her stumble. But every evening, when my father would come home, she would pour herself a drink while preparing dinner. Sherry, I always assumed. And every night, once the dishes were done, she would pour herself another. That changed after the firm's failure. After the collapse, she was drunk more than she was not. Marion and I found ourselves getting our own breakfast a couple of mornings a week. Then most mornings, and then every morning. Some days we wouldn't see Mother until afternoon. When Marion and I would play hide-and-seek in Uncle Thomas's apartment, we would find empty bottles in closets and behind furniture. We didn't know what it meant at the time, but I do now."

Bizzy walked to the window and opened the drapes. Light streamed into the room like a dam bursting, temporarily blinding all three of them and making Lucy recoil from it like a vampire. "Then came January 16, 1919." Bizzy paused a beat to see if either member of her audience understood the significance. When she saw that they did not, she said. "The day the Eighteenth Amendment to the United States Constitution was ratified."

"Prohibition," Wright said.

Bizzy nodded. "I can still recite it. Father, Marion, and I chanted it like a bedtime prayer. 'The manufacture, sale, or transportation of intoxicating liquors within, the importation thereof into, or the exportation thereof from the United States and all the territory subject to the jurisdiction thereof for beverage purposes is hereby prohibited.' Father knew that the actual consumption of alcohol would not be outlawed, but he also knew that once the bottles in the apartment were empty, Mother would have no way to get more. I can still see him turning bottle after bottle up and pouring the clear and brown liquid down the kitchen sink." Bizzy looked out the window, down at 51st Street and the automobiles and pedestrians scurrying about. "I thank God for the Volstead Act."

Bizzy came back to the bed and sat again. "Father and Uncle Thomas vowed to refund every penny that their brother stole. A noble gesture, to be sure, but one that delayed our financial recovery for years. My last name had long since been turned into a slur in Cincinnati, but during the Great War, anyone of German descent had come to be seen as a threat. German language instruction had been banned in school. The playing of Mozart and Beethoven was outlawed. German street names were Americanized. Sauerkraut was called liberty cabbage. German Shepherds became Alsatians. You both remember." Wright and Lucy nodded. "If being a Holtz in Cincinnati was a curse, to be German was to now be a traitor. My father petitioned the court to allow him to anglicize his family name. His request was granted, the offending Z was excised, and at fourteen years old I became Elizabeth Holt."

She reached for the framed magazine collage and looked at herself, the reflection of her face was a ghost floating over her own seductive pout and heavy-lidded gaze staring back. They looked like two completely different people. "I didn't know what I wanted to be when I was girl," Bizzy said. "But I knew I never wanted to be poor again."

Chapter 6

Sands Point, Long Island
Tuesday, June 30, 1931

The *Galaxie* was a hundred and thirty-seven feet long and its diesel engine could propel the steel yacht to a cruising speed of eleven knots. It had been built just last year by Pusey and Jones, the shipbuilders from Wilmington, Delaware who, during the Great War, had delivered fourteen cargo vessels and two *Lapwing*-class minesweepers, the *Elder* and the *Thrush*, to the United States Navy. Since the war, Pusey and Jones had concentrated on building large luxury steam and motor yachts for wealthy patrons. J.R. "Ruly" Conrad had commissioned the *Galaxie* to congratulate himself on his appointment by Irénée Allard to the executive committee and board of directors of Allard Powder & Chemical, the culmination of a career that had begun by getting his foot in the door as a purchasing agent, marrying Irénée's daughter, and then becoming director of Allard's development department, in that exact order.

The Purple Menace and the Tobacco Prince

Upon taking receipt of the *Galaxie*, Ruly Conrad had granted his daughter the use of her, as well as the use of her chief engineer, Bill Blackwelder, to cruise up and down Long Island Sound that summer along with a rotating roster of Broadway intelligentsia.

Wright knew all this because Lucy had spent the last half hour telling him so. Ostensibly she was also telling the half-dozen other guests gathered on the stern deck of the *Galaxie*, but Wright knew this reminder of Lucy's pedigree was aimed his way, despite her loathing of making eye contact with him.

Now Ruly Conrad's boat was anchored a hundred yards off the rock-strewn beach of Sands Point. Lucy had instructed Mr. Blackwelder to stop here so her friends could see the squat, octagonal brownstone lighthouse situated on the peninsula's point. This particular nautical vantagepoint also offered an excellent view of Oyster House, the estate Bizzy had leased for the summer at the behest and, Wright suspected, the financial assistance of Lucy. Wright noted, too, that from this spot in the bay, Oyster House was conveniently blocking from sight the gray cottage he had rented for the season and was sharing with Buck.

Wright moved to the railing, following the migrating shade of the canopy as the yacht lazily yawed around its anchor. The midday sun burned down

144

through a magnifying glass of atmosphere, Wright an ant on a leaf in a puddle. He tugged at the collar of his linen shirt, clammy with sweat and clinging to the nape of his neck. The breeze carried on it the smells of the *Galaxie*'s diesel exhaust, the brackish water of the sound and its mollusks and crustaceans, plus the mess of Atlantic croaker Wright, Buck, and Howard Stahl had caught and Mr. Blackwelder had cleaned, filleted, and breaded with cornmeal and black pepper and was now frying in the galley.

"Let Howard catch a few," Bizzy had whispered to Wright and Buck during the morning's croaker run. Stahl had put together *The Wild Party* and *Three's a Crowd*, and Wright knew Bizzy felt a deep sense of gratitude to the man. Wright did, too. If not for *The Wild Party*, he might be at home with Anne Vogler today instead of on a yacht with Bizzy Holt.

"You know, Howard here came up with the idea for Leo, the MGM lion," Bizzy had said, providing cover for why she had joined the boys and their twitching fishing rods. "Before long he'll move to Hollywood and forget all about us little Broadway people."

Now she joined Wright at the railing, sipping the latest in a long line of Manhattans that could trace their lineage back to breakfast. She was in a red wool Jantzen bathing suit - a belted maillot with a V-back that revealed a vast expanse of skin that still smelled of the orange blossom, narcissus, and vanilla of her tanning oil. Bizzy had discovered the *Huile de Chaldée* in Paris last spring, and this morning Wright had watched her, transfixed, as she massaged the slippery oil into her shoulders. Unable to reach her back, Bizzy had solicited volunteers. Like a pair of duelists, Lucy and Wright faced off, *en garde*, with Wright quicker to the attack. Bizzy had lain face down on the *Galaxie*'s glossy varnished deck and he kneaded the oil by cupped palmfuls into her skin until it glistened. For as long as he thought he could get away with it, he ran his hands over the undulating landscape of Bizzy's body - the rising dunes of her shoulder blades, the riverbed of her spine, the valley at the small of her back, as golden and radiant as the Sahara. Wright imagined his fingertips were a caravan of nomads.

Bizzy elbowed him and pointed toward the shore at a magnificent three-story waterfront house. "John Philip Sousa's shack." She tracked her finger across the horizon until it pointed at another mansion. "Irving Berlin." Her arm swept to yet another sprawling estate. "Foggy lives there." And again. "And that's Bea Lillie's house."

Bizzy saw Wright eyeing the lighthouse. "It's been decommissioned," she said. "They moved it to an automated steel skeleton tower out in the sound." He felt a rueful twinge upon learning why he had yet to see the beacon ignite at dusk. Bizzy explained that William Randolph Hearst had purchased the Sands Point Lighthouse in 1927 and now lived in the keeper's quarters, reserving the adjacent mansion for his mistress and other guests.

Wright's eyes widened. "The *Graf Zeppelin*."

"Beg your pardon?"

"William Randolph Hearst. The *Graf Zeppelin*."

"No, William Randolph Hearst, who owns half the newspapers in the country."

"Hearst sponsored the first round-the-world voyage by an airship. The *Graf Zeppelin*. It was in all his newspapers."

"Touché. Lucy has seen him standing in the lighthouse's lantern room whenever we're out here in the sound, binoculars in hand. Even when we're dressed."

Wright peered at the lighthouse across the water, watching for its would-be keeper.

A different voice said, "I've decided to return the favor."

Wright turned to see Nellie Burnside walking towards him, a snifter of bourbon in her hand. Her slender body was naked, completely and defiantly so, as if she refused to be cowed by the blistering sun. On their two-day drive up from Winston-Salem, Wright had regaled Buck with tales of the celebrated frequency and willingness with which Nellie Burnside was said to discard her clothes. And Nellie had not disappointed. Buck pointed out to Wright after their first weekend aboard the *Galaxie* that Nellie seemed to enjoy being naked even more than Bizzy. Wright had to agree. Except for a sudden summer squall that had drenched the yachters in a cold rain last week and sent her into the cabin to swaddle herself in a fuzzy blanket, Nellie had spent virtually every hour aboard the boat drinking, clowning, and cursing as she prowled the decks without a single article of clothing.

Lucy was descending the steep stairs from the yacht's flybridge. Wright was surprised to see she was no longer shirtless, prompted finally by the reddening of her shoulders and collarbones to retrieve the white knit shirt she had discarded the moment the *Galaxie* had pushed off. She had spent the entire morning as she had every day since Wright and Buck had arrived at Sands Point and, presumably, all summer: stripped naked to the waist in the golden heat, wearing only a pair of snug white duck canvas trousers and tennis shoes.

Lucy was followed down the steps by Eugenia Burnside, Nellie's older sister, her senior by almost exactly one year, and just as naked. They all called her "Sister" and Wright had realized quickly, through a combination of sly asides and his own observations, that everyone except Nellie considered Sister more intelligent, more beautiful, and better company than her younger sibling. Nellie exceeded Sister only in fame and brazenness.

Wright registered suddenly, in a way he had not quite before, that Lucy and Sister's frequent absences from the main deck had coincided all day.

Now Lucy and Sister, along with Bizzy and Nellie, surrounded him, a quartet of women who progressed from half-naked to mostly naked to totally naked. Nellie said, "I purchased a telescope and Lucy has had Mr. Blackwelder mount it on the bridge. Now we all take turns watching whenever Marion Davies comes over for one of her little visits."

"Marion Davies..." Wright said, thinking. Then, "Was she a Ziegfeld Girl?"

Nellie regarded him with admiration. In her baritone, she said, "Now you're learning, *dahling*."

Through the gaps between the women, Wright could see Buck, lounging in a folding canvas deck chair, basking in the sun, an empty glass teetering on his bare chest. The sun was turning the glass into a prism, a kaleidoscope of colors spiking around on his tanned skin. Not unlike the three women, Buck relished any opportunity to exhibit his physique. Wright had playfully chided him about that proclivity since puberty.

The Purple Menace and the Tobacco Prince

Buck's shoulders and arms were still ridged with muscle, his torso still lean and angular despite his final snap on the R.W. Williams High School Demons football team coming a year and a half ago. The women and Fogg had made no effort to mask their admiration. Buck, in return, had stared at the women's bodies, erroneously believing his round-lensed sunglasses prevented them from knowing. Now he was being treated to all their backsides, save for Dorothy Stahl's, lined up in a row. If Wright knew his friend, Buck thought it a smorgasbord for his own benefit.

Dorothy Stahl, unlike Bizzy, Lucy, and Nellie, had not changed into a bathing suit nor stripped to any degree of nudity. Still, in her linen culotte skirt and despite being twice Buck's eighteen years, she, too, had attracted his roaming, indiscriminate gaze, much to Howard's visible consternation. Now she was safely sequestered in the pilot house with her husband, examining the *Galaxie*'s gauges and meters.

Wright, with considerably more subtlety than his friend, took a moment to appreciate the exhibition of beauty before him. Nellie with her incandescent blue eyes and honey-gold waves; Sister and her high, pumice-stone cheekbones; Lucy, with her unblemished milky skin; and, of course, jet-haired Bizzy, with her... everything. Wright blinked and, in the black, saw her stepping onto the stage at the Maryland Theater fifteen months ago, and tried to understand how he had gotten here from there.

Nellie glanced at the lighthouse's lantern room and said, "Mind you, I'm almost ready to throw that telescope overboard. Every time I sneak a peek, all I get is an eyeful of Hearst's hairy ass and tiny pecker."

"My dearest Nell, just because his dick couldn't rub both sides of your cunt at the same time does not mean it is tiny." It was Byron Fogg, emerging from the cabin, his smoking jacket hanging open, clutching Ramona's carved ebony arm to steady himself on the yacht's deck. Ramona had only returned to Sands Point last week after having his employment to Fogg terminated in the wake of a difference of opinion in which Fogg refused to concede Jack Sharkey should have been disqualified for his low blow against Max Schmeling. This was Kimono's week to be fired.

Nellie said, "*Dahling*, if it's not big enough for my snatch, believe me when I say it would find itself irretrievably lost in Marion Davies'."

"They met while she was dancing in the *Follies* at the New Amsterdam Theater," Bizzy explained to Wright. "Hearst sat on the front row every show, eight weeks straight, just to stare at Marion."

"Sound familiar?" Lucy said.

Wright said nothing.

Bizzy ignored Lucy, too, and he realized that he

had not heard the two of them speak directly to one another all day. Bizzy said, "Hearst secretly arranged to have Davies invited to a studio to be photographed in an assortment of costumes. Japanese geisha, virgin bride. While the pictures were being taken, Marion realized Hearst was standing in the shadows of the studio, watching." She paused to watch Wright's reaction. When he exhibited none, she went on. "Scared to death, Marion ran away and locked herself in her dressing room."

"Naturally," Wright said.

"That's three things you and William Randolph Hearst have in common." Lucy counted on her fingers. "Flying around the world, hunting down Broadway girls, and forgetting all about your wives."

"Zeppelins to Ziegfeld," Fogg added. "That's our Wright, the flying circus."

Wright forced himself to laugh.

"Hell, I don't even like cocks," Nellie said suddenly. "What about you girls?"

"Speak for yourself," Fogg intoned.

"Oh, I just *love* those worms," Lucy said, pretending to swoon. "Aren't we all supposed to just adore them?"

Fogg, cinching his smoking jacket, said, "My dear Lady Allard, perhaps therein lies your problem. You've been playing with worms."

Nellie said, "Listen, I don't hate them. I just don't want them bobbing about like they tend to do in my presence. Goddamn divining rods. I think, perhaps, I like the idea of cocks more than the things themselves. Mainly I detest you men's insistence that those things should be sucked upon."

Wright watched Fogg furrow his brow and bow his chest, indignant at the mere suggestion that those things should *not* be sucked upon. Buck sat up in his deck chair, tipping his sunglasses down the bridge of his nose to observe the impending debate. Wright himself wanted to shrink into a mote and be carried away on the Long Island Sound wind.

Cello-voiced Nellie said, "And you devils can always make me want to. With your pleading and your praying, and your invariably broken promises of reciprocation. Damn it all, I'll want to. I'll want to get drunk off it. All the way up until the exact moment I do it. Then I'll want nothing to do with it." She laughed that deep gurgle of a laugh of hers.

Next Nellie said, "I once watched Louise Brooks service Harry Wagoner." Then, to Wright, she clarified, "Production chief at Paramount Pictures. Right there in his office on Melrose. I figured she was doing it just to get him ready, you know? The short before the feature. But after a few minutes, it became obvious that this *was* the feature. I'll never forget it. The hem of that

153

bob haircut of hers swinging back and forth between her nose and earlobes. *Dahling*, she made it look like art."

Nellie paused, maybe to make sure she was remembering it correctly. Or simply just to remember. "She gave him the best blowjob of his life, I know it. Louise Brooks made herself the center of Harry Wagoner's universe, if only for those five minutes."

Rapt, Nellie's impromptu audience leaned closer. "When I understood that she intended to see it through to the bitter end, so to speak, I felt a very strange mixture of titillation and dread. The idea of it repulsed me, but at the same time thrilled me."

Buck was out of his deck chair now, joining the semicircle of listeners.

"I can still see the look on her face. I never saw a drop of it, though. Down the hatch. And if she hadn't genuinely wanted to, she did a goddamned good job of pretending she did." Nellie looked down at the last of her bourbon and finished it off with a gulp. "I was envious. Not because it was her and not me. I was glad it wasn't me, darling, believe me. But I wanted to be like her. I wanted to be that dirty. And not just to be that dirty, but to like being that dirty. I knew it was impossible, though. I knew, just as Harry did, that Louise was acting. She didn't do it because she liked it. She did it to get a contract with Paramount." Nellie stared down at the empty snifter. "But that didn't stop me from getting excited by it."

Everyone listened for a moment to the slapping of waves against the *Galaxie*'s hull and the distant harbor buoy bell. And then Bizzy said, "Tell me, men, what is the appeal? It doesn't feel better, does it, when we swallow? Men?" She looked at Wright, Fogg, even Ramona, in turn.

"It's a show." Buck, with a scholarly clearing of his throat that almost made Wright laugh, said, "The silk stockings, the high heels - all of it. We don't get off on the actual shoes. We get off on you wearing the shoes." Wright would have laughed at the hyperbole, but he had heard this before. Buck continued with the fervor of a stumping politician. "An awful lot of what y'all do in the bedroom, or in the backseat -"

"Or on a yacht," Bizzy said.

Buck nodded at her. "Or on a yacht, is a show."

"Each another's audience," Nellie added.

"I always say, a good blowjob is ten percent technique, ninety percent enthusiasm," Fogg proclaimed. "You wouldn't spit out the champagne after a toast. The insult would be staggering."

Wright was watching Bizzy. Like the tumblers of a lock clicking into place, he could see it suddenly making sense to her. "Or the wafer after communion." She laughed a little and added, "Says the Jewess."

The Purple Menace and the Tobacco Prince

"Now, I ain't stupid, Miss Holt," Buck said. "I know that neither Miss Brooks nor Mr. Wagoner got any real pleasure from the way she... *uh...*"

"Closed her performance," Nellie helped.

Buck nodded. "But that's beside the point. The best thing about a girl swallowing your load is the fact that a girl swallowed your load."

There was an assortment of coughs and laughs at the abrupt turn away from euphemism and innuendo toward the blunt. Fogg said, "My boy, you are a fellatio savant."

The others seemed as surprised as Fogg at the astuteness of Buck's philosophy. Wright, though, was not. Despite Buck clearly having never heard the word 'fellatio' before that moment, Wright knew if there was anything his friend could elucidate, it was sex. The *only* thing, perhaps. For the duration of their friendship, Wright would hold forth on aviation, automobiles, industry, and Buck would simply listen and nod. When the subject turned carnal, however, the roles were reversed.

Suddenly Mr. Blackwelder emerged from below deck, balancing a large tray piled high with golden fried croaker. Howard and Dorothy rejoined the group, Lucy retrieved a stack of plates from the galley, everyone but Nellie got dressed, and they all sat cross-legged on the shaded deck and ate lunch. Wright could not help but notice that Bizzy and Lucy did not sit together.

*****

The western sky over Manhasset Bay had become a watercolor smear of pink and mauve. The sun was dropping behind the trees on the far shore, casting mottled shadows and orange patches of light across the *Galaxie*. Along the beachline, lights in mansions had been blinking on for half an hour until they made a pair of shimmering diamond necklaces around the rim of the bay, one above the water's edge, another reflected below it.

Wright stood at the bow alone, listening to a symphony of overlapping sounds drifting on the balmy evening breeze: Lucy's portable phonograph back on the stern deck, playing 78s by Gus Arnheim's Cocoanut Grove Orchestra, Duke Ellington and His Cotton Club Orchestra, and the Mills Brothers; burbling laughter from above on the flybridge; the faltering rhythm of bare feet padding drunkenly up the promenade deck.

Bizzy appeared, stepping into a spear of light streaming from a porthole in the yacht's dining room. She was still in her Jantzen maillot, her hair sculpted into a black chrysanthemum by the salty harbor wind. Wright watched her as she made her way toward him, slowly, planning each step, making sure he got an eyeful. Shamelessly he gazed. Bizzy flashed a flattered smile, and Wright could not help but return it.

She sauntered in a lazy circle, hips rocking back and forth, faltering every few steps to preserve her balance on the swaying deck. The last glow of dusk lit her skin, framed by the red bathing suit. Wright wanted to go to her, get his hands on her somewhere, but before he found the courage, she was weaving toward him. When she arrived, she folded her arms around his neck and pulled his mouth to hers, kissing him deeply. The taste of it was whiskey and vermouth, her lips warm and sweet, dispatching opioids through Wright's bloodstream. He was euphoric, his pulse a kettledrum in his ears. He prayed for that blood to pump elsewhere.

Bizzy unbuttoned his linen shirt and opened it, fingertips dancing across his chest. She nibbled at his jawline, lowering her head to kiss his throat, peeling away his shirt to kiss his shoulders. Wright's breath was fleeing him in bursts. Bizzy's tongue flitted across his nipple and he tensed, a groan slipping awkwardly from him. He could feel her lips smiling against his skin. His fingers tangled in her black hair and he drew her face back to his. She was pushing her tongue into his mouth before their lips met. And then she pulled back, stepping away to allow Wright to look at her again. She turned her back to him, watching him over her shoulder as she walked to the railing.

Wright stepped to her and, with trembling hands, gathered her wool shoulder straps between his thumbs and forefingers, pulling them aside and down to her elbows. He eased the suit down, making it bunch and roll down her back until the channel between her buttocks came into view.

"Keep going."

The tight suit squeezed at Bizzy's hips and she wiggled as Wright inched the bunched hoop of wool over them. Her ass slowly came into view like the buck moon that was rising over the sound. Her cheeks looked like Neapolitan ice cream, Wright thought. Vanilla white where her bathing suit had covered, the brown of her tanned legs, and the fresh strawberry pink of the sunburn on her hips.

Wright's eyes traced her body's lines, starting high above her violin hips and following the contours of the indented hollows beneath her hip bones, over the swells of her buttocks, and down the crevasse between. The shape of her languid curves all seemed to funnel his line of sight like floodwater down to that delta.

Bizzy smiled over her shoulder at him. With the heels of her palms, she pushed the bathing suit down until it fell and pooled around her ankles. She stepped out of it, teetering precariously on one foot before righting herself. Blinking and lightheaded with desire, Wright simply stared. When he realized that Bizzy was watching him, he saw that her smile was gone, replaced by something intense and needful.

She said, "Are you just going to look at it?"

When Wright made no move, Bizzy spun to him, again almost capsizing before clinging to his forearms. Her hands fumbled between his legs. With a huff, she let the air out of her lungs, discovering that Wright's cock had not deemed her nakedness and her drunkenness, and her willingness an occasion worth rising to.

"I'm sorry." He gave his unresponsive penis a punitive swat.

"Don't say that."

Wright's shoulders slumped. Bizzy tilted his chin up until he was looking into her eyes. Holding his face in both hands, she kissed his forehead and smiled.

Together they walked to a wicker settee beneath one of the dining room's portholes. They sat and listened to the bay lap at the steel hull. And then Wright said, "Marry me, Bizzy."

He watched her eyes flutter shut. "I thought we had reached an understanding."

"We used to chase lightning bugs when I was boy, Walt and Buck and me, just like you and your sister did in the mountains. We would run after them,

160

laughing, reaching for them under the pecan trees and the muscadine vines. We'd catch them and then watch them crawl up to our fingertips and fly away." Wright looked at his hands and then up at Bizzy. "These nights with you - Paris, New York, here - these nights have been like lightning bugs, lit up for just a second and then gone, flashing again just out of reach." He took her hand. "I promise I won't put you in a jar."

Bizzy stared at Wright for a second and then laughed, loud and percussive, echoing across the water. "You're certifiable." She took her hand away from his and patted his wrist. "What's your favorite thing in the whole world, Wright Williams?" Before he could open his mouth to say *you*, Bizzy said, "And don't you dare say me." Not giving him a chance to reply, she said, "Mine is being looked at. It's why I've ever done anything. Anything I've ever worn. Anything I've ever taken off. Every song I've sang. Every dance I've done. It's all been to get looked at."

Bizzy absentmindedly reached for a pack of cigarettes that would not have been in her pocketless bathing suit even if she still had it on. Wright tugged his shirt back into place and pulled a pack of Taxis from his chest pocket. He watched the flame's reflection dance in her eyes as he lit a cigarette for her.

"The first time I stepped on stage," she said, white smoke jetting from her nostrils, "the first real stage, with a real audience, was at the University of Cincinnati. We were doing a musical comedy called *Wet Paint*. I was playing 'the aesthetic flapper.'" She laughed at the memory. "During the curtain call, I didn't know what to do. My castmates on either side of me were bowing. I had never taken a bow in my entire life. I hedged my bets by barely doing it all, figuring I'd rather look disinterested than an overzealous freshman obsessed with the minutia of it all: Was I bowing deeply enough? Staying down long enough? Like the stupid nineteen-year-old I was, I cared.

"At Hughes High, I had joined the Quills, our women's drama group. I sang in the girls' glee club. But I never seemed to feel the need for the applause like the others did. It felt indulgent. But after that opening night of *Wet Paint*, I learned there was something tangible about need. It feels good to need."

Wright wondered if Bizzy was talking about herself or him.

"On the second night, the aesthetic flapper was ready to take her bow. She took it again and again. I must have looked like one of those drinking birds you can win at Coney Island. I didn't care. I just wanted to hear the applause. I didn't care that I was sharing it. Some of it was mine. I felt high. I haven't been able to get it again, no matter how much of a show I put on."

Wright thought maybe that was his cue to

retrieve Bizzy's bathing suit from the deck, but he could not be certain, so he stayed put.

She took a drag and said, "I think I've become one the dope fiends I used to sneer at in the alley behind the Selwyn. We'd see them, crawling back to where they scored their last hit, promising themselves there wouldn't be a next, but knowing damn well there would be."

"Let me watch you," Wright said suddenly, casually, hoping it would sound like the thought had just then come to him.

Bizzy laughed. "Watch me do what, Wright?"

He could not bring himself to say it. Instead, he said, "Perform."

"A duet, I presume?"

Wright nodded.

"With *whom*?" She elongated the last word, letting it buzz and fade just as she did the final syllable of a song lyric.

"You know."

Wright could see Bizzy trying to read his face, trying to determine if he was being serious. She said, "You know, if you were smart, you would just forget this. These things never end well, you know that. Fantasies never translate to the real world. Expectations don't get met. Or worse, expectations get exceeded and someone likes it too much. Then someone gets jealous.

Feelings get hurt. Bad things. Believe me."

Wright knew she was right. But it did not matter.

"Let's say I do it," Bizzy went on. "Let's say young Mr. Moore wants to."

"He'll want to."

"And we go through with it. What if you regret it? What if I regret it? What if tomorrow I hate myself for doing it? What if I hate *you* for wanting me to?"

Wright had thought of all those possibilities and then some.

"Or," Bizzy said. "What if I love it? What if all of us love it, all three of us? What then? Itch scratched? People behave in strange ways when they get what they've wished for, Wright. What if it's the highest any of us will ever get? What if you knew, right now, that would be the case? Would you still do it? Knowing full well it would be all downhill from here?" Bizzy let what she was saying sink in. "Or is better that it's a fantasy?" she said. "Could it be that the wish is sweeter than the granting?"

It was a good point. They were all good points, Wright knew. "I don't care."

Bizzy watched him for a moment. "You're drunk."

"No, you're drunk."

She laughed a little and then said, "Oh, yes. That's right." Now Bizzy laughed in earnest, falling against Wright's arm until finally it subsided. Once she had caught her breath, they sat without speaking for a while. Then she said, "Why in the world do you love being married so much?"

"I hate being married right now."

"Yet you cannot wait to do it again. That's R. Wright Williams in a nutshell, isn't it? He loves what he hates and hates what he loves." Bizzy was laughing again. "But I know what you want."

"Good, because I sure as hell don't."

"What if I say yes?"

Wright eyed her carefully, hopefully.

Seeing the wish in his eyes, Bizzy hastily clarified. "Not that, Wright. I'm not getting married. I'm talking about the other thing you want me to do." He stared at her. "What if I say yes?"

"I would say alright."

"Alright. But it has to be by my rules."

"Alright."

"This is my show. But you get to be in the audience."

Wright was nodding in agreement.

"Three rules," Bizzy said. She extended her index finger. "Number One: No fucking." She watched him, perhaps expecting to see a cloud of disappointment darken his eyes. When she did not, she said, "I save that for when I'm in love."

Wright nodded.

"Rule Number Two: You have to watch."

"I will."

Bizzy stood; the latticework of the wicker settee imprinted on the cheeks of her ass. She inhaled the last of her Taxi and flicked the lipstick-rimmed butt into the Long Island Sound. "And Rule Number Three: Don't ever ask me to do it again."

Before Wright could make any addendums or amendments, Bizzy began to walk away. "Wait in the dining room. Turn off the light."

"What about Lucy?"

"What about her?"

It was the answer Wright was hoping for. He watched Bizzy's naked body as it passed alternately through the yellow beams of light from the dining room's portholes and the inky blue shadows in between, disappearing finally into the darkness down the promenade. After a minute, he could hear the voices on the stern deck raise in boisterous salutation as they welcomed her back to their end of the yacht. He did not hear Lucy.

Wright stepped to the doorway of the brightly lit dining room, surveying it quickly before switching off the light. Scanning the deck in both directions, making sure he was unnoticed, he ducked inside. He carefully moved past the long dining table to the head of the room. In the darkness he could barely see the place settings Mr. Blackwelder had meticulously arranged before Lucy informed him that she and her guests would be dining on the stern deck. Wright positioned himself near a porthole and looked out at the moonlit foredeck through the glass, empty save for Bizzy's discarded bathing suit. The risk he was taking suddenly sank in. He could be discovered at any moment, by anyone. Mr. Blackwelder could return to put away the tableware and utensils, Fogg and Ramona might enter in search of some privacy, Howard and Dorothy Stahl might seek refuge, a sanctuary away from the giggling and gossip. Wright banished his fears of discovery, planning to plead ignorance of the *Galaxie*'s layout and an inebriated loss of his bearings if need be. He held still and watched and waited.

As he had in Florida last Easter, when he sat in the floating Savoia-Marchetti, Wright began to suspect that Bizzy had grown weary of his company and had easily eluded him with a promise she never intended to keep. To allay those fears, he envisioned the scenario playing out on the stern deck at that very moment. In his mind he saw Buck, shirtless still, wearing only his snug wool trunks, standing at the railing. Wright saw nude Bizzy approaching, sashaying, sidling up to him, a hand on his bare shoulder, whispering an invitation directly into his ear. He imagined Lucy eyeing the exchange suspiciously and contemptuously. Nellie would be watching, too, with a blend of admiration and envy. Wright pictured Fogg, smirking slyly, pleased that Bizzy had selected Buck over his unctuous friend. He saw Howard and Dorothy exchanging awkward glances, regretting they had ever accepted Lucy's invitation.

Wright heard footsteps, two sets of them. He shrank into the shadows, motionless. The first porthole went black, the pale blue glow of the night outside occluded for an instant as two figures walked past. The next porthole was darkened by the silhouettes, then the next. Wright watched out his window as Bizzy led Buck onto the foredeck, glancing over her shoulder at the darkened dining room. With Buck in tow, she moved to the center of the deck. She spun on the balls of her bare feet and let Buck take her in his arms. Wright could see Bizzy's lips moving but could not hear her voice through the glass. Whatever she had said made Buck laugh, genuinely, the sound of it barely audible in Wright's hiding place.

Bizzy and Buck swayed with one another, not quite dancing but not simply counteracting the gentle rise and fall of the deck. She held onto Buck's shoulders, testing their firmness before letting her fingers follow the ridges of his biceps. He was already breathing heavily, Wright could see. Then Wright realized that he was breathing heavier still. His heart was a boxer's speed bag being worked over. He let out a little laugh as he pictured himself and Buck both keeling over from the excitement. Wright imagined that Fogg would be the best candidate to concoct a cover story for the ambulance that would arrive at the marina shortly after the *Galaxie*. He could almost hear Fogg's immaculate diction, explaining to the medics that, yes, that's correct, both of these young men seem to have gone into simultaneous cardiac arrest stemming from acute cases of *mal de mer*.

Wright shook the thought from his head and refocused on what was happening on the foredeck. Bizzy glanced at the black window he lurked behind. He could see in her eyes the same giddy frisson he was feeling. She laced her fingers through Buck's hair and then slid her hands onto the back of his neck, over his shoulders and down onto the expanse of his bare chest, palms pressed flat against his skin. Wright felt a familiar pang. But it was not jealousy, he told himself.

He could see them talking to one another, smiling, giggling, and he wished he could hear them. Buck moved his hands to Bizzy's waist and then let them glide down onto the rolling curves of her hips. She did not resist when she leaned in to kiss her mouth.

And here, Wright admitted to himself, he began to have a problem. Yes, he wanted this to happen. He had asked for it, both explicitly and indirectly. He wanted to watch it all. But what he was watching was not what he had expected. He had envisioned locking limbs and pinned wrists, saliva, and gnashed teeth. Gasps, clenched fists, and gurgled moans. But Bizzy and Buck were being patient, deliberate. Intimate. And it felt more transgressive to Wright than anything Bizzy's rules had forbidden. But if he felt an impulse to stop it, it passed as quickly as it came. He did not, he told himself, set the terms for this encounter. He did not say to Bizzy, do this, but do not do it personally. That the show was surprising him was to be celebrated, he convinced himself.

He peered through the porthole as her hands roamed over Buck's ridged abdomen, her fingers drifting lower until they could toy with the waistband of his bathing suit. With measured, confident movements, Bizzy loosened the belt. Wright could see her eyeing the conspicuous fist-like bulge straining against Buck's trunks. He smiled down at her, expecting her to be impressed. If she was, she did not show it. Not yet.

Bizzy glanced quickly at the dining room's porthole, as if giving Wright one final opportunity to call this off. It was obvious she was prepared to make this happen. He was almost nauseous with a frothy blend of fear and thrill. He had a last, panicked thought for his relationship with Bizzy, such as it was, but whatever worry he had, it stood no chance against his tortured need to see this happen.

Bizzy looked back at Buck, her lips curling in a grin as she lowered herself to her knees. She leaned forward and mouthed the shape of his member through the tight wool of his trunks. Even from his removed vantage point, Wright could discern Buck's penis, lengthening and stiffening, responding to Bizzy's attentions. She seemed to almost flush with pride at being the cause of it.

She reached for the waistband and folded it down over Buck's erection, freeing it to spring forward, bobbing until it was aimed directly at Bizzy's face. It was obscenely large, almost disproportionate to Buck's lean frame, and looked painfully hard. From their earliest days of prepubescent comparisons, his penis had always been larger than Wright's. Now, as young men, the difference was even more pronounced.

The *Galaxie* pitched and rocked Buck half a step forward, the tip of his erection brushing against Bizzy's chin. She opened her mouth and allowed it to move inside, stretching her lips around it and working them down until they were sealed halfway to the base. Buck inhaled deeply, his chest rising as he tangled his fingers in Bizzy's black waves. Her eyes suddenly seemed to lock with Wright's, but he knew he was unseen. Her excitement was plain to see. She was excited to be doing this. She was excited that he was watching.

At this point he finally confessed the lie he had told himself. He was jealous. He was so goddamned jealous. And he recalled perfectly what it had felt like in the dressing room of the Maryland Theater when Bizzy was so unattainable and there was a jungle of orchids from admirers and a queue of them two dozen deep in the hallway, and he wanted nothing more in the world than the nerve to make her his. That was what this felt like. Because at that exact moment, she was Buck's.

Like a buoy bell that was ringing in a dream before surfacing in reality as an alarm clock, Wright slowly became aware of his erection, pushing almost painfully against his swimming trunks. With a quick glance about the dining room to verify his solitude, Wright unbuckled his slender belt, withdrew his cock, and began to masturbate.

Everything seemed suddenly amplified, the moonlight brighter, the shadows deeper. Wright stared at Bizzy and Buck, memorizing them, cataloging everything about them in his mind, making sure he would not forget a single detail of this. Bizzy swept her hair away from her face, making sure Wright's view was unobstructed. She pulled back, smiling up at Buck as she playfully dragged her incisors over the ridge of his head. Buck's eyes were squeezed shut, his chest heaving. He reached for Bizzy's hand and held it tightly, that gentle act somehow more objectionable to Wright than what she was doing. Wright could see Buck saying something to her, and Bizzy nodding her head in response.

The entire yacht shuddered as the twin Gardner diesels Lucy had boasted about earlier grumbled to life in the engine room beneath the stern deck. In the pilothouse, Mr. Blackwelder was throttling up the big motors, feeding them fuel and dispatching tremors throughout the *Galaxie*'s teak superstructure. With a lurch, the boat moved forward, sending Wright fumbling to balance himself against the dining table. When he staggered back to the porthole, he saw Bizzy and Buck in the process of righting themselves, repositioning feet and knees as they clumsily regained their equilibrium. She chased Buck's erection with her open mouth, catching it and closing her lips around it again.

Buck tangled his fingers in her hair, raven tufts of it sprouting between his knuckles. Wright could see his mouth moving, saying something inaudible to Bizzy. Her eyes flashed at the porthole for just a moment. Wright stared helplessly, clamping his fist around his own shaft and pumping himself as he watched. She worked her mouth over Buck's erection until she realized he was driving at his own rhythm and all she needed to do was hold still as he thrust through her lips. Wright could see the imprint of the crown of Buck's cock against the inside of Bizzy's cheek, stretching and distorting it as it passed back and forth underneath.

As if he had been stabbed, Buck's body froze. His back arched and he grasped for Bizzy's shoulders, squeezing so tightly he left marks on her. His abdomen clenched and spasmed. She snapped back, startled at the force of his orgasm, recoiling from it as if it had scalded her tongue. Buck's body convulsed, twitching like a silent movie death scene until his climax finally faded into a series of trembling aftershocks.

In the darkened dining room, Wright's own rhythm faltered. The muscles in his calves bunched into knots. With just enough presence of mind to know that staining Ruly Conrad's Persian rug would be uncouth, Wright reached for a linen napkin from the dining table. Mr. Blackwelder's thoughtfully arranged silverware clattered to the floor as Wright sheathed his penis in the cloth. With a heave, he came, helplessly pulsing into the napkin, his erection dissolving into fever-hot liquid. Behind clenched eyelids, he saw aurorae and flames.

Finally, mercifully, it subsided. The foredeck slowly swam back into focus for Wright, his breath fogging the porthole as he panted. Before returning the napkin to the table, he unfolded it and looked inside. It was the first time he had seen his own semen in two years.

Through the porthole, he saw Bizzy rising to her feet. Like an actress on stage who had been front-lit during a monologue and was now lit obliquely, her face now looked subtly but undeniably different to Wright.

He slumped into a chair, his arms hanging heavily at his sides. His body felt twice as heavy as normal, like lying in the bathtub after the water had drained. Wright felt suddenly ashamed and confused at how easily this had all happened, frightened at how easily Bizzy had agreed. He wondered if she was feeling it as well.

Through the frame of the chair, Wright could feel the vibrations of plodding footfalls outside of the dining room. He could see Buck's shape pass by each porthole as he stumbled, dazed with dopamine-soaked satisfaction, back down the promenade toward the back of the boat. He had the stunned and exuberant look of a cripple who had been miraculously cured by a tent-revival preacher.

Bizzy's silhouette seemed to materialize in the dining room's doorway like a Marian apparition. She slipped silently into the room. In the shadows, Wright could see her chest rising and falling as she caught her breath. The full moon made the room's windows radiate like cathode-ray tubes, the blue nightglow

175

gleaming on Bizzy's sweaty skin.

She moved closer, watching Wright, eyes narrowing to white slits as she smiled at him. She stepped into a moonbeam, a spotlight on her face. Her mascara had streamed in tributaries of black tears down her cheeks, her lipstick a crimson smear. Wright thought she looked like some kind of lurid expressionist painting, like an obscene Edvard Munch.

Bizzy's eyes flitted between the undone belt of Wright's trunks and the wadded napkin on the table. When she understood what had happened in here, she smiled at him, slumped in his chair like a beaten prizefighter in his corner.

When one of them finally spoke, it was Bizzy. "May I assume from the state you're in that you liked it?"

Despite there being only two possible answers to her question, Wright could not decide between them.

Bizzy said, "Let me guess. You loved it, but…" She waited for him to finish the sentence. Finally, she did it for him. "But you also hated it."

She loomed over Wright and reached into his shirt pocket for a cigarette, only to discover she had smoked his last one before going to fetch Buck. He breathed in the aroma of Bizzy's Huile de Chaldée, her sweat, the rye whiskey on her breath, cut through now with the bleachy scent of Buck's semen.

"I liked that he told me how I was doing," Bizzy said. "A real review. It was like I was sucking Sime Silverman's cock and he was writing his piece for *Variety* at the same time. Most men are hopeless in that regard. They're so happy just to be getting blown, they don't pay any attention to the performance." She started again to reach for a cigarette and then remembered they were gone. "Buck paid attention."

Wright had paid attention, too, and wanted to tell Bizzy so, but knew it would sound like an afterthought.

She asked, "Is he seeing anyone?" Wright began to suspect Bizzy was trying to impart a lesson about being careful what you wish for. She chuckled. "I just remembered the cross-stitched thing that hung in Mother's kitchen. It said, 'If you love something, set it free.'"

And then, Wright broke Rule Number Three.

Chapter 7

Sands Point, Long Island
Wednesday, July 1, 1931

The mid-afternoon sun glinted off the Romanesque fountains and hand-carved Rosso di Verona marble basins as Wright strolled with Bizzy through Oyster House's gardens. Despite the sweltering heat, he thought it felt like the day after Christmas. He could not quite believe it had come and gone already. He had dreamed and wished and anticipated for so long. And now it was over, and Wright was instantly nostalgic about it. Just like Christmas.

When Bizzy finally answered the door, everything about her looked the same as it had when he carefully deposited her in this spot last night. She was still in her red Jantzen bathing suit, her hair a jet-black bramble. Bloodshot eyes peered out at Wright from the centers of dark hurricanes of blurred mascara.

179

The Purple Menace and the Tobacco Prince

They looked at one another with what he thought was a mix of disbelief and curiosity. Wright knew he had been quite drunk last night but not enough, he believed, to alter his recollection of the evening's events. Nonetheless, he had begun to question the veracity of his memories as he drove the yellow Rolls Royce to Oyster House. Maybe it had been a dream. Maybe Ruly Conrad's maritime liquor stash was stronger than Wright was accustomed to and his fantasy had manifested itself as a lucid and particularly vivid dream.

But he could still smell Buck on Bizzy's breath. And he could barely make out bruises, phantom outlines of Buck's fingers on her shoulders, faint purple handprints.

As they walked through the gardens, they listened to the babbling arcs of water spouting from the pursed lips of stone cherubs until Bizzy said, "I suppose if we don't regret it by now, we won't ever." Wright did not reply. Then she announced, perfunctorily, that she decided to regard the previous evening as something she could look back on when she was too old to care about such things and be proud that she was once young and adventuresome.

Wright looked at her. Bizzy's face was suddenly alight with the thrill of what she had done. "It was theater," she said with a flourish of her hand. "I was on the stage, in the moment with another player, performing for an audience." She glanced at that audience now. When she realized Wright had said nothing since beginning their walk, the light in her eyes dimmed. "What's the matter?"

He would only shake his head.

"Don't say you're jealous, Wright Williams. Don't you dare." The look on Bizzy's face had morphed from thrill to anger and then to something else, something harder for him to read. It was not quite pity, but something akin to it, he thought. "You wanted this."

"I know."

They stopped walking to turn and face one another. "Do you wish I hadn't done it?"

"Do you love him?"

"What? God, no, Wright." She almost laughed at the idea. "No."

"Do you think about him?"

"It was just last night. What do you want me to say? Of course, I think about him. Do you think about Anne?"

"We're not talking about Anne and me. We're talking about you and Buck."

"There is no 'me and Buck.' This was your idea."

"It was our idea."

Silence.

Wright said, "Did you like it?"

"I told you last night I did."

"Tell me again."

"Wright, don't do this."

"Just tell me."

"Yes, alright? I liked it." If Bizzy had felt any pity, it had been displaced again by anger. "Was that not the point? You wanted this, don't forget that."

"Tell me."

"Fine. I liked sucking his cock. Is that what you want to hear me say? Does that excite you?"

Wright did not answer.

"Does that turn you on?"

"Yes."

"Fuck you."

Not with anger, or even hurt, Wright turned and began to walk away, simply resigned to the fact he was no longer welcome in Bizzy's presence. She watched him for a few steps and then said, "Wait. Wright." He stopped and listened. "Where are you going?"

"The Mauser is in the cottage. Buck is, too, if I can't do it myself."

"Oh, Wright, don't be a child. You know how I detest it when you bleat and whimper so."

"Let him go," came a shout from Oyster House. Wright saw Lucy standing on the front stoop. "He won't do it."

"Wright," Bizzy began but seemed to not know what to follow it up with.

Lucy called out, "If he had the nerve, he would have done it one of the dozen other times he's threatened to."

Wright turned again and resumed his exit from the garden. Behind him, he heard Bizzy's angry footsteps, crunching away from him toward the house on the crushed stone walkway. Then he could hear Bizzy and Lucy, raising their voices at one another but he could make out none of it.

The Rolls Royce was waiting in the driveway and Wright climbed in. He sat for a few minutes, staring at the automobile's gauges as if oil pressure and water temperature could help him diagnose what was wrong with him. As he reached for the starter button, the passenger door unlatched and swung open. Wright's heart gladdened and he tried to conceal his smile as he turned and watched for Bizzy to slide into the Phantom, a change of heart softening her face. Instead, he saw Lucy.

She dropped into the seat and pulled the door shut. Like Bizzy, Lucy was still dressed in her boating attire from the day before. She ran her hand across the curved dash, caressing the Birdseye maple. "Hello, Elizabeth. Long time, no see." Lucy peered out of the windscreen, over the long yellow bonnet. "She's something, isn't she? Our Elizabeth."

Wright nodded and squeezed the steering wheel. "Seven-point-seven-liter straight-six, overhead valves, crossflow cylinder heads."

"I wasn't talking about the car."

Wright saw Lucy watching over the prow of the Phantom, across the gardens at Bizzy as she disappeared into Oyster House. He said, "Shouldn't you be in there with her?"

"I was politely informed that I would need to procure other accommodations for the evening. I think it was that last jab about your broken promises to off yourself."

Wright and Lucy regarded each other for a moment, and then he fired up the Phantom's big engine. They pulled away and left behind the mansions of the peninsula's northern shore and drove into the forest of sugar maples and red oaks, bisected by Middle Neck Road, a pale ribbon of compacted sandy soil. Wright watched the speedometer needle sweep past sixty.

"The *Spirit of Ecstasy*," Lucy said suddenly.

Wright thought the sentiment a little florid for Lucy, but he agreed with it nonetheless and replied, "I love speed, too."

"No, her." Lucy pointed to the chrome figure poised atop the Phantom's radiator, canted into the wind. Wright took a second to admire the hood ornament's silver shape, her fluttering robes frozen behind her. The afternoon sun gleamed off her plating, making her sparkle almost magically.

"Eleanor Thornton," Lucy said. "That's her name. I like her even more than Isadora Duncan. Eleanor was a young woman with beauty, spirit, and intelligence. Not unlike someone else we know. But Eleanor lacked the social status to marry the man she loved. John Montagu-Scott, Second Baron Montagu of Beaulieu. But Baron Montagu was already married. Not unlike someone else I know. But that did not stop him from getting Eleanor pregnant. Like you, Baron Montagu was a Rolls Royce man, and with no way to publicly declare his love for Eleanor, he commissioned the creation of a mascot to adorn the radiator of his 1909 Silver Ghost, a commission filled by one Charles Robinson Sykes, a London sculptor and close friend and confidant of John. There's a sharp curve in the road up here."

Wright heeded Lucy's warning, geared down the Phantom, and took the sweeping righthander at a still-too-fast forty miles per hour. The slender tires sprayed a sleet of pebbles against the underside of the fenders like buckshot. Wright wound back through the Phantom's gearbox until the speedometer's needle skittered past *seventy*.

The Purple Menace and the Tobacco Prince

"Charles knew of John's love affair with Eleanor and chose the young secretary as his model for the sculpture. Like the lovers themselves, Charles used the utmost discretion as he worked. He named the original piece of art *The Whisper*, having sculpted Eleanor with one forefinger against her lips, symbolizing their forbidden affair. Subsequent sculpts, sans the secret gesture, were rechristened *Spirit of Ecstasy* and Eleanor's likeness has graced every Rolls Royce since. But poor Eleanor didn't live long enough to see it."

Wright and Lucy both stared out at Eleanor, her arms cast out behind her like wings. Wright asked, "What happened to her?"

"Cop," Lucy said matter-of-factly.

"A cop?"

"Cop." Lucy pointed ahead. Wright followed her gesture up Middle Neck Road and saw, hidden behind a cluster of shrubs and betrayed only by a glint of chrome, a Harley-Davidson lying in wait. It was straddled by a New York State Trooper.

"Shit."

As Wright and Lucy blasted past the trooper, they both craned their necks to see him. His motorcycle sat crouched and poised, its muscular shape punctuated by swooping fenders and a bulging gas tank. Its flathead V-twin engine spilled forth from its frame, bristling with chrome-plated implements of speed.

Lucy turned her attention to Wright, waiting for him to use the brake pedal to bring the speeding Phantom to a stop. His eyes were locked on the rearview mirror, watching for the trooper to give chase.

"Don't try it," Lucy said. "Surely your daddy's name can get you out of a simple speeding ticket. If yours can't, mine can."

In the mirror, Wright saw the motorcycle emerge from its hiding spot, a red light strobing on its front fender. It bounded onto the road, veering wildly before righting itself, then, with rear tire spitting silt and gravel in a rooster tail, launched into pursuit of the Rolls.

Lucy braced herself as he yanked back the shifter and kicked the gas pedal to the floor, pumping fuel to the thirsty engine and sending them fishtailing down the road.

"Wright!" Lucy shouted over the full-throttle roar.

He ignored her, watching the trooper in the rearview, cloaked in the sandy cloud swirling in the Phantom's wake. The Harley-Davidson was sailing across swells and ridges in the road, shimmying through ruts, the beam of its headlamp shooting all around in the dust, down at the road below, and then into the tree canopy like a searchlight. Lucy glanced at the passenger-side mirror just as it clipped a low-slung maple branch and was amputated, sent flying in a rain

187

of shattered glass.

Lucy vaulted from her seat, springing to her knees, and turned to watch through the Phantom's rear glass. In the mirror, Wright could see the trooper gaining on them, his jodhpurs fluttering in the wind. He pressed the accelerator into the carpet, trying to push it right through the floor. "Come on, Elizabeth," he begged. The Rolls Royce clawed at the sand, digging for speed.

Beacon Hill Road loomed, a quarter mile ahead on the left. Wright knew, no matter its horsepower advantage, the big car could never outrun the lighter, nimbler motorcycle. He downshifted, braked hard and sawed at the steering wheel, sending Lucy's body slamming against the door. Wright aimed the *Spirit of Ecstasy* down the narrow lane and pinned the accelerator to the floor again.

Lucy scrambled back into place and resumed her lookout through the rear window. "Go," she said.

Beacon Hill Road headed straight toward Hempstead Bay before making a hard right and running parallel to the shore. They were close enough to smell the salt on the wind that was blasting through the Phantom's open windows. Through the windshield, looking down toward the bay, the road was a lazily winding white snake, slipping silently into Long Island Sound. Wright knew if he could make the curve, they had a chance.

"Go, go," Lucy was chanting.

Fifty miles an hour on Beacon Hill Road would have been dangerously fast. Sixty was palms sweating. Seventy was tunnel vision and Wright's peripheral vision smeared. The Phantom's hefty four thousand pounds were exacerbated by the shifting, slippery sands of the track beneath it. At seventy miles per hour, the focus and reflexes it took to keep from accidentally killing Lucy and himself were exhausting. Seventy miles per hour was what it would take to get to the curve before the cop could.

"Go." Lucy was smiling now, eyes dancing and bright.

Wright scanned the road for corrugations and furrows that would shunt the Phantom from its path. He strangled the wheel, knuckles white, sensing every bearing and spring shackle, the vibrations and tugs telling him what Beacon Hill Road was doing underneath him. His saliva tasted like a mouthful of pennies. The speed of the car became secondary now to the speed of the approaching waterline.

Wright geared down, braked, tapdancing on the pedals as he yanked the wheel and dove the car into the curve. The growl of the engine was bass to the yowling treble of the tires gouging into the dirt. Lucy hugged the seatback. Wright looked in the rearview mirror and saw the Harley-Davidson skidding across the road, both wheels locked and sliding. The motorcycle slumped into the drainage ditch and then ramped out of it in a lazy arc, frame buckling as it crashed back to Earth. The motorcycle pirouetted, pieces flying off it, ejecting its New York State Trooper in a somersault and sending him slaloming across the road on all fours until he came to rest in the opposite ditch.

Wright watched along with Lucy as the trooper clambered to his feet, legs wobbling, shaking his fist in the air as the Phantom sped away.

Lucy let out a whoop and spun to flop back in her seat, clapping her hands. "Wright," she said, calmly at first, then frantically. "Wright! *Wright!*"

He turned around in time to see a crabgrass-covered berm filling his field of view. With a whomp, the Rolls Royce was suddenly airborne. The indigo horizon of Long Island Sound loomed beyond the bonnet. The car arced over the beach, lifting ever so slightly to the starboard side. Wright and Lucy floated away from their seats; gravity gone for the briefest of moments. And then it returned, violently, the Phantom's wheels embedding in the soft sand at the edge of the sound with a concussive impact, launching a fan of water into the sky and tumbling its occupants like a pair of dice in a cup.

Wright pried the driver's-side door open with his

legs, the warped hinges shrieking in protest. He climbed out, feet splashing in the waves as he skirted the Phantom's flanks to extract Lucy. They helped one another out of the water and up the beach, examining each other's limbs for breaks or lacerations and finding only scrapes. Wright turned his attention next to the Rolls Royce, resting axle-deep in Long Island Sound, quickly ascertaining that the car was stuck and there was nothing to help it.

Together, Wright and Lucy sat on a dune and stared at the car.

"Poor Elizabeth," Lucy finally said.

"What happened to Eleanor?"

A wave broke against the Phantom's radiator, spraying the chrome hood ornament. "She drowned," Lucy said.

"No, the real Eleanor."

"Yes, she drowned," Lucy said. "Along with hundreds of other passengers - and a large quantity of gold and jewels belonging to the Maharaja Jagatjit Singh - when the *SS Persia*, on which she was sailing through the Mediterranean, was torpedoed without warning off the coast of Crete by a German U-boat."

They sat in silence for a while, listening to the waves and wind and birds. Then Lucy said, "Why'd you let her do it?"

"Let who do what?"

"I know what happened on the boat last night."

"No one *lets* her do anything," Wright said. "She does what she wants. You know that."

"Why did you want her to?

He was quiet as he thought about the answer to that question. He finally told the truth. "I don't know."

"It's a hell of a boost to the ego, isn't it? Knowing that Bizzy Holt likes you. Knowing the woman that everyone wants to fuck, wants you. I know, trust me. It makes you feel like Paul Bern at the premiere of *Hell's Angels*, doesn't it? Walking the red carpet at Grauman's Chinese Theater with Jean Harlow on your arm."

Wright was nodding.

"Only thing is, Bern hated it. He couldn't stand all those men taking pictures of his date. He resented the fact that Harlow left his side at the first sight of a microphone to publicly thank Howard Hughes for giving her the role."

Wright nodded still, commiserating with Mr. Bern. Then he said, "I haven't slept since the night before last. Not a wink. All I can think about is what happened on your daddy's boat. Too many reminders. Buck snoring like a bear in the next room all night long. That damned buoy bell in the bay. Every time it rang, I felt a little twitch."

Lucy said, "The first time she ever let me go

down on her, she dabbed a little Shalimar on the insides of her thighs." Wright watched her eyes close briefly, reliving the moment. "She was the first girl that ever let me do that. Now, whenever she wears it, cue the waterworks down there." Lucy glanced at her lap. "It's like Pavlov's cunt."

They both laughed. Wright blushed. Then he said, "I wanted to feel that again."

"A wet pussy?"

They laughed harder.

"That first permission," Wright said. "And not knowing where the limits were."

"But hellbent on finding out."

He nodded again.

"So, what now," Lucy said. "What happens next?"

Wright shrugged his shoulders. "I suppose I hire a wrecker."

"With you and Bizzy, I mean."

"I don't know."

"I can tell you what happens. Next time she'll have to go a little further to give you that same high. What she did last night won't be enough next time." Lucy gave Wright a chance to say something. When he did not take it, she asked, "When will it be enough?"

"I may have already found out."

They listened to the breakers for a few minutes.

Wright said, "What about you? You and her?"

"Father's sailing the *Galaxie* to Havana next month. Bizzy and I have done nothing but quarrel this summer. I think it's time for a vacation. And don't think for a second that it has anything to do with you."

Lucy stood, brushed the sand off the seat of her white ducks, and began the long walk back to Oyster House.

Chapter 8

Somewhere over the Atlantic
Friday, July 10, 1931

Two hours ago the lights of Manhattan had vanished, blinking out below the horizon, candles blown out by the curvature of the Earth. Wright's altitude had prolonged the sunset, but his easterly course had hastened it. Now the Savoia-Marchetti S.56 was centered in a disk of black, the inky void of the depthless Atlantic Ocean stretching to the horizon in all directions. Above was a hemisphere of midnight blue, studded with innumerable stars, diamonds sprinkled across velvet, the shining pearl of the moon situated in the middle. To the south, a squall line of thunderheads, anvils ten miles tall, glowed in the moonlight like lumbering, ghostly giants. Sheets of blue lightning flickered and danced deep within them.

Wright could feel a sense of movement, but not of forward motion, like he was in a model aeroplane hung from the ceiling of heaven. Mac had told him it

195

would be like this. When he rented the Sands Point cottage, Wright had brought Mac McDonnell with him and arranged for his employment at Port Washington's airport. The veteran aviator had spent the summer preparing Wright for his round-the-world flight, both the joys and the risks.

Night was a seductress, Mac liked to say. Wright had not understood what the old pilot had meant at the time, but now, with the moonlight glinting off the Savoia's silver wings and the placid Atlantic glittering five thousand feet below, he got it. At night the air was calmer, glycerin smooth. The haze of the day was gone, visibility was so good he thought he could have seen Portugal if the Earth were flat. Arrayed across the vault of the sky were Hercules, Virgo, and Libra. Then, as he slipped into the ionized air beneath the thunder clouds, Wright was hypnotized by the liquid fire named after Saint Elmo, a luminous electrical discharge like that in a neon tube, forking across the Savoia's windscreen in blue jets.

There were dangers, too, peculiar to night-flying and transoceanic journeys. The aeroplane doesn't know it's dark, Mac would say, nor does the plane know it's over water. If something goes wrong, it will not be because of either one of those things. Night-flying is contrary to human behavior. Our circadian rhythms tell our bodies that night is the time to sleep. The drone of the engine and the vibration of the airframe can lull you into drowsiness. Your instruments are more difficult to see in a dark cockpit, yet an accurate reading of them is more crucial. Landmarks were nonexistent, and even if they were not, they would be invisible. If the worst happened, Mac told Wright, and you have to ditch, an emergency flare could be seen three or four miles away and for only about thirty seconds—provided you survive the landing, were able to get your raft deployed, succeeded in climbing aboard, did not suffer hypothermia, and did not get eaten by sharks—so make sure you saved it for when a ship was visible.

But Wright would not be using his flare. He had no intention of surviving the landing. He wanted to die, but he wanted to do it upon impact with the ocean, not by drowning in it. Four hours ago, he had careened onto the airfield at Port Washington, eyes flooded with tears, barking at McDonnell to fuel the Savoia, declaring his plan to end it all by flying out to sea until the gas was gone. Before the big radial engine had even warmed up, Wright was airborne, having ignored Mac's protests and admonitions, reminding McDonnell that he was an employee and if he wished to remain one, he would stand aside. Wright had clumsily brandished the Mauser when Mac asked whose employee he would be after Wright dove into the Atlantic.

He had flown east until the airfield was a dot

over his shoulder, receding along with everything else that had happened that evening. He exhaled for what felt like minutes and imagined himself no longer flying an aeroplane but instead at the controls of a time machine. Behind him was the past. Out there, framed within the Savoia's windscreen, was the future, what was left of it. And all he had to do to get there faster was open the throttle.

The aeroplane could not fly backward, though. If it could, Wright would have traveled six hours in reverse and not answered his telephone when it rang in his cottage that evening. He would not have listened to Bizzy's slurred voice on the other end of the line.

"It's me," she had said, almost before Wright could get the receiver to his ear.

"Where are you? I tried calling your house."

"Bea's. A party. Bea Lillie's"

"Is everything alright?"

"Nellie's here."

"What?"

"Nellie's here. She's going to..."

"What? Bizzy?"

Wright could only make out every few words. "I'm... the phone down now. I hope... enjoy..."

"Bizzy? Bizzy?" He had pressed his ear to the receiver, straining to hear, listening for any type of sound that would tell him what Nellie Burnside was doing. But he could hear nothing. "Bizzy?"

The telephone came back to life, and Wright heard what sounded like a muffled giggle. He heard Bizzy's voice, laughing, saying, "Stop," before the receiver fell silent again.

"What's going on? Bizzy?" She was drunk, that much was plain to hear. Seconds of silence accumulated into minutes. She would not do this, Wright told himself. *Rule Number Two: You have to watch.* Not without talking to him first. But what if that was why she had phoned?

He pressed the receiver tightly against his ear and tried to hear something, anything. Five minutes passed. Then ten. With a struggle that bordered on panic, Wright had tried not to imagine what was happening at Beatrice Lillie's mansion. And then he tried to picture exactly that. In his mind, he saw a parade of images like a series of Kodak photographs, each one accompanied by the crash and crackle of a flashbulb. *Flash.* The partygoers forming a loose circle with Bizzy and Nellie in the center. *Flash.* Bizzy on her back, on the floor, skirt bunched around her waist. *Flash.* Nellie on her knees, Bizzy's thighs clamped around her head. *Flash.* Nellie's blue eyes glittering up at her, wanting to be told what to do and how long to do it.

Then, like a carousel slowly churning to life, the images began to connect and string together until they became a flickering movie in Wright's head. He saw the crowd closing in, vying for position, craning their necks to see better. They watched, riveted, respectfully hushed. Nellie gazed at Bizzy, golden-red waves sweeping across jutting hipbones. A run of staccato gasps burst from Bizzy's mouth as tremors of pleasure rippled through her body. Only then did the crowd erupt in riotous applause.

And then the line went dead. Wright listened to the dial tone for a moment before realizing the telephone had been hung up. He set the receiver in its cradle.

Before departing the cottage for the airfield, Wright had left a note, meaning it this time.

To Richard Walton "Walt" Williams Jr., I bequeath my share of it, he had scrawled, meaning the forty-million-dollar inheritance that he would have come into when he turned twenty-eight, nine years hence. To Buck Moore, he left the Mauser semi-automatic, his talisman, the thing he'd held the closest, longest, save for his friendship with Buck. To Lucy Allard Conrad Jennings he left *unfettered access to our shared Dream*. And to Elizabeth Lloyd Holt, he left *all my love, my Darling Angel*.

But now, with the Savoia's tank half-empty and three hundred miles of ocean behind him, Wright was having second thoughts. Not because, as Bizzy had assured him, he was calming down and accepting the fact that Bea's "hen party" was not, as he initially suspected, the latest salvo in her circle's ongoing effort to sabotage their relationship, a campaign Bizzy was abetting by refusing to lobby for his invitation to the party. Wright's reconsideration of his self-scripted demise was the realization that if he went through with it, he would never see her again. Up until then, he had framed his suicide in his mind as her punishment, not his. He wanted to wrack her with the guilt that would accompany the knowledge that had she only chosen him over them, he would still be here. He wanted to rob her of his presence. Now he was understanding that what he was planning to do would accomplish the converse. If he were dead, Wright would never get to be in Bizzy's company ever again.

He yanked the joystick and kicked at a pedal, ailerons and rudder responding instantly. Wright jammed the throttle wide open, the engine singing at full throat. The Savoia banked into a turn that ended with the time machine pointed back to New York. The needle of his fuel gauge vibrated over the tick mark midway between E and F. He should have enough.

Wright suddenly remembered an early flying lesson with his brother. Walt had told him about Zeno's Dichotomy Paradox as they flew from Raleigh to Winston-Salem in a Curtiss TS-1 biplane Walt had borrowed from Mac. "Point A to Point B, right?" Walt had called to his little brother over the roar of the Lawrance J-1 radial engine. Wright nodded. "Nothing to it. All we have to do it keep cutting that distance in half and we'll get there eventually." He nodded in agreement again. "If we can just get to the halfway point, that leaves just the other half. So, we do it again. We cut the remaining distance in half. Reach the next halfway point, right? But if we keep going like this, there will always be some distance left. Only going halfway every time means we'll never get home." When Walt saw the concern behind Wright's goggles, he laughed and said, "Don't worry, algebra is our copilot. We'll get there." Wright had not known what Walt meant, but if his brother said they would get home, he believed it.

He peered into the darkness, watching for the glow of New York City to delineate the horizon as he cut the distance in half.

Chapter 9

WESTERN UNION

CABLEGRAM

Received at

66FL F 19

PORT WASHINGTON NY 390V

AUG 27, 1931

TO: ELIZABETH HOLT

DARLING ANGEL. ALTERCATION
WITH CAPTAIN OF CUNARD LINER
BERENGIA DELAYED LOADING OF PLANE
AT 47TH STREET PIER. 5-DAY VOYAGE TO
SOUTHAMPTON ENGLAND. BY END OF
JOURNEY WILL HAVE TRAVELED 17000
MILES BY AIR, 12000 BY SEA.

LOVE,

WRIGHT

THE QUICKEST, SUREST, AND SAFEST WAY
TO SEND MONEY IS BY TELEGRAPH OR
CABLE.

WESTERN UNION

CABLEGRAM

Received at

55PS S 53

LONDON 153B SEP 4, 1931

TO: R. WRIGHT WILLIAMS

DEAREST WRIGHT. MY
LINGERING MEMORY IS OF YOU IN YOUR
PLANE, BUZZING MY BEACH AND
STREWING THE SAND WITH YELLOW ROSES.
NELLIE SAYS IN YOUR FLYING JACKET YOU
NO LONGER LOOKED THE SULLEN YOUTH.
I TOLD HER THERE IS A SECRET TREASURE
BURIED DEEP INSIDE YOU. SHE SAYS
SOMETHING SEEMS TO HAVE MADE A MAN
OF THE BOY. I AGREE.

FAITHFULLY,

204

BIZ

THE QUICKEST, SUREST, AND SAFEST WAY

TO SEND MONEY IS BY TELEGRAPH OR

CABLE.

WESTERN UNION

CABLEGRAM

Received at

74PJ B 68

NEWARK NJ 547P SEP 7, 1931

TO: ELIZABETH HOLT

ARRIVED AT SOUTHAMPTON

AND FLEW TO LONDON. STAYING AT

MAYFAIR HOTEL. I HAVE BEEN SICK. I

DON'T KNOW WHAT'S THE MATTER.

DELAYING FLIGHT TO PARIS. I HAVE NEVER

FELT MORE LIKE DYING IN A LONG TIME.

LOVE,

WRIGHT

THE QUICKEST, SUREST, AND SAFEST WAY

TO SEND MONEY IS BY TELEGRAPH OR

The Purple Menace and the Tobacco Prince
CABLE.

WESTERN UNION

CABLEGRAM

Received at

55PS S 53

LONDON 153B SEP 12, 1931

TO: RWW

IF YOU ARE SICK, I URGE YOU TO COME HOME. THE PROVINCIAL TOUR OF THREE'S A CROWD BEGINS TOMORROW. FIRST STOP CLEVELAND. LUCY SAILING TO HAVANA ON THE GALAXIE.

FAITHFULLY,

BIZ

THE QUICKEST, SUREST, AND SAFEST WAY TO SEND MONEY IS BY TELEGRAPH OR CABLE.

WESTERN UNION

CABLEGRAM

Received at

13SW F 01

CLEVELAND OH 214G SEP 17, 1931

TO: ELIZABETH HOLT

DARLING ANGEL. I BELIEVE I
HAVE CONTRACTED A VIRUS. I HAVE BEEN
IN BED TWO WEEKS. WHY RETURN HOME
NOW? MEET YOU LATER—BUT SUICIDE IS
PREFERABLE. THIS IS THE LAST CABLE.
GOODBYE.

LOVE,

WRIGHT

THE QUICKEST, SUREST, AND SAFEST WAY
TO SEND MONEY IS BY TELEGRAPH OR
CABLE.

WESTERN UNION

CABLEGRAM

Received at

55PS S 53

LONDON 153B SEP 20, 1931

The Purple Menace and the Tobacco Prince

TO: RWW

I ATTRIBUTE YOUR DESPONDENCY TO LONELINESS. I AM LONELY TOO. I HAVE SHOWN YOUR CABLES TO NELLIE. SHE SAYS YOUR TRAGIC EXPOSTULATIONS ARE SILLY AND BOYISH. PLEASE COME HOME. SISTER BURNSIDE HAS ASKED TO MEET YOU IN PARIS. THREE'S A CROWD IS IN PHILADELPHIA NEXT.

FAITHFULLY,

BIZ

THE QUICKEST, SUREST, AND SAFEST WAY TO SEND MONEY IS BY TELEGRAPH OR CABLE.

WESTERN UNION

CABLEGRAM

Received at

33TD D 81

PHILADELPHIA 927S SEP 25, 1931

TO: ELIZABETH HOLT

208

DARLING ANGEL. WILL CABLE
SISTER. FEELING BETTER. FLYING TO PARIS
IN THREE DAYS.

LOVE,

WRIGHT

THE QUICKEST, SUREST, AND SAFEST WAY
TO SEND MONEY IS BY TELEGRAPH OR
CABLE.

WESTERN UNION
CABLEGRAM

Received at

52JR E 12

MALLORCA, SPAIN 212F SEP 25,
1931

TO: EUGENIA BURNSIDE

DEAR SISTER. BIZZY HAS
RELAYED YOUR MESSAGE. I AM FLYING TO
FRANCE IN THREE DAYS.

YOURS,

209

R. WRIGHT WILLIAMS

THE QUICKEST, SUREST, AND SAFEST WAY
TO SEND MONEY IS BY TELEGRAPH OR
CABLE.

WESTERN UNION

CABLEGRAM

Received at

55PS S 53

LONDON 153B SEP 26, 1931

TO: R. WRIGHT WILLIAMS

MOTHER HAS SHIPPED MANY SILVER
HEIRLOOMS TO ME IN PARIS. I AM UNABLE
TO CARRY THEM TO MY HOME IN
MALLORCA AND HOPE TO PERSUADE YOU
TO DO SO FOR ME. I DO NOT TRUST THE
SPANISH MAILS.

YOU SHOULD KNOW THAT
LOVING BIZZY IS LIKE LOVING
CHOCOLATE MOUSSE. SWEET TO THE
TONGUE, BUT THE PLEASURE IS FLEETING.

210

AND ALL YOU WILL GET FOR YOUR
TROUBLE IS A BELLYACHE.

I SHALL AWAIT YOU IN LE HAVRE ON
A MOTOR LAUNCH WITH MY HUSBAND, A
WIND-UP VICTROLA, AND TWO BOTTLES OF
KRUG '29.

WARMLY,

SISTER

THE QUICKEST, SUREST, AND SAFEST WAY
TO SEND MONEY IS BY TELEGRAPH OR
CABLE.

WESTERN UNION

CABLEGRAM

Received at

33TD D 81

PHILADELPHIA 927S SEP 27, 1931

TO: ELIZABETH HOLT

I WOULD GLADLY COME HOME
IF YOU WERE NOT GOING ON WITH THE
SHOW. I'LL GLADLY GIVE UP THIS TRIP OR

ANYTHING I HAVE TO DEVOTE ALL MY
TIME WITH YOU, IF YOU DO THE SAME FOR
ME. IF I GET TO THE POINT WHERE I SIMPLY
CANNOT STAND IT WITHOUT YOU FOR
ANOTHER MINUTE, WELL, THERE'S THE
OLD MAUSER WITH A FEW CARTRIDGES IN
IT. I GUESS I'VE HAD MY INNING. IT'S TIME
ANOTHER TEAM WENT TO BAT. LET US
MEET IN HONG KONG.

LOVE,

WRIGHT

THE QUICKEST, SUREST, AND SAFEST WAY
TO SEND MONEY IS BY TELEGRAPH OR
CABLE.

WESTERN UNION
CABLEGRAM

Received at
55PS S 53
LONDON 153B SEP 28, 1931

TO: RWW

I WISH TO HEAR NO MORE TALK OF YOUR TOY PISTOL. NELLIE HAS FINALLY STOPPED FOLLOWING THE TOUR. HOWARD STAHL SAYS A DAY AWAY FROM NELLIE BURNSIDE IS LIKE A DAY IN THE COUNTRY. BYRON FOGG HAS ASKED AFTER YOU AND I TOLD HIM I WAS PROUD OF MY AVIATOR. CINCINNATI IS NEXT.

BIZ

THE QUICKEST, SUREST, AND SAFEST WAY TO SEND MONEY IS BY TELEGRAPH OR CABLE.

WESTERN UNION

CABLEGRAM

Received at

52JR E 12

MALLORCA, SPAIN 212F OCT 1, 1931

TO: EUGENIA BURNSIDE

DEAR SISTER. PLANE SANK.

LOVE,

WRIGHT

THE QUICKEST, SUREST, AND SAFEST WAY
TO SEND MONEY IS BY TELEGRAPH OR
CABLE.

WESTERN UNION

CABLEGRAM

Received at

11RC S 70

CINCINATTI OH 411H OCT 1, 1931

TO: ELIZABETH HOLT

DARLING ANGEL. I AM
DISCONSOLATE AND UNABLE TO FLY
FURTHER. I HAVE A DISEASE OF THE
MASTOID. MY FRENCH DOCTORS ASSURE
ME I REQUIRE IMMEDIATE SURGERY. HONG
KONG POSTPONED. I SAIL FROM
SOUTHAMPTON TO NYC ABOARD THE

AMERICAN LINER LEVIATHAN NEXT WEEK.

PLEASE HAVE BUCK MAKE THE

ARRANGEMENTS. IF HE WISHES TO

CONTINUE TO RECEIVE A SALARY AS MY

SECRETARY HE NEEDS TO EARN IT.

LOVE,

WRIGHT

THE QUICKEST, SUREST, AND SAFEST WAY

TO SEND MONEY IS BY TELEGRAPH OR

CABLE.

Chapter 10

Winston-Salem, North Carolina
Saturday, October 24, 1931

Piloting a Waco 10 Whirlwind was not like flying the Savoia-Marchetti S.56. Wright once believed the Savoia was fast. Never was he more convinced of that than on his first test flight of the seaplane. He had flown her north to Pilot Mountain, the distinctive white quartzite knob that crowned it visible from Winston-Salem, rising fourteen hundred feet above the landscape like a circus tent. Aiming the aeroplane directly at the craggy cap, Wright flew toward the mountain at full throttle until the sheer rock wall filled his windscreen.

Wright had pulled the Savoia's joystick into his groin with all his strength, the Kinner B-5 howling, its wooden propeller trying futilely to claw higher into the air. But the altitude could not be gained, the peak was too tall, so he banged the stick against his thigh, sending the spindly plane careening to the right. Eighty, eighty-five miles per hour now. The mountain was right there, close enough that Wright thought he could reach out of the cockpit and trail his fingers across the treetops. A vertical wall of hickory and oaks flanked the plane's port wingtip; a quarter-mile drop was off the starboard. Ninety miles per hour now. Still the plane banked. Ninety-five miles per hour. The Savoia's wake turbulence shook the trees like baby rattles, the pale undersides of the leaves flashing at Wright. He squeezed his eyes shut and chanted a parting prayer, unheard even by himself over the banshee wail of cyclone and motor, certain the plane would lose its grip on the wind and slam into the side of the mountain. But it did not. At the last second, the ailerons had bitten into the air, the engine snarled, the gap between the belly of the plane and the trees doubled, and then doubled again. One hundred miles an hour. Wright's heart was pounding. He had made it. Thank God, he made it. God, that was fast.

No, it was not. That was not fast, he told himself as he eased the Waco's throttle forward. The Savoia was not fast at all, he now understood. The S.56 was a ninety-horsepower amphibian with a wooden hull and fabric skin. The bright red plane he was flying this morning was snatched through the air by a Wright R-760 Whirlwind, a seven-hundred-fifty-six cubic-inch displacement, seven-cylinder radial engine that made two-hundred twenty-five horsepower. The R-760 lived by inhaling eighty-octane poison which it compressed and detonated to hurl slugs of forged steel with enough force to cut a man in two. It was a jagged, saw-toothed ring that encircled the shark nose of the Waco 10. Even resting on the runway, the plane looked like it was breaking speed records. Its fuselage was sleek and muscular, tapered like a bullet. Its knife-edged wings spanned thirty feet, outstretched like a bird of prey.

Wright checked the airspeed indicator and leaned toward Bizzy in the copilot's seat. "One-forty!" She nodded, forced a smile, and gave him an *OK* with her gloved fingers and thumb.

After ten minutes of flight, Wright slowed the plane as Winston-Salem came into view through the morning haze. The air was hot and humid and swirled with the sweet, warm aroma of dried tobacco from a hundred warehouses. He relinquished control of the joystick for a moment to gesture with looping waves of his hands beneath his nose, his chest swelling as he inhaled the scent, nudging Bizzy to do the same.

Now he banked the Waco, titling her earthward so she could take in Winston's maze of brick and glass-blocked cigarette factories. The city teemed with automobiles, electric streetcars, pedestrians, men and women who owed their livelihoods to Wright's father, going to work in buildings with his last name on them. He and Bizzy flew over smokestacks and steeples, rooftops and water towers, high above the grid of streets and sidewalks below but still close enough to hear the occasional *ahooga* of a Model A's klaxon. The sun glinted off their windshields, moving like glistening beads of water on a giant spiderweb.

And at the center of the web, the Williams Building rose three hundred fourteen feet above the city, dominating the skyline, its twenty-one floors of limestone, copper, and one thousand windows set aglow and golden by the rising sun. Wright pointed the aeroplane at the skyscraper and began to arc up, climbing in the sky until they soared past the graduated top floors and the sixty-five-foot-tall flagpole that capped the building, the Stars and Stripes snapping in the breeze.

"Two and a half million dollars," Wright had told Bizzy before takeoff, knowing he would have to shout to be heard over the Waco's throbbing engine. "It won the American Association of Architects award for best building in 1929. The tallest one between Baltimore and the Miami-Dade County Courthouse. It's the inspiration for the Empire State Building. Same architects."

"Yes, so you've said."

Wright promised to give her a tour of the interior

before Bizzy rejoined the traveling production of *Three's a Crowd*. He boasted of radiating sunbursts of marble from Hauteville, France in the lobby, bronze-clad doors with zigzagging grilles, crystal chandeliers, black Belgian marble in the elevator lobbies, gold leaf on the ceilings.

"Nothing happens in Winston-Salem," Wright said, "unless it's first approved on the nineteenth floor of the Williams Building."

Now he put the sun behind them and flew west, away from downtown. On the horizon lay the smoky silhouette of the Brushy Mountains, rolling like sleepless-night bedsheets out of the Appalachians down to the lazy brown waters of the Yadkin River.

Wright called suddenly over the drone of the engine. "Anne has sued me for divorce."

Bizzy watched him through her goggles and waited for the rest.

"She likes big parties and I like small ones."

"Certainly grounds for dissolving the union."

"She is charging incompatibility, as well as alleging that I continually nag her."

Now Bizzy had to bite her lip to keep from laughing. "Wright Williams, a nag? Say it ain't so."

Wright shot her a sideways glance. "She says I make her feel 'terribly nervous and upset.' That I have 'assumed so domineering an attitude that she is terminally distraught.'"

"Did she lie about anything?"

Another pointed glance. "She is insisting that we expedite the process and I have consented to travel to Reno, Nevada. Walt says it's the Divorce Capital of the World. You must only live there six weeks to become a citizen. Anne will be staying on a dude ranch owned by Cornelius Vanderbilt Jr. After a month and a half, we'll get our divorce and come home."

"How much?" Bizzy called over the wind.

"How much what?"

She rubbed her thumb over her index and middle fingers.

"Half a million," Wright said. "When I come into my trust. Small price to pay." Then, pointing to a clearing among the loblolly pines and magnolias, he said, "There."

Bizzy peered over the wing and saw a verdant half-mile-long corridor of grass, encompassed by a thousand acres of crimson and gold leaves and blue-green needles. Meandering white paths and weeping Japanese cherry tree allées converged at the end of the lawn, where stood the house that Wright's mother and father built when he was six years old. R.W. and Lillian Williams had modestly described their home as a bungalow, and Wright had done the same with Bizzy. Now she was seeing the truth that he lived in a mansion on a sprawling country estate.

Wright let the Waco shed altitude and then guided it in a swooping arc over Peace Haven, giving Bizzy a look at its white Tuscan columns, French doors, and green clay-tiled roof. They soared overhead and she looked down at the formal gardens with their fences, arches, and trellises, the greenhouse and its domed palm house, the vineyards, golf course, and tennis courts. And beyond the manor, sparkling in the sun, was a lake.

"Lake Lillian," Wright called to Bizzy over the engine's exhaust note. "Named after my mother." He eased the aeroplane into a lazy circle above the lake. "Sixteen acres. They dammed Silas Creek to make it."

Bizzy could see clear water cascading over a spillway into a concrete swimming pool and she remembered Buck's tale of Bessie Nifong.

"Mother had sixty thousand daffodil bulbs planted around the lake. On some Sundays, the church uses the pool for baptisms."

As they climbed into the cloudless blue sky away from the estate, Bizzy said, "It's even more sumptuous than Montchanin." Wright hoped it was Lucy's home that she was referring to, but he dared not ask.

They flew for a long while without speaking, and then Bizzy called across the cockpit, "I must confess something." He eyed her cautiously. "The tour of

The Purple Menace and the Tobacco Prince

Three's a Crowd has been a failure. It's the damned Depression. We were lucky to be one of the shows that recouped its initial investment. And I know that I'm lucky to be working. Most singers and actors and begging for work. Hell, even the Shubert brothers are in dire financial straits.

"In Newark, Dwight expected a gross of thirty grand," Bizzy said. "The show grossed nine. When the same thing happened in Philadelphia, and again in Cleveland, Dwight told the whole cast we would have to take a drastic pay cut."

"How drastic?"

"I had been making fifteen hundred bucks a week on the road. Now I'm making fifty."

Wright knew anything he said about money would seem either crass or patronizing, especially considering the fact he'd just flown over his palatial estate in his aeroplane. Instead, he said, "Here's my confession: I can't stand the theater. I didn't always hate it, but that was before Baltimore; before I saw *The Wild Party*; before you walked onto the stage at the Maryland Theater and sang 'Moanin and Sore.'" He looked at Bizzy. "My life is split in two, before and after. Before that night in April last year, and after. Before that night, I could go to the theater, see a show, and be entertained. Laugh. Tap my foot. I could watch and listen and not be reminded that the theater has the thing I want more than anything else in this world: your heart."

"Wright, I - "

"Marry me, Bizzy. Be with me. Here. This can be your home."

"It's beautiful, Wright, but -"

"Don't answer. Not yet. Please."

Bizzy looked out the aeroplane's wing and said, "No."

At the edge of Lake Lillian, Wright watched the party. He stood on the porch of the boathouse and, to himself, counted the attendees mingling on the grassy bank. He had made two dozen telephone calls that afternoon, and he now had two dozen guests, in addition to the one he had invited them all here to meet tonight.

On the crisp autumn air drifted the sweet scent of the chopped barbecue they had for dinner and the still smoldering hickory coals Buck had used to smoke the pork shoulder. Everywhere Wright looked, he saw friends, gathered in a circle around Bizzy, listening, watching, smiling faces glowing orange in the torchlight. Behind them their shadows jigged and swayed, black columns stretching away until they were absorbed by the night.

Bizzy was perched on a wrought-iron table, her shapely calves dangling over the edge, bare toes sweeping the grass. Wright had asked her to stay clothed and, so far, she had, shedding only her canvas-top tennis shoes. She was still in the snug sailor-button shorts and polo shirt she had worn earlier to beat Wright four to six, six to three, six to four, seven to six. The pristine white of her outfit contrasted vividly with her scribbled black hair and lustrous olive complexion, her skin shimmering in the low light of evening. In response to their requests for some show tunes, Bizzy was singing "Body and Soul." Her voice went out into the dark like a famished vixen emerging at dusk to begin her nocturnal hunt.

In the flickering firelight, Wright saw the faces of his friends, all entranced by his Yankee girl, if for different reasons. In Judge Wharton's admiring gaze, Wright saw only appreciation for Bizzy's talent and the seeming ease with which she controlled her lush voice. Wright could see that Charley Hughes was starstruck, almost in awe, that a world-famous Broadway star was here in Winston-Salem. Elizabeth Dillard seemed to recognize in Bizzy the confidence of someone who knew exactly who she was and what she was meant to do. Geraldine Slater was more interested in Bizzy's sportswear than in the singer herself. In Annette Wall's sneer and squint, Wright could see the unmistakable disdain and thinly veiled envy the puritanical always felt toward a libertine. And in Buck Moore's leer, he saw only lust and the memory of that night on the *Galaxie*, a feeling he was certain he had seen reciprocated in Bizzy's frequent, furtive glances Buck's way.

It was well past midnight when the partygoers staggered up the hill away from Lake Lillian. Judge stumbled close and awkwardly shook Bizzy's hand, profusely thanking her for singing, and told her she was one of the most beautiful women he had ever seen. In the glow of Peace Haven's rear portico, Wright saw, perhaps for only the second time ever, Bizzy blush. She kissed Judge on the cheek, making the young man blush in return. Wright could tell by Bizzy's flattered smile that she did, indeed, feel beautiful here.

*****

In Peace Haven's open-air sleeping porch, she and Wright lay in the shadows and listened to a symphony of crickets and treefrogs. Everything in the room was the same as it had been since he had slept here as a child, as if time had stood still when his mother died. The wicker daybed, the ferns and bamboo palms, and the sheer linen curtains that levitated like specters in the October breeze. But with Bizzy lying amongst it all, naked and languid, Wright's familiar surroundings had been utterly transformed, as if a blurry memory had suddenly been brought into sharp focus.

"What if I say yes?" Bizzy said.

Wright watched her eyes glint in the dark. "To

227

what?"

"If Anne Vogler can get half a million out of Wright Williams, who's to say Bizzy Holt couldn't get five million?"

He propped himself up on his elbow and stared at her now. "Are you saying yes?"

"Are you still asking?"

"Yes."

"Then yes."

Wright pressed his smiling lips to Bizzy's and kissed her. He could feel her smiling back.

Chapter 11

Macao
Wednesday, April 13, 1932

If Wright kept his eyes open, he could stay in the present. He could stay afloat on this current of fragrance—the wet, green perfume of newly opened lotus blossoms on the pond, the intoxicating scent of Bizzy's naked body lying next to him in the opium den, and the pungent cloud of smoke enveloping him. With his eyes open, he could stay here, lie here on this woven bamboo mat, and watch the tentacles of smoke twist and curl around him, suffused in their warm embrace. But he could not keep his eyes open. The current became an undertow, as strong as the Pearl River, and pulled him beneath the surface again. Wright's eyelids slumped shut and he was no longer here or now.

Behind the veil of consciousness, he found himself standing in the parlor of Fred Schoepfer, justice of the peace. Through the magistrate's French doors,

The Purple Menace and the Tobacco Prince

Wright eyed the steel gray waters of Lake Erie being churned into a cauldron of waves by the late November gales. It had been only three days since the divorce decree had been issued. Anne Vogler had departed Vanderbilt's ranch on a stretcher, blaming rheumatoid arthritis and exhaustion, but Wright knew it was her alcoholism. The next day, he met Bizzy in Michigan, the only state in the country where a minor could get married without a guardian's consent. Together they drove to Monroe, an inconspicuous hamlet halfway between Toledo and Detroit, the previous and next stops, respectively, for the road production of *Three's a Crowd*.

Wright could not stop smiling as he watched his new bride sign her name. *Elizabeth Williams*. She had listed her occupation as *at home*, and her age as *twenty-five*, both lies. He had signed *Richard Wright Williams*, calling himself a student, but told the truth when he wrote *twenty*. The Honorable Fred Schoepfer had no idea who they were.

Wright and Bizzy spent one night together, in a small hotel in Toledo. They took turns telephoning the family and friends to whom they deemed worthy of revealing their secret. Bizzy did not relay their reactions to Wright but through the receiver he overheard the tinny voices of Nellie Burnside accusing her of finally wearying of his indefatigable efforts, and Howard Stahl calling the marriage "an irrational knot." Bizzy had smiled and replied innocuously, hoping to not betray their criticisms to Wright by defending herself. She did not call Lucy, telling him she would cable her in the morning.

The next day, bride and groom parted ways, Bizzy to rejoin *Three's a Crowd*, Wright bound for New York City, where he would watch his Savoia-Marchetti being hauled aboard the S.S. *Paris*. With vows to meet on April 1 the following year, at the Repulse Bay Hotel in Hong Kong, where they would celebrate the culmination of Wright's long-delayed round-the-world flight and finally enjoy a proper honeymoon.

Now Wright resurfaced, slowly, mentally reoccupying the Macao opium den his physical form had never left. He lifted his heavy head and, with a great deal of determination, focused on Bizzy's face. The reflection of the heating lamp flickered in her glassy eyes as she guided the bamboo smoking pistol to her O-shaped lips and sucked on it. Almost immediately, the weight of Wright's eyelids became too great and he let them fall shut again.

He saw himself writing now, in *The Log of Aeroplane RS-597B*. A detached observer, he did not know what he had written until he saw his hand form the letters on the page.

I arrived in Plymouth Dec. 7 and proceeded to London.

231

The Purple Menace and the Tobacco Prince

In London, I have encountered much delay due to flying permits, and after the short test flight today, a fitting on the undercarriage gave way due to corrosion. The weather has been cold and foggy.

In Wright's mind, he saw the log's pages flutter by like a pale moth's wings, a hundred days. In his own handwriting, he saw *Paris, Marseilles, Milan, Rome, Tunis, Tripoli, Cairo.* The names began to entwine, like the exotic locales themselves had that winter, until they were a string of firecrackers, rolled and tied by the young Macanese girls in the streets outside the opium den. One by one, the names of the destinations burst and exploded into colorful camelia blossoms before coalescing into the places they represented. On the screen of his mind, Wright saw a shimmering Technicolor travelogue, silent save for the whir and chatter of the imaginary projector's shutter. He saw himself awestruck by the Pyramids of Khufu, Khafre, and Menkaure. He saw the Savoia, shining silver in the sun as it descended into Gaza, Baghdad, and Karachi. His own audience, Wright watched himself, climbing onto and under the amphibian at every stop, diagnosing a myriad of mechanical maladies, using his hands, head, and heart to coax the troublesome craft back into the air. He saw the plane flying fifty feet above desert and jungle, skimming dunes and treetops, where a sudden downdraft would have meant the end of both machine and man. He watched the aeroplane's cross-shaped shadow tracking railroad spurs and rivers. In the movie in his mind, Wright's Savoia swept through narrow passes and valleys, the aeroplane's lack of oxygen and cabin heating forcing him to duck the higher altitudes of the easier paths over the mountains. He saw himself with the maharajah in Jodhpur; in Agra, touring the Taj Mahal by moonlight. Rangoon, Bangkok, Hanoi, Haiphong. Through courage and skill in the air and pluck on the ground when he needed a spare part, a square meal, or a roof over his head, Wright worked his way east toward the Orient.

Again, he saw his own hand, scrawling entries into the logbook. *...the devilry of the weather ...plane almost went under in Swiss lake ...street of prostitutes in Tunis ...yellow fever in Egypt.* The pages turned. *Stranded in Afghanistan ...almost jailed in Calcutta ...fortuneteller in India. But here, I am only a flyer, not an heir.*

And then the color bled from the image until it became only a flickering black-and-white nickelodeon show, halting and jerking as Wright frantically tossed cargo and luggage overboard in a desperate attempt to lighten his ailing aeroplane's load. Cut to Wright, safe on the ground, circling the Savoia, kicking at the landing gear in frustration. Forced to abandon the crippled craft at Fort Bayard in French Indochina, eight days overdue and still two hundred and seventy miles from his Hong Kong finish line.

The Purple Menace and the Tobacco Prince

The scene changed and in the dream movie, Wright saw Bizzy checking into the Repulse Bay Hotel. There was a closeup of the concierge, followed by a silent movie title card. *We have no news of your American fly-boy!*

Now an image of Wright's older brother, Walt, filled the mental screen. He looked directly at the camera and when he spoke, his voice was distant and imperfectly synchronized with his mouth, like the talkies Bizzy and her Broadway friends so reviled.

"Promise me, Wright. Fly her. Fly her within an inch of her life. Then replace the things that fall off. Then fly her some more. This is, after all, her calling in life. You do an aeroplane no higher honor. Could she speak, she would thank you."

As if sinking into murky waters, Walt's face rippled, receded, and vanished into blackness. In its place, Bizzy's face surfaced, beautiful and serene. Wright watched her through his eyelashes as she drew on the opium pipe. She smiled and sighed, smoke curling from her nostrils in white ringlets like a sleepy dragon.

Wright could hear voices speaking Cantonese. Then they were speaking English. And then Wright realized one of them was Bizzy's voice. She was telling Wright, in a languid drawl that only manifested itself when she was high, that on the day she departed

Vancouver for Hong Kong, the newspapers had reported the kidnapping of Charles Lindbergh's twenty-month-old baby. Slurring, and laughing about it, she talked about the war that had just begun between China and Japan, and how the streets of Hong Kong were crowded with foreign soldiers. She recounted how her landfall had coincided with an outbreak of influenza and how she had been quarantined on the ship for twenty-four hours before being allowed to disembark. "Everything was… *wrong*. Ill omens and portents."

Bizzy and Wright bobbed together on the rolling surface of consciousness, she talking only when her head was above water, he only able to listen likewise, the two occurrences overlapping rarely. When she spoke with any coherence, and Wright was awake to comprehend, he pieced together the story of how Bizzy had whiled away his two-week tardiness. He heard about the Repulse Bay Hotel's wisteria-cloaked entrance and lavish gardens with their canopies of bright orange flame-of-the-forest. He listened to her describe, with oscillating lucidity, the Hong Kong avenues and alleys, teeming with refugees, merchants, and hagglers. She spoke of a Chinese street urchin she had befriended after thwarting his initial attempt at fleecing her as he had other oblivious tourists. She told Wright how the boy had been her guide and interpreter, and how two days ago he had bounded into the Repulse

Bay's lobby, announcing that an American pilot had fallen from the sky and come into the bay on a ship. At the waif's suggestion, because of the war, he helped Bizzy disguise herself as a coolie-hatted peasant and she sailed into the harbor on a rented junk.

"You were there," she cooed, "standing on the deck in your white linen suit. Do you remember?" Despite the recency of the event, Wright could scarcely recall. He closed his eyes and saw gelatin silver prints of the harbor, dotted with bat-winged junks, hundreds of them like giant brown autumn leaves being blown gently across the water; himself proudly on the prow of a lumbering Gulf Oil freighter, Bizzy shouting and waving from her boat. Then, vividly, Wright remembered deigning to return a perfunctory nod to the excited woman under the wide-brimmed hat, graciously acknowledging his admirer, before realizing her true identity.

"On the dock," Bizzy half sang, "do you remember?"

He did. Wright could hear himself, declaring to her that civilians were prohibited from carrying cameras or guns in Hong Kong, and then producing one of each from his jacket pockets, brandishing both the Kodak Six-16 and the Mauser semi-automatic in the air defiantly. With sudden immediacy, he remembered how he had felt in that moment. He had just flown around the world and married the most exciting woman in it. No one could stop him.

Bizzy said, "But now that my hero, my dashing aviator is here, everything is good again."

She smoothed his damp hair to his scalp with her palm, and her soothing touch submerged his brain again. Beneath the surface of consciousness, Wright found himself in the room at the Repulse Bay Hotel he shared with his wife. *His wife.* The ceiling fan drew the humid night air in through the louvered door and stirred it with Bizzy's Shalimar and the smoke from Wright's Taxi. He watched as she glided naked to the camphor-wood dresser. He had not anticipated being stunned by her beauty, but upon their reunion, he was. It had been almost five months since he had seen her, and now he refused to take his eyes off her.

She lifted the lid from the flat cardboard box that had been sitting on the dresser all evening, taunting Wright with its Havana return address, daring him to investigate its contents. He had been steadfast. Bizzy carefully folded away tissue paper, read the card, smiled at it, and then set it aside. Then, like magician's scarves, she pulled first one smoky length of stocking from the box, and then after a considerably arduous extraction, a matching length. She held them up, one in each hand, so diaphanous that the ceiling fan lifted them and made the flattened legs dance on their own like Peter Pan's rogue shadow.

As Wright watched, silently and intently, Bizzy sat on the edge of the bed next to him and began rolling the stockings onto her legs. "Pointex," she said. The fabric whispered as she scissored her knees together. Wright ran his hand up her thigh, the texture of the stockings speeding it along on its way. "A wedding gift. From Lucy."

That they were a gift from Lucy, Wright had no doubt. That the gift was in honor of Bizzy's marriage to him, he knew was a lie. He discerned from her delay in adding the stocking's origin that Bizzy was apprehensive of his response. It was the first time she had mentioned her erstwhile lover's name as a married woman. Wright simply nodded and said, "He did it," more impressed with Uncle Pierre Allard and his chemists than he was worried about the niece.

Bizzy stood and swiveled her calves, bending to straighten the seams, mapping the contours of her legs with her hands as she went. Then, taking a circuitous path to give her new husband a nice, long look, she walked back to the dresser. She picked up the card and read Lucy's words aloud. "'I promised John I would have my girlfriends try them out. I would do it myself, but you know I can't stand anything on my feet.'"

"Wait," Wright said suddenly, bounding from the bed and reaching into the pocket of his jacket, withdrawing the Kodak. He stepped back, unfolding the camera and holding it flat against his chest, squinting down at the viewfinder as he aimed it at Bizzy. Before she could pose, Wright pressed the exposure lever and took a picture. With a lacquered fingernail, Bizzy pointed at the darkened band around the top of her stocking. Still reading from Lucy's card, she said, "This is called the welt. It's a reinforced double-thickness of pointex that the garter belt attaches to." Wright turned the Kodak's winding key and snapped another exposure. "And this," Bizzy was pointing now at the lighter transitional band between the welt and the leg of the stocking, "is the shadow welt."

She looked at Wright. He was watching her through the camera's finder, smiling stupidly. Bizzy swayed her hips a little, side to side, smoothing the pointex to her skin with her palms. He took another photo. She pivoted on the ball of her foot and pointed at the teardrop-shaped gap at the back of her stocking's welt. "This is the keyhole. 'A function of the manufacturing process,' Lucy says. 'A finishing loop, needed for the seaming machinist to be able to finish the back seam by turning the welt of the stocking in a circle and allowing the needles to be withdrawn.'" Wright took another snapshot.

"'Denier is the term they use to describe the

thickness of hosiery. The lower the number, the more sheer the stocking. The higher, the opaquer.'" Bizzy slipped her hand behind the sheer pointex, down onto her thigh, fanning out her fingers. "'Ten denier or less is ultra-sheer, giving the illusion of bare legs. Forty denier or more is opaque. Ballet tights, for example. Your stockings here are a Twenty.'" Wright stepped closer, snapping open the Kodak's shutter and advancing the film.

"'The heel and toe have a denser weave to improve wear and prevent runs.'" Bizzy rocked her foot back and forth. "'The Cuban heel, like this one, is a design in which the reinforced part climbs the back of the heel and finishes in a square top. There are also Havana heels. And French heels taper to a...'"

Bizzy's voice echoed and dissipated. Like a drowning man breaching the surface, Wright was back in the opium den, back in the now, for just a moment. He futilely tried to focus on Bizzy's face only to watch it dissolve into expanding concentric ripples. Now he was riding in a rickshaw, jostling over a cobbled street, two hours ago. She was seated next to him in a mandarin-collared cheongsam, its vermilion brocade tight as a corset, a flock of red-crowned cranes taking silken flight across her body. The dress closed on the side Wright was seated on and his eyes marched up and down the open slit, the pankou knots undone to Bizzy's thigh. Her hair was swept into a raven wreath, skewered by a single silver icepick of a hairpin. A pink Bengal rose was tucked behind her ear.

Rua dos Ervanários mirrored Wright's mood. Like his thoughts, the crowded street pulsed with possibilities and potential. Pagoda-roofed shops, ornamented balconies, and draped awnings, a thousand paper lanterns, flags with brightly painted Hanzi, all vied for his attention. Sidewalk soup restaurants, tea, and rice cake stands, jewelry shops. Locals at folding tables playing mahjong with their neighbors. Temples with full-moon entryways.

Wright had not known which way to look. Here, street peddlers with rabbits, cats, and chickens in spherical wire cages. There, a temple procession with a street orchestra, led by embroidered and bejeweled banners, followed by bouquet-laden shrines dedicated to strange gods. Trailing the parade was a lion-headed dragon, gyrating and contorting in a serpentine dance, frightening away any evil spirits that might be following.

From doorways drifted the sultry smell of joss sticks, or the smoky aroma of horseshoe-shaped Portuguese alheira sausage hanging in butchers' windows. From the alleys came laughter and groans from the Fan-Tan players in the gambling parlors and the high-pitched, childlike vocals from the Shidaiqu jazz clubs.

Bizzy slid a hand onto her hip and deftly unfastened the braided closure at the point of the dress's slit, the red silk parting further, revealing the top of her coffee-colored stocking and a triangle of bare thigh above. She was watching Wright, her eyebrows raising when his gaze met hers, red lips curling in a sly smile. She slipped her fingertips into the cheongsam's slit and hooked the hem with her thumb.

Bizzy pulled the dress up, revealing the clasp of an elastic garter biting into the pointex. The need to touch his wife overwhelmed Wright and he laid his hand on her exposed leg. He ran his fingers over the stocking, crossing the border between the synthetic texture of the hosiery and the pebbled flesh of Bizzy's naked skin above. Wright glanced at the rickshaw puller, making sure he was concentrating on the busy foot traffic ahead, then he dipped his hand between Bizzy's thighs, making her inhale sharply, her breath whistling through her teeth.

"Beco das Caixa*sss*," Bizzy called to the rickshaw puller, hissing the final syllable as Wright slipped a finger through the seam of her vagina. Wright rocked his wrist back and forth in syncopation with the cobblestone bumps. "Number... eleven." It was the address of the opium den Bizzy's street urchin had recommended when she told him that she and her

242

husband "wished to opiate upon his arrival." The puller nodded and began to trot now, circumnavigating a line of farmers in conical bamboo hats, each man his own beast of burden, baskets of fish or bundles of firewood balanced on long poles slung over their shoulders. The increased speed of their cart bounced Bizzy on the woven wicker seat, her lap the jiggling lid of a pot about to boil over.

She was breathing through her mouth now. "Wright…"

"Yes, Mrs. Williams?"

"Wright…" Her voice was becoming unreliable. She looked down into the hollow between her thighs and watched Wright's hand, his fingers dancing there. She could not keep her legs still, her knees opening and closing like a bellows. Now Bizzy gazed at him, mouth hung open, cheeks flushed a rosy pink.

Wright saw her fingernails claw at the basket weave of the seat and then she reached overhead, clutching at the ribs of the rickshaw's canopy. Her body convulsed, legs coiling in and then springing back out, her body a splayed letter X pinned to the bench by Wright's hand, like she was being branded by it, immobilized and trembling at the spot where a red-hot iron was pressed onto her. Finally, she slumped, her body sagging, a puppet whose strings had been suddenly scissored.

The Purple Menace and the Tobacco Prince

Now Wright's eyelids opened with the almost imperceptible pace of a sunrise. Something big and alive was croaking in the trees just outside the opium den's open window. He watched Bizzy for a long while.

*****

Later, sober, back at the Repulse Bay Hotel, Wright would confess to her that those final, uncompleted two hundred and seventy miles had negated his grand adventure. He hid *The Log of Aeroplane RS-597B* in his steamer trunk and proclaimed there would be no Slick Carpenter-penned account of his risky journey syndicated in the nation's newspapers. He had failed, he told Bizzy. He was not the conquering hero she believed him to be. She swiftly informed Wright that she would have no truck with such nonsense. She spent the next two weeks making him feel as he had on the dock upon his arrival. The couple waltzed beneath crystal chandeliers at the Peninsula Hotel, toured Kowloon, bet on the ponies at Jardines, and sipped gimlets by moonlight on Victoria Peak.

The following month, aboard the *Empress of Russia*, in the Hong Kong harbor, with the repaired Savoia on deck and the liner preparing to depart for British Columbia, Bizzy would agree to a one-year sabbatical from Broadway and be his wife - and simply that - in Carolina.

Chapter 12

Winston-Salem, North Carolina
Sunday, July 3, 1932

I f there was one place on Earth where Wright felt
more himself, more in control, than in the womb of
an aeroplane's cockpit, it was Peace Haven. The
brainchild of Wright's mother Lillian and architect
Charles Buxton Sugg, the design and construction of
the bungalow and the surrounding thousand-acre estate
began in 1912, when Wright was an infant.

Just before Christmas 1917, R.W. Williams,
Lillian, their four children, and a platoon of butlers,
cooks, housemaids, laundresses, nannies, tutors,
handymen, gardeners, groundskeepers, stable hands,
and nightwatchmen left their Queen Anne-style
Victorian mansion on West Fifth Street—downtown
Winston-Salem's "Millionaire's Row"—and moved to
the sixty-room country mansion Lillian had christened
Peace Haven, far from the city's noise and bustle.
Wright had just turned six, but the memory of first

stepping into his new home was etched into his memory.

Even upon that first entry, Wright felt the space fit him as comfortably as his clothes. The Reception Hall was the center of the house, a large, open, two-story expanse, ringed by a cantilevered gallery and dominated by an enormous white marble fireplace recessed in an inglenook. A glittering chandelier loomed over the space like a brass and crystal octopus. Loveseats, broad sofas, and lounging chairs formed hedges and divided the hall into smaller provinces, each boasting its own distinctive furnishings: English reading tables, Chinese floor vases, Persian carpets, Flemish tapestries. In a far corner was the console of a built-in Aeolian pipe organ with four manuals and a pedalboard. Two thousand five-hundred sixty-six concealed pipes occupied portions of three floors and an elaborate system of chambers and flues carried the sound throughout the Reception Hall, the notes emanating from ornate grilles in the ceiling and walls.

Flanking an eighteenth-century grandfather clock was a pair of oil portraits, one of Wright's mother, the other of his father. The newlyweds had sat for French photographer and painter Eugène Pirou during their 1905 honeymoon in Paris. A pubescent Wright would delight in passing along to his friends - namely Buck - the tale Walt had related to him about how

Monsieur Pirou had produced a moving picture called *Le Coucher de la Mariée* (*Bedtime for the Bride*, per Walt), one of the first erotic films ever made. According to Wright's older brother, the movie's plot revolved around a lecherous husband's attempts to surreptitiously watch his new bride undress on their wedding night. Wright and Buck had spent many a teenaged afternoon giggling about it.

On their first night in Peace Haven, the children, in order of birth, had picked out their bedrooms on the second floor. Wright's was on the East Wing, spanning its entire width, double-hung windows on each side that overlooked Lake Lillian to the rear and the half-mile-long lawn to the front, which, in the coming years, would double as a landing strip for both Walt and Wright. Beyond a dressing room and bathroom was Wright's sleeping porch, capping the end of the wing, tucked among the magnolias, Southern smilax climbing its exterior walls so rapidly that Lillian swore you could sit and watch it grow.

Pancreatic cancer killed Wright's father eight months after the family moved into their new home. At the time, R.W. Williams Tobacco Company was producing more than twenty billion cigarettes a year, allowing R.W. to leave each of his four children twenty million dollars to be held in trust until their twenty-eighth birthdays. Six years later, when Wright was twelve, Lillian died of a brain embolism. Wright, the youngest of the Williams children, was doted on by his siblings and a cadre of aunts, governesses, nursemaids, and housekeepers—chief amongst them Pluma Washington, his favorite—who did their best to give the sullen boy a happy childhood.

Despite their attempts to shield him from his mother's death, Wright regularly eavesdropped on his brother, sisters, and their guardians as they discussed matters impenetrable to him in the library on the house's main level. During his initial explorations of his new home, he had discovered an accident of acoustics: he could stand beneath one of the pipe organ's speaker grilles on the gallery above the Reception Hall and hear conversations from below as clearly as if he were part of them. In the immediate aftermath of his mother's death, when banished to his bedroom so the adults could speak privately, Wright would secretly listen to the voices emitting from the ceiling.

Now, as an adult, he was doing it again. He and Bizzy had returned from their Hong Kong honeymoon in May. Back in New York City, the tabloids quickly learned of Bizzy Holt's covert nuptials nearly six months prior. Declining all invitations from Bizzy's friends keen to celebrate, Wright held his wife to her word and immediately extracted her from Manhattan and drove all night down the East Coast to Peace

Haven. He had spent the remainder of spring lurking on the gallery above the Reception Hall, lingering beneath a grille and listening to Bizzy's conversations from below.

Initially, their marriage seemed as idyllic as its setting. Except for the servants and staff, the couple had the sprawling estate to themselves. Trying to make Broadway seem not so far away and improve her odds of keeping the promise she had made to him about staying a year in North Carolina, Bizzy rehearsed regularly with the Dean of Music at Salem College. She invited her friend Blanche Hruska - a Czechoslovakian actress who had struck gold directing a revival of *Goose Chase* at the Shubert brothers' 49th Street Theatre in New York City - for an indefinite stay. Blanche had brought with her a play by Czech-Jewish playwright František Langer called *Periferie*—in English, *The Outskirts*. The play had been directed in Vienna by the legendary Max Reinhardt and dealt with the motifs of adultery and murder on the fringes of society. Blanche felt Bizzy would be perfect for the lead role of a prostitute who seduces a younger, married architect who ends up murdered in his studio. The two women spent the muggy June afternoons lounging in the shade of Peace Haven's flowering magnolia trees, reading and rereading the script. Wright had hoped Bizzy's New York connections would make life in the rural South more tenable, but they only served to make him all the more aware and trepidatious of his wife's yearning to be elsewhere.

Husband and wife spent their days swimming in the spring-fed pool, playing tennis, eating muscadines on the banks of Lake Lillian, riding horseback along the miles of trails, golfing on Peace Haven's nine-hole course in plus-four knickerbockers and argyle socks. In the evenings, there were parties and dances to host for Bizzy's visiting theater cronies - Blanche, Bea Lillie, Spring Byington, Byron Fogg, of course - and pig pickins and horseshoes for Wright's local set - Charley Hughes, Jim Baggs, Charles "Fat Charlie" Wilson. The couple prudently prevented their respective circles from intermingling; only Buck Moore was welcome in both worlds.

At virtually every gathering, Bizzy was implored to sing. Wright's young friends, especially, were thrilled to hear in person the smoky-voiced torch songs they had heretofore heard only on record or the radio. For all except Buck, it was the first professional vocalist they had ever seen perform in real life. Employing the pipe organ's music rolls, or Byron Fogg as organist, Bizzy sang in the Reception Hall as her guests watched and listened, spellbound.

Bizzy threw herself into the role of lady of the manor with the same relish she had portrayed ladies of the night on Broadway. But it was just that, Wright feared: a portrayal. He pressed her for a confession that she missed the city, the stage, the spotlights, the speakeasies. When no such admission was forthcoming, he remembered the Aeolian organ's speakers.

When Fogg, Blanche, or Bea stayed at Peace Haven for long weekends, Wright would excuse himself and skulk upstairs to the gallery, where he loitered under the grille in the ceiling and waited for the discussion on the main floor to turn candid in his absence. Wright overheard Fogg relaying to Bizzy the latest gossip from the Great White Way. Howard Stahl was preparing a new revue he was calling *Flying Colors*, Fogg's disembodied voice said through the speaker. Fogg himself would star, naturally, alongside Imogene Coca, Buddy Ebsen, and Tamara Geva. Cole Porter's *Gay Divorce* was set to open in November, Fogg said, and rumor had it that its star, Fred Astaire, was considering offers from Hollywood, to which Bizzy audibly scoffed. Wright overheard Bea Lillie saying Vernon Duke had promised her that she would sing "April in Paris" when *Walk a Little Faster* opened at the St. James Theater in December. Noël Coward's next musical, *Words and Music*, was having a Manchester Opera House tryout in England this August. Bizzy never said it, but in her silence, Wright could hear his wife's longing to return to that world.

He had also heard Bizzy and Buck, their exchanges coded, trading thinly veiled innuendos even when alone.

One evening at a party by the lake, Fat Charlie had requested Cole Porter's "Love for Rent," trying, Wright knew, to embarrass Bizzy by asking her to sing the scandalous song that all in attendance knew had been banned from the radio. Head held high, Bizzy serenaded his friends.

> *I've got love for rent,*
> *There's a vacancy.*
> *Love for rent,*
> *Come up and see.*

Wright had receded into the twilight shadows to watch. Depending on their proximity to their girlfriends or wives, his friends either gazed lustfully at Bizzy or futilely pretended not to. The women stared, too, with either disgust or barely concealed jealousy. Wright let the cover of night hide his burgeoning erection, waiting for it to inevitably wane so he could return to the party and subtly but sternly whisper instructions to Bizzy to sing something less suggestive. Lake Lillian's attendant navy of bullfrogs preempted her performance before Wright could, however, croaking so vociferously that she bowed and gestured with a wave of her hand for the noisy amphibians to take it away, much to the amusement of her audience.

Back at the house, with the guests dispersed save for Buck, Wright crouched on the galley and listened, hoping to hear his friend repeat to Bizzy the surreptitious pronouncements of infatuation by the men, doubtlessly confessed to Buck on their way up the hill from the lake after the party. Wright was simultaneously ready to be angered by those same sentiments.

Through the pipe organ's speaker, he heard Bizzy and Buck laughing, she lamenting her lack of the microphone she would have needed to overpower the frogs. Then she began to sing the verse they had robbed her of.

Love for rent,
Single occupancy.
I've got love for rent,
Available immediately.

Wright closed his eyes and imagined his wife, sauntering around the library below, trailing a fingertip over the Steinway baby grand. "Have you ever sung into a microphone, Buck?"

"No, ma'am."

"There's a technique, you know. It's not as easy as it looks."

"Oh yeah?"

"First off, you have to know how to hold a

microphone," Bizzy said. "You must find a comfortable grip, so your hand doesn't get tired. If you shift your fingers around too much while you're singing into it, you can cause unwanted... spikes in sound. You want a mic that suits your hand—not too thin, not too thick—so that you can hold it comfortably for a three-minute song."

"Is that so?" Buck asked. Wright could picture his eyebrows raising.

Bizzy's voice was lower now. "The proper position is off to one side but pointing at the center of your mouth. Did you know that?"

"No, ma'am, I didn't know that."

"And you want to keep it about one or two inches from your lips. If you keep moving the microphone around, the timbre of the sound changes. Keeping the correct grip, angle, position, and distance lets the mic pick up the true sound of your singing voice."

"I like the way you sing, Miss Holt."

"I know you do, Buck. And it's Mrs. Williams."

"Mrs. Williams," he echoed.

"It helps, too, to pull away during high notes, to keep from overwhelming the microphone. When you know you're going to sing louder, you just ease the mic away from your mouth to compensate."

"Yeah." Wright pictured Buck nodding like an

idiot.

"Just as important is drawing the mic closer to your mouth for low notes. It takes a lot of practice."

"I bet."

"You must be careful, though. You don't want to eat the mic."

"You don't?"

"If you press your lips directly against it, it can increase the volume suddenly, and the sound you'll get is all... buzzy."

With that, Wright had rapidly descended the staircase into Reception Hall to make his presence known.

On another occasion, he heard Byron Fogg's voice, reciting an article to Bizzy. "Listen to this," Fogg had said. Wright could hear a newspaper snapping open. "*Sunday Times*, New York." Fogg cleared his throat. "'Whirligig, speed, faster, crazier, champagne cocktails, corn liquor straight, pour it on, step on the gas, shoot the works, gin, rye, bourbon, sex. Dizzy dames. Dizzy Bizzy Williams' house parties. Moonlight dips. Dances. Joyrides. Speed. Chasing a new thrill today. Tiring of it tomorrow. Nowhere to go but places. Nothing to do but things. Speed with youth at the throttle, millions to spend, and bored stiff. Life's blah. The world's a phony. The whirligig spins on.'"

Bizzy replied, "That's a bit of an exaggeration."

"Only slightly."

And then Wright had heard the sound of his wife's sobbing through the ceiling grille. She was tearfully confiding to Fogg that she knew her husband's older relatives hated her. They had been polite, she said. "Of course they have," Fogg snorted. "They're Southerners. They're genteel to a fault, even as they murder you." Bizzy told Fogg that she had overheard Peace Haven's staff laughing about the fact that Wright's aunts referred to her as "that damned Yankee Jewess." When Fogg asked her what Wright had said when she confronted him about it, Bizzy replied that she had not. "It would only cause more strife. And we have had enough of that already. He's become paranoid, Foggy. The Lindbergh case has made him deathly afraid of being kidnapped for his money. He hears footsteps. He sleeps under the bed, worried someone will sneak into his bedroom at night."

Fogg told her, "Try to have pity on him, my dear. He was raised without parents by nursemaids and servants. He has been given too much money, far too soon. Perhaps you or I would have turned out similarly."

"I never told you about Nellie Burnside and the White Russian," Bizzy said. Wright, too, had never heard this tale.

Fogg said, "You've told me about Nellie and

Mercedes de Acosta. Nellie and Greta Garbo. Nellie and Isadora Duncan. Nellie and Eva Le Gallienne. And Marlene Dietrich." Wright could hear Bizzy laughing now. "And Ona Munson, Tamara Karsavina, Pola Negri, Sally Cornell. But never, my dear, have you told me about Nellie Burnside and any White Russian."

"Nellie and I visited a fortuneteller in Paris, an old White Russian woman. I can't remember now what the woman told me, but days later Nellie admitted to me what the fortuneteller had told her. Nellie said the White Russian asked her if she was fond of me, to which she had said yes. Then the old woman said, 'I dare not tell her, but she is in some way going to be mixed up in a violent death with a man she will marry.'"

"That's ridiculous," Fogg scoffed. "Fortunetellers."

"I thought so, too. For the longest time."

"Now who's being paranoid, my dear?"

Just last night, Saturday, Wright had overheard Bizzy in conversation with Blanche Hruska. When Blanche asked her if she had seen Lucy since she had returned from Havana, Wright rose on his tiptoes to inch closer to the speaker grille. "Yes," Bizzy replied. "Yesterday. Here." He—listened intently. "She and Foggy and Bea arrived together. Wright's gang were already here. We had hoped to finally integrate our friends this weekend. When mine arrived on Friday afternoon, his were already drunk and behaving like the children they are. Even though he knew to expect her, the sight of Lucy was so threatening to Wright that he withdrew to his beloved balcony and aimed that goddamned pistol of his through the railing and began shooting the crystal ornaments from the chandelier while his drunk friends egged him on. It took the poor maids an hour to collect all the shards."

In the Bohemian accent she had inherited from her parents, Blanche could only say, "Oh, my." Even alone in the gallery, Wright could feel the heat radiating from his reddened face, mortified to hear his petulant behavior so plainly put.

Bizzy said, "Lucy had planned to stay for the Fourth of July but Wright's displays so appalled her she could not bear to be around him. I begged her to stay, but she wouldn't hear it. She's never approved of the marriage, you know that, but I believe she had begun to accept it. She's always thought Wright a child, but now she's convinced he's a danger. To himself. To others. To me."

And now, on the Sunday afternoon before Independence Day, Wright was leaning on the balcony's railing, eyes skipping sightlessly over the Reception Hall's treasures as he listened to the words spilling from the overhead speaker.

"You want a drink?" Bizzy asked. He could hear

the neck of his cut-glass decanter clinking against a tumbler.

"Won't you join me?" a man replied in a deep voice that Wright did not recognize.

She objected, "You know I never touch the stuff."

"You want me to drink alone?" The voice did not belong to Fogg or Buck, nor was it Fat Charlie or Baggs or Wilson. There was a brief silence and then the anonymous man continued, "Why don't you do something better with your life? You wanted to be a singer."

"Something better? I've got 'em lined up, baby, with their wallets out. You at the front."

Another pause, then, "It's been so hard, not seeing you."

"Well, you better get used to it," Bizzy snapped back with venom. "After this, we can never see each other again."

Wright's heart rate suddenly accelerated.

"We'll make it look like an accident," the man said. "Drag the body into the street. Make it look like he got run over."

Bizzy responded, coldly, "I don't care if they know it's murder." Now Wright's heart drummed against his ribcage so violently he could see his shirt front fluttering. "They'll send me away! Don't you know I'm in love with you?"

"No, you're not."

"Yes, I am! I was willing to kill for you!"

"That's not love."

Lightheaded, Wright staggered away from the speaker, losing his balance momentarily, bracing himself against a tapestry. When his equilibrium returned, he straightened himself and walked calmly and deliberately down the hall to his and Bizzy's bedroom, where he opened the drawer of his marble-top side table drawer and withdrew the Mauser. With a practiced and familiar motion, he pulled back the semi-automatic's slide, revealing the shining copper-nickel casing of a .32-caliber round in the chamber. Tucking the pistol's short barrel behind his belt and concealing its grip under his untucked shirttail, Wright went back the way he came.

Passing under the speaker grille, he heard the unknown man's voice again, imploring Bizzy not to abandon him. Wright descended the staircase into the Reception Hall, weaving between vases and armchairs as he made his way toward the library. The voices grew louder, along with a dissonant thrumming in his ears, the closer he got.

When Wright entered the wood-paneled library, he saw three people. His wife was lounging on the leather sofa, still in the red and white bathing suit she had worn for her after-lunch swim with Blanche. Blanche was standing by the fireplace, a shoulder leaning against the mantle. By the window stood a man, roughly twice Wright's twenty years. Gimlet eyes squinted behind a pair of wire-rim glasses. Black hair streaked with silver was slicked straight back. He had a handsome face with an aquiline nose, skin tanned and smooth. All three library occupants held in their hands matching bundles of paper, hole-punched and bound by brads, folded over to read from the same page.

Upon seeing Wright, Bizzy sprang from the sofa and kissed him on the cheek. She pulled him by the wrist toward the bespectacled man. "Louis, this is my husband. Wright, this is Louis Batchelor."

At the same time, both men said, "Bizzy's agent," and shook hands. Wright subtly palmed the Mauser's handle, making sure it was well hidden.

"Louis is down from New York to read the play Blanche brought me," Bizzy said.

"And to see your magnificent home," Batchelor added with a slight bow. He paused, seemingly to wait for a welcome from Wright.

A wordless beat passed, and then another. Bizzy staved off the next by interjecting, "Yes, well, shall we continue our read? Walt? Blanche?"

They nodded, each clearing their throats and scanning the scripts for their places. Blanche began.

"Young lady! We have no place here for a girl of your sort."

Batchelor read, "Gather your belongings. You're through."

Bizzy returned to her spot on the sofa and patted the leather beside her. Wright sat next to her as her character replied to Batchelor's. "Mr. Lumley, it wasn't my fault. He followed—" Wright sunk deep into the settee, the cushion creaking noisily as it swallowed him, the sound smothering Bizzy's words and forcing her to stop and start again. "Mr. Lumley, it wasn't my fault. He followed me into the washroom. He's my employer. A girl has to earn a living, doesn't she?"

The trio quickly rediscovered the rhythm Wright's entrance had interrupted and efficiently worked through scene after scene. Blanche settled into an armchair while Louis preferred to stand or pace. Bizzy eventually reclined, folding her legs beneath her, and laying her head in Wright's lap as she read. His hand lit on her bare leg. She flinched, so slightly that he was unsure he had not imagined it. Then, not as subtly, she closed her hand over his and moved it away. Hiding her face from Blanche and Louis behind the script, Bizzy mouthed to her husband, "We have *company*."

Wright stood, unceremoniously dumping her from his lap. "I'll be upstairs."

Without looking back, he exited the library,

retraced his path through the Reception Hall, and climbed the stairs to the gallery. As he walked under the organ's speaker grille, he heard nothing.

In his bedroom, Wright stood in front of the dresser's mirror. In it, instead of a man, he saw a twelve-year-old boy who had just learned he had been orphaned and was refusing to accept that fact and therefore robbing the truth of its dominion. He pulled the Mauser from his belt and cradled it in his hands. With his fingers, he outlined the barrel, the sight, the trigger guard. He massaged the pad of his thumb into the sharp diamonds of the checkered walnut grip and then, with a sharp metallic snap, flipped the safety off. He curled his index finger around the trigger and watched in the mirror as he raised the pistol and pressed the muzzle against his left temple.

With a clatter, Wright tossed the Mauser onto the dresser, watching it spin on the marble top until it slowed to a stop, aimed at his reflection. He turned and walked back down the hallway, sitting with his legs crossed on the gallery floor beneath the speaker. He could hear his wife reciting a prostitute's pleas of innocence.

Chapter 13

Winston-Salem, North Carolina
Tuesday, July 5, 1932

Wright was relieved when he counted only two empty shot glasses on the table between Bizzy and Bebe Walker Belk. After watching just one round of the contest, though, he realized his relief was premature. The women were drinking a concoction he recognized as one of Buck's inventions, a part-cocktail, part-game called a dive-bomber. Wright watched as Bizzy performed the ritual just as Buck had devised. First, she pulled a dark amber bottle of homebrew from a galvanized washtub on the boathouse's concrete patio, flipped the bail on the porcelain stopper, then poured the beer into a glass. Next, she filled her shot glass from the spigot on the five-gallon oak keg perched on a masonry wall. She tipped the smaller glass over the lip of the taller one and dumped one-hundred-proof corn liquor through the foamy head of the beer. And finally, the object of the game: gulp down the entire mixture before the moonshine had time to settle to the bottom of the glass.

Now Wright saw the collection of empty bottles in the tub—he counted eight, four for Bizzy, four for Bebe—and realized how deep into the contest his wife was. She drained the glass, aiming its base at the dusk sky and swallowing the last suds before banging it down on the tabletop to the rowdy cheers of the other partygoers.

Bebe Walker Belk politely applauded her opponent, giving Bizzy a lopsided smile and respectful nod.

"You said you could hold as much liquor as any man." Bizzy leaned forward and said in a mock whisper, "I'm a woman."

Bebe reached for another bottle of beer, prompting the small crowd to hoot and clamor, waving dollar bills above their heads, placing bets. Bebe fumbled for her shot glass and sloppily refilled it, obliviously tilting it at a precarious angle, spilling the precious liquor onto the concrete. As Wright's guests shouted, Bebe shakily deposited the moonshine into the beer. She lifted the glass to her lips and began to tip it back, hinging her head until she was staring at the clouds. Then, like an axed tree, she began to slowly fall backward, her body plank straight, saved from a crash against the patio by an attentive Buck, who shot forward and caught Bebe under her arms.

Wade Beauchamp

The crowd roared its approval of the victor and Bizzy waved her arms in the air, acknowledging their cheers. With laughs and pats on the back, they all returned to their own drinks and conversations that had been paused for the duration of Bizzy and Bebe's contest.

The boathouse party, ostensibly, was to celebrate the twenty-first birthday of Charley Hughes, Wright's best and oldest friend save for Buck. Like Wright, Charley was a skilled pilot. His father had married into the same Vogler family from which Wright had divorced, making Charley one of the most eligible bachelors in Winston-Salem. The timing of his birthday was incidental. In reality, Wright was throwing the party for himself, hoping that a boisterous evening spent in the company of his Southern friends would inoculate him against an interminable summer surrounded by Bizzy's Northern ones. She agreed.

Wright drew up a guestlist of twenty names, in addition to Charley's. Some invitees were out of town during the week of July the Fourth. A few of his friends were unable to finagle permission from their parents to attend what was sure to be another wild evening at Peace Haven that would be gossiped about in Winston-Salem's diners, markets, and salons the next morning, always a popular pastime in town, but one pursued with renewed vigor since the arrival of Broadway's Dark

The Purple Menace and the Tobacco Prince

Purple Menace.

In addition to the party's hosts and Buck and Blanche, who had spent the weekend at the estate, Wright's only friends to *répondez s'il vous plaît* in the affirmative were Fat Charlie Wilson, Mac McDonnell, Jim Carpenter, and Billy Harper.

The guest of honor, Charley Hughes, was accompanied by twenty-three-year-old Virginia Burke, a former classmate and friend of both of Wright's sisters. The Burke family-owned Winston-Salem's largest laundry company, Rosendorf, named for the lavish Rosendorf Hotel that had burned to the ground on Thanksgiving Day 1892 in a fire that marked the end of the city's dream of becoming a renowned resort destination in addition to a tobacco hub.

Mac McDonnell, now the owner of Winston-Salem's only airport, arrived solo, as did Billy Harper, a Charlotte radio salesman who had flown in the Great War. Fat Charlie, too, came stag, despite his prominent position at Moravia Loan and Trust—the largest trust company between Baltimore and New Orleans—typically affording him the clout to arrive at any party with at least one beautiful debutante on his corpulent arm.

Art gallery owner Jim Carpenter—Slick's cousin—brought as his date twenty-eight-year-old widow, Bebe Walker Belk, who worked at Montaldo's, the closest thing Winston had to the type of department stores New York City boasted, albeit on a much smaller scale. Her husband, Dewey, had been burned to death just a year earlier.

Those eleven people, in ever-mutating configurations of pairs, trios, and quartets, mingled now on the patio of the boathouse on the bank of Lake Lillian. The sun was going down and they were serenaded by the bullfrogs, crickets, and, occasionally, Bizzy Holt. Pluma Washington and the other servants trekked continuously back and forth to the main house, up and down the hundred-yard slope between the lake and the colonnaded rear portico of the bungalow, carrying silver trays of canapés and other hors d'oeuvres. The guests drank White Rock Sparkling Water -the same brand Charles Lindbergh had used to christen the *Spirit of St. Louis* - beer brewed in Peace Haven's basement, and, of course, the corn liquor.

The moonshine had been procured by a newly industrious Buck, who seemed to Wright to be finally taking his employment more seriously. Buck and Jim Baggs had driven to Lewisville, a small farming community ten miles west of Peace Haven, on the banks of the muddy Yadkin River. In the shadow of the Brushy Mountains, in the woods away from the roads, were men who squeezed their livings from hot copper tubes. When the liquor became illegal in North

Carolina, the Revenuer Man came tromping through the trees with his axe and baying hounds, and the fox ran his corn mash in souped-up Tin Lizzies down to Winston-Salem, High Point, and Salisbury. In search of one such fox, the boys drove Buck's Plymouth Sport Roadster to the dead end of a deeply rutted dirt road, where a weathered man in faded denim bib overalls and skin like cracked boot leather greeted them. In accordance with the customary caution of his trade, the bootlegger informed the youths that he did not make the white lightning himself but knew the man who knew the man who had. For fifteen dollars, Buck and Baggs bought five gallons and the keg rode back to Winston-Salem on the roadster's rumble seat, arriving at Peace Haven an hour before the guests.

Those guests had consumed all five gallons by sunset. The beer was almost gone now, too. Birthday boy Charley and his date, Virginia, had sequestered themselves in a corner of the patio. Virginia was bobbing and weaving like Jack Dempsey to avoid Charley's attempts to kiss her, playfully letting him land one every few jabs. Mac and Billy were on the lawn, watching the lake's mallards and swans paddle toward their nests for the night. Wright resisted the urge to join their conversation about the operating range of air-to-ground radio. Fat Charlie was trying to impress Blanche with news of his appointment as the first president of the Winston-Salem Jaycees, she countering with a report on her recent Broadway turn as Helen of Troy in Shakespeare's *Troilus and Cressida.* Jim was sitting with Bebe, caressing her shoulders, trying to persuade her to drink some soda water in the aftermath of a vomiting session at the water's edge. Buck hovered nearby, ever vigilant for an opportunity to offer the young widow some comfort of his own.

Wright watched Bizzy cinch the sash of her white flannel lounging pajamas and leap onto a wooden crate of White Rock. "Let's sing!" she shouted to Bebe from her soda pedestal, who gamely got to her feet, shrugging off Charley, and began to teeter toward Bizzy. Before the drunken duet could begin, though, Bizzy stumbled, the crate pitching to one side, bucking its rider and loudly jangling the bottles inside. Bizzy and Bebe tumbled into each other's arms, laughing, dancing a maladroit tango until each found their balance and laughed louder.

Pluma arrived with another wide platter of hors d'oeuvres, which was instantly descended upon by the ravenous partiers. The steadfast housekeeper who had once changed Wright's diapers exchanged a glance with him, each recognizing the disgust in the other's eyes.

Now Buck orbited near Bizzy and Bebe, who had released their embrace and spun away from one another. Wright watched Buck sniffing the air in Bebe's wake. Bizzy had seen, too. "Bebe!" she called after her. Bebe returned. Bizzy reached for the other woman's forearm and, cradling it in her hands lifted it toward Buck's face. Bizzy pressed the inside of Bebe's wrist to Buck's nose. He inhaled.

"Chanel No. 5," Bizzy said.

Bebe eyed her and Buck in turn, and then nodded.

"Of course, you know its story," Bizzy said, surrendering Bebe's arm. Buck shook his head. "As with most things credited to Coco Chanel - suntanning, the little black dress - the inception of Chanel No. 5 is shrouded behind a veil of acopro... acop... *apoc*rypha."

Bebe stood by silently, visibly confused.

To Buck, Bizzy said, "The creation myth of No. 5 begins in 1920 with Coco challenging the French-Russian perfumer Ernest Beaux to formulate a scent that would make its wearer," Bizzy affected an aristocratic French accent. "'Smell like a woman and not like a rose.' As the legend goes, when presented with a selection of numbered glass vials of scents to sample, Coco chose number five." Bizzy breathed deeply, gesturing for Buck to do the same. "What do you smell?"

Buck shook his head and shrugged. "Flowers?"

Bizzy said, "Thank you, Bebe. You're dismissed." Bebe blinked, stood motionless for a moment, and then wandered away. Bizzy smiled at Buck. "Chanel No. 5 has an olfactory bouquet of notes that include ylang-ylang, may rose, sandalwood. It's clean. Like fresh laundry."

Buck sniffed and nodded. "Clean." Had Wright's mood been lighter, he would have chuckled at his friend's predictability. He knew it had been foolish to invite Buck to Peace Haven tonight. He knew he would be unable to leave neither his friend nor his wife unchaperoned with one another at any point during the evening. But no matter how wary of the pairing he was, he did nothing to separate them now. He moved closer.

Bizzy said, "Before Chanel No. 5, there were only two types of perfumes. So-called upstanding women wore fragrances that smelled like a flower. The rest of us in the demimonde preferred a scent more…" Buck shot Wright a glance that betrayed the fact he had no idea what 'the demimonde' was. Wright was unsure as well but offered Buck no comfort by way of a commiserate shrug or shake of his head. Buck was on his own. "Provocative," Bizzy continued. "Musk. Jasmine. Smells that attract the male of the species. By blending the amina… *anima*listic and floral, Mademoiselle Chanel and Monsieur Beaux created a perfume that appealed equally to flappers and courtesans alike and dispelled the notion that a woman had to choose between being sexy or pure. Now they could be both."

Buck nodded and stared at Bizzy. Wright did too. She looked like a bronze snake, glinting eyes charming its victim into paralysis, ready to swallow it whole. Neither Buck nor Wright could take their eyes off her.

Bizzy reached and cupped her hand around the crown of Buck's head. She pulled his face down to nuzzle her neck. Wright could see Buck's chest rising as he breathed in the scent on her throat.

She released him and he straightened himself. "That's Shalimar," she said. "Another glory of French perfumery. Created by Jacques Guerlain in 1921, his tribute to the love story of the Emperor Shah Jahan and his wife, Mumtaz Mahal."

Buck's eyes widened at the mention of such exotic names.

Wright said, "The Taj Mahal of perfumes."

Bizzy cut her eyes at him. "Quite literally." Then, staring at Buck, she said. "The base is…" She drew in a breath. "…almost lewd. A little indecent. Don't you agree?"

Again, Buck simply nodded.

"It's been said there are three things a respectable woman does not do: smoke in public, dance the tango, and wear Shalimar."

Bizzy's eyes narrowed as she smiled at Buck.

And here Wright saw it again, that Bizzy Holt magic. The same sorcery she so effortlessly worked night after night on spotlighted stages. The same spell she had cast on him in Baltimore. The trance she had put Lucy in. The same thrall she had held over Buck on the *Galaxie*. Even as an observer, Wright felt it now, that aching desire to be elevated by her, transfigured by her. In her dark eyes, between her lips, you saw an intercessor, a messenger, an intermediary between the human and the divine. She would relay your prayers, but you might not like the answer. She was a psychopomp. She was Anubis. Charon. Valkyrie. She would open for you a portal and offer you passage. And a deal: She would ferry you to paradise. In return, you would forfeit your soul. "Shalimar is sexy precisely because it smells a little obscene."

Wright could see Buck's cheeks redden. Buck's cock had been in Bizzy's mouth, but she had not relinquished her power to reduce him to a blushing schoolboy. Buck held her gaze as long as he could before dissolving into giggles and looking down at his bare feet. Wright, too, could take no more and stepped away from the patio, out onto the lawn and into the summer night.

Hands stuffed into the front pockets of his ducks, Wright wandered to the edge of the lake, the unmown blades spritzing his socks with dew. A chorus of bullfrogs ringed Lake Lillian, ceaselessly advertising for mates with their resonant, almost bovine calls. As he always did whenever under the stars, Wright recalled his first lesson in celestial navigation, given to him by Walt on the front lawn of Peace Haven. Wright looked skyward and located the Big Dipper, then its pointer stars, Merak and Dubhe, the two points of light the water would run off if one could reach into the heavens and tip up the dipper. He traced an imaginary line through the pointers and followed it until it intersected with Polaris, the North Star. True north. Around this twinkling pinprick, the entire dome of the sky revolved. Wright thought he could stay out here all night and watch it happen.

His solitude was short-lived. He heard the sluicing sound of footsteps through the wet grass and turned to see the hourglass silhouette of his wife walking away from the boathouse. The smooth skin on her bare shoulders reflected the moonlight. Wright watched until her shape was absorbed by the mottled shadows beneath the trees as she made her way up the hill toward the main house. He exhaled the breath he did not realize he had been holding. He was surprised by Bizzy's early retirement - the sky above the western horizon was still in the twilight afterglow of sunset - but was relieved to know she was done drinking for the evening.

No sooner had Wright turned back to the glassy lake than he heard another set of steps kicking through the tall grass. This time he saw Buck's lean figure, following the path Bizzy had taken just minutes before.

Drawn like a magnet, Wright trailed in Buck's wake, keeping his distance, lagging far enough behind to ensure that his tracking would go undetected. Halfway up the hill, Wright realized he could no longer see Buck's shape and had lost the trampled trail he had been following. Still,, Wright ascended toward the brightly lit manor until he heard the faint burble of laughter emanating from beyond the woods to his left.

Wright changed course, following the laughter, now accompanied by the sounds of splashing. As he neared, he could see the underside of the canopy of tulip poplar trees aglow with turquoise light from Peace Haven's spring-fed outdoor pool below. Wright slowed his approach, crouching now, creeping closer. He could smell the fresh, aquatic scents of the hyacinth and waterlilies that kept the pool naturally filtered and oxygenated. Closer still, Wright stole. Now he could clearly hear Buck's laugh, the same one he had elicited a million times since they were boys, followed by Bizzy's, throaty and melodious, and much rarer to Wright's ears.

The rectangular pool was surrounded by concrete coping and a narrow patio, which in turn was bordered by a low stone wall over which English ivy cascaded. The wavering aquamarine light from the pool's submerged lamps shimmered in the trees overhead like restless spirits searching for an escape through the leaves. Through a gap in the tree trunks, Wright saw Bizzy's flannel pajamas in a pile on the patio. He craned his neck to look for his wife, so focused on the glowing pool that he stumbled into a bramble of kudzu. The vines tangled themselves around Wright's ankles and almost sent him tumbling.

Cursing under his breath, he freed his feet with a few kicks and edged closer to the swimming pool. Bizzy and Buck's voices carried across the water, but Wright could not decipher their words through the din of crickets, rustling vines, and the slosh and spatter of the pool. Kneeling in a dense undergrowth, he got his first unobstructed view of the swimmers.

Bizzy was in the middle of the pool, bobbing, her head seeming to float in the mist of white vapor that hovered above the water's plane. Buck was reclined against the edge, arms draped across the coping, his erection protruding proudly from his lap. Bizzy let herself sink into the water to her nostrils, her black hair fanning across the surface and trailing behind her as she swam to Buck. Like a pair of hunting alligators, his hands slipped off the pool's rim and into the water, moving to clasp onto Bizzy's waist.

Buck kicked off the wall, buoying himself and Bizzy out into the center of the coruscating pool. Wright's head felt as weightless as their bodies. They revolved around one another until Buck released her body to drift toward the wall. Bizzy turned and reached out for the concrete apron with her hands and pulled herself close, vaulting out of the water with extended arms, elbows locked. She hinged her hips and let Buck take a long look, her body glistening wet, the water beading into glittering diamonds on her skin and running off her in rills. She watched Buck over her shoulder, pushing her ass out behind her and twitching it like a mischievous cat's tail.

Buck dipped beneath the water and propelled himself like a torpedo toward Bizzy. He broke the surface at speed, hands reaching ahead, fingers hooked like talons. He dug into her soft buttocks and she arched her back to push them into his palms. She tightened the halves into clenched bunches and then let them relax into full, supple globes for Buck to knead. Wright's pulse throbbed in his temples.

Bizzy smiled and said something to Buck that Wright could not hear. Buck lowered his mouth to her ass and pressed his lips to it, kissing it all over, painting it with broad strokes of his tongue. He squeezed and parted it, pushing his face into its seam. Bizzy arched her back, threw her head back laughing. Over her shoulder, she looked down at Buck. Wright heard her ask, "You like?" Buck nodded his head enthusiastically; a boy being asked if his birthday cake was good. He bit into the softest part, hard enough to leave reddened teeth marks, making her yelp and giggle.

Bizzy unlocked her elbows and let her body splash back into the pool, spinning to face Buck. She drew a deep breath, filling her lungs with humid night air, and then slipped silently beneath the illuminated blue water. A hot breeze rustled the poplars and Wright used the noise to cover his own sounds as he moved closer, shuffling through the ivy. He could see Bizzy's undulating shape dolphin-kicking toward Buck's penis.

Buck stared down through the water as she closed her lips over his erection, along with a mouthful of water. Wright could see Buck's body shudder, could see his hips moving. He could hear him moan.

Bizzy suddenly broke the surface, gasping. With lungs refilled, she dove under and took Buck's turgid member into her mouth again, nodding her head. Wright could see her dark hair swirling under the water as if she were caught in a slow hurricane. He could see her face now, looking up at Buck, distorted and refracted through the ripples. She sucked until Wright was certain her lungs were on fire, and she pulled free and burst above the surface once more, gulping down a chest full of air.

Buck inclined onto his back, drifting away and rising until his erection emerged from the water like a periscope. He floated that way, making sure Bizzy looked as long as she wanted to at his rigid young body and cock, blatantly proud of both. She swam to him and lapped at the full length of his shaft, giggling as she made it sway and lurch. She closed her mouth over its crown and Buck knotted his fingers into her damp locks and extended his lean torso to its fullest.

Wright's heart thumped heavily against his ribs. Bizzy pulled back, glancing toward the trees and, unknowingly, directly at Wright. With a splash, Buck righted himself and took her by the arms, guiding her through the water and backing her against the lip of the pool. She parted her legs as Buck swam between them. She held onto him by his wet shoulders, the long muscles flanking his spine flexing and tightening. Wright saw her eyes flutter and close and Buck entered her.

Under the water, Bizzy wrapped her legs around Buck's waist, locking her ankles together behind his back. Wright heard her breath hiss out of her in a long sigh. Buck kissed along her jawline and down her slender neck. Bizzy tilted her head to the side, her dark, wet curls draping across Buck's shoulder as he nipped at her jugular. She seemed to be trying to say something, but the words came out only as halting gasps. Buck was gathering momentum, churning the water into choppy waves all around them, splashing onto the pool's patio.

Again, Bizzy looked toward the poplars, this time fixing her gaze on Wright's hiding place. She seemed to be staring right at him, wanting him to see what this looked like, wanting to burn this image into his brain. She was heaving against Buck now, meeting his every thrust, spreading her legs wide to accommodate him. She seemed suddenly hellbent on giving Buck the night of his young life. The night to which he would compare every other one. Bizzy was making sure Buck would never fuck anyone ever again without thinking of her.

Buck gazed in astonishment at the grown woman in his arms, as did her boy-husband. Wright prodded and pawed at his penis, distended now and pushing painfully against his canvas trousers. Tomorrow, he knew, after he had slept, after he thought about this, he would be appalled. At Bizzy, at Buck. At himself. But right then, that did not matter at all.

The woods filled with their sounds: Buck's growls, Bizzy's moans and strangled gasps, the constant slapping of waves against the coping. She clung to Buck's arms, her face buried in his chest. Mewling and sobbing, Bizzy came, her orgasm seeming to radiate out of her like a tsunami. In his head, Wright could hear her reciting her rules on the deck of Lucy's yacht. *Rule Number One: No fucking. Rule Number Two: You have to watch…*

Wright turned and trudged noisily back through the tangled kudzu, uncaring now if they heard him. He climbed the slope toward the main house, drawing a nod and an "Evening, Mr. Williams," from W.E. Fulp, Peace Haven's night watchman, who was standing with one boot on the running board of his Model A Ford parked on the back lawn. Wright ambled over and knelt for a moment by Mitzi, Fulp's German Shepherd, as much as to give her some gentle scratches behind her pricked ears to conceal his erection and perhaps force it into remission before entering the house. Then he resumed his walk, the yellow lights of the bungalow a beacon to guide him.

*****

When Buck entered the Reception Hall shortly before midnight, Wright watched him silently take inventory of the guests. Jim and Bebe had gone for a night drive but were back now, lounging together in an armchair, Bebe's head slumped on Jim Carpenter's shoulder. Blanche was yawning on an ottoman, arms stretched over her head, announcing it was past her bedtime. Guest of honor Charley Hughes was long gone, having left the same way he had arrived, to a round of "For He's a Jolly Good Fellow" and with Virginia Burke on his arm. Billy Harper and Fat Charlie Wilson had departed, as well. Mac McDonnell was in the process of leaving, escorted by Wright and listening to instructions to repair the landing lights on the Savoia-Marchetti tomorrow as he intended to take her up for an evening flight the following day.

Duke Ellington & His Famous Orchestra's *Moon Over Dixie* was spinning on the Victrola, the needle hissing and popping through the shellac grooves. When Wright returned to his remaining guests, only he, Jim, Bebe, Blanche, and Buck were present. He watched his oldest friend survey the room, looking for someone in particular but hesitant to ask where she was. Mercifully, Wright finally said, "Bizzy's not here."

Before Buck could reply, Blanche again delivered a performative yawn and stretch, this time standing and bidding the others a good night. "See you all tomorrow," she said as she climbed the staircase.

"Yes," Jim said next, "I believe it's time to get this Cinderella home before my Chevrolet turns back into a pumpkin."

"Let her stay here tonight, Carp," Wright said. "You, too. There's an extra guestroom or three on the second floor."

Jim shook his head. "I couldn't impose, thank you. But if you're certain you don't mind, I'll assist Miss Belk upstairs and be on my way." He stood and gently gathered the sleeping Bebe into his arms and ascended the stairs.

Alone now, Wright and Buck stood and watched one another. He knew it must have been otherwise, but Wright could not remember a time it had been just the two of them since sharing the cottage on Sands Point last summer. He tried to see the man across from him as some kind of villain, to see Buck as his enemy. But try as he might, all Wright could see was the boy he had grown up with, the friend who had been by his side through the peaks and valleys of a very strange life. The only friend who was not drawn by his wealth, the only one not repelled by his eccentricities. The only one not held by the promise of lavish gifts and free liquor. The only friend that had not been chased away by his capricious moods and dark emotions.

Wright knew, too, that Buck had no more chosen his proclivities than had he himself. Buck could not help what he wanted any more than Wright could. If Wright could not repress his own urges, how could he expect Buck to?

Jim was returning to the Reception Hall down the staircase now. As he began to issue his report on how angelic Bebe looked asleep, Mitzi began to bark loudly out on the back lawn. Grateful for the distraction, Wright and Buck stepped outside and ventured into the dark toward the sound of the German

Shepherd. W.E. Fulp called to the boys, announcing he was "coming up with the madam."

Fulp materialized in the glow of the house lights, Bizzy clinging to his forearm. She was in the white flannel pajamas again, a deep green grass stain smeared across one knee. The nightwatchmen held her shoulders, steadying her as she loped and staggered toward the bungalow's rear portico. Fulp remanded Bizzy into her husband's care and, with a respectful nod, faded back into the night.

With Buck at one elbow and Wright at the other, the two men guided Bizzy into the house. Her head lolled to Wright's side and she gave him a lopsided, salacious grin. Once inside the Reception Hall, she brushed away her escorts, wanting to prove to them she was clearheaded and capable of walking without their help. Wright, Buck, and Jim watched, cautiously encircling Bizzy as she moved slowly to the center of the room, ready to spring into action if she began to founder.

In the center of the hall, directly under the chandelier, she stopped and began to extricate herself from her pajamas, only to have her nascent striptease thwarted by the knotted sash. With a singsong, "Is there a doctor in the house?" she looked to each man in turn, hoping to solicit help solving the puzzle. Buck and Jim exchanged nervous glances but neither budged. Wright watched silently, unwilling to help his erstwhile ecdysiast but showing no interest in stopping her, either.

Bizzy grappled with the sash until finally, its ends fell free. She turned her attention next to the buttons on the pajama's blouse, fumbling with the top one before suddenly grabbing the lapels and giving them a swift yank, the buttons bursting off one after the other like kernels of popcorn. As the men watched, Bizzy shuffled the top down her arms until it hung from her wrists. She held the flannel to her chest, swaying to the Ellington Orchestra's "Mood Indigo" on the phonograph, then dropping her arms to let the shirt slump to the floor and displaying her buoyant breasts.

In Wright's mind, a tug of war was being waged between his pride and his jealousy, those eternally and equally matched foes, the ever-shifting centerline pulled one way and then the other, but never decisively toward either.

Bizzy began to push down the waistband of her pajamas, swirling her hips, eyeing all three men in sequence, making sure she had their attention. Once over the swell of her hips, she let the flannel pants fall around her feet. Naked now, she danced to "Tricky Sam" Nanton's plunger-muted trombone, waist swiveling, arms spiraling over her head like wisps of smoke. The glow from the chandelier bathed her body in a halo of light, limning the crescents of her breasts and the circumference of her hips. A smile had stretched across Buck's face from ear to ear.

Wright moved to Bizzy and clamped his hands over her shoulders, steering her toward the staircase. She did not resist. Wright maneuvered her forward, her bare feet slapping against the polished hardwood floor as they wove their way through the Reception Hall. He aimed her between the banisters and steadied her as she began to climb the stairs, each riser requiring two or three clumsy attempts to ascend. A teetering transit of the gallery followed with Bizzy careening back and forth between the wrought iron balustrade and the wall, clawing at a centuries-old tapestry, practically swinging on it to maintain her balance, threatening to rip it down from its hanging rods. Wright finally shepherded her into the bedroom, where he told her to put on some clothes.

Bizzy lurched into her dressing closet while Wright rested in an armchair and massaged his temples with the heels of his palms. Minutes passed and just as he rose to retrieve her, she reentered the bedroom. She was dressed in a peach-colored negligee, the shape of her body beneath the sheer chiffon almost as apparent as it had been when she was naked.

"Where did you get that?" Wright demanded.

Bizzy watched him for a moment and then slid

her hands onto her hips, smoothing the gauzy material to her skin as she swayed proudly. "It was a gift," And then, with a wink, she added, "From a special someone."

"And did you model it for him?"

Bizzy looked at Wright as if he had shot her. "You gave it to me. *You.*"

Now Wright remembered. He had bought it for his new bride at the little boutique in the Wan Chai section of Lockhart Road on their honeymoon in Hong Kong. "I'm sorry, darling angel." They faced one another and simply stared.

Finally, Bizzy turned away and walked, with a slight starboard list, to the dresser, where she began raking the stiff bristles of her silver-handled brush through her jungle of black hair. "So," she said to Wright's reflection in the mirror. "Did you enjoy the show?" Wright held his breath, just long enough for Bizzy to glean that she had the upper hand. "Did you like what you saw in the swimming pool?"

Wright said nothing.

Bizzy let out a laugh, tilting her head as she yanked the hairbrush through a nest of tangles. "Wright Williams, the boy who loved to be hurt. The aviator who liked crashing. The daredevil who wanted his bones broken."

"I don't like being hurt," Wright offered, barely

289

loud enough for Bizzy to hear.

"You love it, Wright!" She spun to face him, teetering back against the dresser. "It's your goddamned occupation!"

"Bizzy…"

"You just want to see who would weep at your funeral! But martyrs don't get to attend their own wakes, dear."

"Darling, please, we have guests downstairs."

Bizzy raised her voice even higher. "I'm not one of your aeroplanes that you can fly around and then expect me to stay in the hangar when you're not showing it off!" She threw the hairbrush at Wright, making him duck but sending it wide to crash into the wall and clatter to the floor.

Wright stood, gave a sharp tug at his shirttail, and walked past Bizzy out of the bedroom. As he descended the stairs, he saw Buck, alone, still in his bathing suit, flitting from door to door, locking each one now that Jim Carpenter had departed, leaving only the guests who would be spending the night at Peace Haven.

"You've just lost your situation," Wright said.

"What do you mean?"

Without answering, Wright stepped outside. The night air was saturated with the scent of honeysuckle nectar. The rear porch that once seemed to overlook half of North Carolina now felt claustrophobic. The pallid light from inside the house threw shadows behind the columns out into the lawn, spokes on a giant wagon wheel, Wright alone at the hub.

He patted the front pocket of his canvas trousers to gauge whether the pack of Taxis next to his wallet was mostly full or almost empty, ready to affix some symbolism to either outcome. He withdrew the flattened pack, shook it like a pair of dice in his palm, and then lipped out the cigarette that sprouted through the opening, the last one. He tucked it into the corner of his mouth, lit it, and inhaled deeply, coaxing the smoke into every lobe and bronchiole of his lungs, burning the cigarette down like a fuse.

Wright pinched the cigarette between his thumb and forefinger and blew a pillar of white smoke into the night. He looked to the stars, found Polaris, and then shut his eyes. The scene from the swimming pool was there—had been there the whole time—just waiting for Wright to blink. This was no monochromatic photograph, no garish Technicolor spectacle, and more than a memory.

Wright watched, again, in his mind, as Bizzy fucked Buck, propelling one another through the water. Her eyes were clenched, white teeth gnashed behind swollen crimson lips. Now he saw the party guests gathering, surrounding the swimming pool, the glowing waves illuminating their features with turquoise light.

The Purple Menace and the Tobacco Prince

There was Jim and Bebe, Mac McDonnell, Billy Harper, and Fat Charlie Wilson; Blanche Hruska; Charley and Virginia. Then Wright saw others. Pluma Washington and W.E. Fulp joined the crowd, followed by Dwight Forbush Daub. Then came Noël Coward, Howard and Dorothy Stahl, Bea Lillie, Nellie and Sister Burnside, Byron Fogg with Ramona and Kimono. The final opening in the circle of spectators was filled by Lucy Allard Conrad, in her tuxedo, monocle, and top hat.

The crowd closed in, vying for position, craning their necks to see better. In the dark of his shut eyes, Wright looked at the faces of the spectators one by one. Some were smiling and nodding in approval, others were clearly scandalized, clutching at strings of pearls in shock. Only Lucy exhibited no outward reaction, staring stone-faced at the mating pair in the pool.

Buck's body snapped and writhed like an electroshock patient, the water roiling around him, washing torrents of it over Bizzy's body. Drunk on endorphins, he rested his forehead against hers as the two panted in one another's arms. Their audience burst into applause.

Wright opened his eyes, banishing the vision, and flicked his cigarette into the night, a looping orange dot against the black. He turned and reentered the bungalow, stalking past Buck toward the stairs. Halfway up, he dug into his front pocket and flung his wallet down at him, bills fluttering like moths. "You can have that. Consider it your severance."

The bedroom was empty when Wright returned. He found Bizzy standing on the adjacent sleeping porch, her expression placid, the negligee swaying in the breeze. He opened his mouth to speak but realized he was utterly unsure of what to say.

Bizzy turned to face him. For a long while she simply stared at him. And then she said, "I've missed my period, Wright. Two weeks now."

He said nothing.

"I'm pregnant."

"But... I..."

Bizzy shook her head. "You didn't."

The sound of the midnight air whispering through the porch's screens rose in Wright's ears until it was a deafening cyclone. The world seized on its axis and only he was unanchored, his centrifugal force throwing him to the floor. Bizzy revolved above him, Ursa Minor wheeling around the pole star. Her eyes were black pools.

Wright pulled himself to his feet, legs wobbling. The porch had stopped spinning, tidally locked now, but its floor was still canted at a precarious angle. He stared at his wife until she, too, held still. In a voice that sounded to him like it had come from elsewhere in the room, he said, "Do you love him?"

Bizzy shook her head. "I don't love him, Wright."

"Do you still love me?"

"I've never been in love."

Wright slowly began to shake his head. "No," he said, shaking his head harder, violently now as if he could sling her words from his ears. "No, you're wrong. You love me."

"You're a child, Wright. If I loved you, it was as your mother."

"You love me!"

"The only thing I've ever loved is what you dragged me away from!"

"Then why are you here?" Wright yelled. "Why are you in my house? Why did you marry me?"

"Because you wouldn't leave me alone, you goddamned terrier!"

Wright stomped to the nightstand and snatched the top drawer open, its contents tumbling to the carpet, He dropped to his knees and shuffled through the digests and papers until he felt the cold angles of the Mauser. Squeezing its handle until his knuckles went white, he rose and turned to Bizzy.

"What are you going to do now, Wright?" She was up on her toes, her face inches away from his, so close he could feel her hot breath as she shouted. "Are you going to shoot me? Shoot Buck?"

Wright clamped his eyes shut, beads of tears forming at the seams. He raised the gun and pushed the muzzle against his temple.

"You're going to shoot yourself? Do it! Do it, Wright, and finally stop talking about it. Do it and stop holding my goddamned feelings hostage."

Husband and wife stared at one another.

"Wright!" Buck shouted from the porch entry.

Even as he was lowering the pistol, Buck charged him, the ball of his shoulder driving into his sternum. The boys stumbled across the floor, careening into the wall, grappling and struggling. Wright freed the arm that held the Mauser and pried it away from Buck, waving it in the air. Buck finally captured the arm by its wrist and wrenched it almost completely around, using his lean torso as a fulcrum and leveraging Wright off the floor.

A loud pop made Buck freeze, fearing he had snapped his friend's humerus. He released Wright and stepped away, expecting to see the broken left arm dangling uselessly at his side. Instead, he saw Wright's body fold to the floor with a thump, his shirt speckled with bright red droplets of blood.

As if across a nautical mile of ocean, Wright thought he heard Bizzy shriek but it was quickly drowned out by what sounded like the rhythmic thrum of a radial engine. The smells of the sleeping porch -

honeysuckle, Bizzy's perfume, the alcohol on her breath - gave way to salty sea air, gasoline, and leather. Wright felt the spray his aeroplane's propeller was kicking up, pooling and trickling down his neck in a warm rivulet.

"Wright!" This time it was Buck's voice across the vast expanse of water.

Then Bizzy again, screaming, "Wright!" And then only the roar of the wind and the Kinner B-5.

The porch was suffused in bright daylight now, the walls rippling and dissolving into clear blue sky. The painted wood floorboards had become a steel floor pan. Wright looked about the Savoia's cockpit, scanning for the Mauser so he could put it away, back in its place in the nightstand drawer. He should have stayed downstairs, he thought. He should turn the plane around. So often it was those small decisions, Wright thought, where if you had listened to one more song or one less, the world would be a much more different place. The wind would smell like Shalimar again, and not liquor and blood. The sky would be dotted with blinding white cumuli instead of blotched with shadows, propagating like inky raindrops in a puddle.

Wright lifted his goggles and rubbed his eyes with his gloved knuckles. When he opened them again, the cockpit had grown larger, twice as spacious as it was before. The joystick was almost too far away to reach, his arms extended to their full length. Now his goggles slumped loosely down the bridge of his nose; his leather flight helmet flapped against his scalp, too big for his head. Wright straightened his legs, stretching for the aileron and rudder pedals but could not find them with his feet. He looked down and saw that they were precisely where they should have been, only now they were impossibly out of reach. He sat up, straining to look over the instrument panel.

The wind and the engine faded to silence. Wright heard only his own halting breaths, and soon not even that. He fixed his eyes on the horizon. He knew all he had to do to get there was cut that distance in half.

Epilogue

Wilmington, Delaware
Saturday, August 20, 1949

Dick's ticket was for *King of the Rocket Men*, easily his favorite serial the Arcadia Theater had shown that summer. Today's matinee was bittersweet, though, being the twelfth and final installment, bringing an end not just to the story but, unofficially, summer as well.

Still, Dick could barely contain his excitement. Last Saturday, Doctor Vulcan had stolen from the Science Associates their most dangerous invention, the Sonic Decimator, and would destroy New York City if Rocket Man could not unmask him in time and bring him to justice. All photographed, as always, by intrepid reporter Glenda Gleason.

The usher tore Dick's ticket in half, handed him back the stub, and pointed him to the right. Dick dutifully walked toward the porthole-windowed door beneath the lighted marquee that read *Rocket Men*.

Behind him, he heard a gasp, followed by an exasperated, "Billy, *honestly!*"

Dick turned to see a small boy standing dejectedly over a pile of spilt popcorn on the Arcadia's carpet. Upon seeing the usher distracted by his impromptu custodial duties, a switch of some sort seemed to flip in Dick's mind and, without thinking twice, he changed course and headed toward the other screening room, the one used for second runs and revivals. He shuffled briskly under the marquee that read *Reckless*, checking over his shoulder the whole way, making sure his detour had gone unnoticed. He slipped into the first empty seat he found and sank as far into its cushion as he could.

Dick had been unfamiliar with *Reckless* until that morning. As he had lain in bed, awakened by the smoky aroma of bacon frying downstairs, he could hear his mother and Lucy talking. Typically he could hear them, especially on Saturday mornings when they raised their voices above the sizzling pans and clattering silverware. But this morning was different. Their voices were hushed, which perked Dick's ears in a way their normal conversation would not have. The women were not quite whispering, but he could tell they meant to not be overheard. He tiptoed to the bedroom door and made sure they would be exactly that.

"I can't believe they're showing that filth in this

town," Mother hissed.

Dick could hear Lucy reply, "To be fair, it did make it past the Hays Code."

"You would feel differently if you were me." Dick's mother could no longer control the volume of her voice. "You're not in the damn thing."

"Neither are you, Bizzy."

The pop and sizzle of the bacon abated as it was removed from the pan and plated. "At least it was a flop."

Now Dick sat in the darkened theater as the whir of the projector supplanted the murmur of the audience. He fidgeted in his seat, anxiously awaiting the filth his mother had unknowingly tipped him off to. A *March of Time* newsreel began, much to Dick's consternation, narrated as always by Westbrook Van Voorhis and his Voice of Doom. This month's episode was titled "Farming Pays Off," and he had to fight the urge to retreat to Rocket Man and Doctor Vulcan. But he knew that if he could just withstand fifteen minutes of wholesome Midwestern values as purveyed by the hardworking farmers from Lincoln County, Ohio, and evidenced by grainy black-and-white footage of potato mountains and mounds of surplus wheat, he would be rewarded with… something. Dick had no idea what, but he knew it was scandalous enough to upset his mother.

The Purple Menace and the Tobacco Prince

Right as Westbrook reliably delivered his closing catchphrase - "Time... marches on!" - a man flopped into the seat next to him. Neither moviegoer acknowledged the other.

On the screen appeared the words:

THIS PICTURE APPROVED
BY THE PRODUCTION CODE
ADMINISTRATION OF THE
MOTION PICTURE PRODUCERS
& DISTRIBUTORS OF
AMERICA
CERTIFICATE NUMBER
736

Dick knew this must have been the Hays Code he overheard Lucy mention that morning. The MGM lion roared and snarled. Then, as *Metro-Goldwyn-Mayer presents...* appeared in a sleek, slender Art Deco typeface, the man next to Dick leaned to him and whispered, "Ever seen this one?"

Dick simply shook his head and kept his eyes on the screen.

Jean Harlow

"Oh, you'll love it. It's a classic."

William Powell

The man took another look at Dick. "Say, how old are you?"

in "Reckless"

302

Dick weighed for a moment how much exaggeration he could get away with, but before he had to lie, the man smiled. "It's okay, son. Your secret's safe with me. I was only fifteen when I snuck in to see this very picture on its first run in '35."

The movie began with an almost slapstick scene of a matronly woman browbeating a New York City sports promoter into helping spring her granddaughter from jail. That exchange played out without so much as a bare shoulder, exposed ankle, or any hint at all of what so offended Mother. Just as thoughts of Rocket Man once again began to tug at Dick, a barred cell door opened on screen, and through it ran who he could only assume was Jean Harlow. An unfamiliar pang stabbed at his chest. Harlow was a prominent member of the exceedingly small pantheon of Hollywood actresses Mother and Lucy seemed to respect, an atavistic avatar of a time "when movie stars could *act*." But Dick now understood that he had never actually seen Jean Harlow. Not really. Not like this.

She loomed, twenty feet tall in pristine silvers and deep, sooty blacks, a crown of snow-white cotton candy waves framing her porcelain face. She was the kind of woman that would intimidate and fascinate Dick when his mother's friends came to visit. She had the confidence of Aunt Nellie and the icy beauty of Miss Greta. But she was warm, like Miss Baker. And she seemed like the kind of person, like Uncle Foggy, who would be unafraid to use their walking stick to rap the windshield of a city bus that got too close as they crossed the street. Dick decided all this before Harlow's first closeup.

"I like her too," the man next to Dick whispered to him. Dick could feel the blood rushing to his face and kept his eyes affixed to the screen. "You know what this story is about?"

Still watching the movie, Dick shook his head.

"Every culture takes pride in its own folklore, you see? It doesn't matter if it's the Irish or the Chinese or the goddamned Italians. Anytime a group of people with similar backgrounds get together, stories get told. And retold. And sooner or later, the stories take on a life of their own, you see? It's like the telephone game; you ever play that one? Where you line up ten people in a row and whisper something in the ear at one end and by the time it gets to the other end, it's a completely different story?" In the movie, Harlow took to the stage in a shimmering satin pantsuit, an orchestra in its pit at her feet. "Broadway ain't no different, son, trust me. They got their own stories, Lord knows. And by the time this one got whispered all the way to Hollywood," he gestured at the screen, "it came out as *Reckless.*"

Still watching the movie, Dick said, "What's it about?"

"Well, Jean Harlow up there, she's playing a character called Mona Leslie. But Mona Leslie ain't really Mona Leslie. She's really Bizzy Holt."

Now Dick turned to look at the man, expecting to see Uncle Foggy or Uncle Noël, carrying out a truancy mission to tail him and catch him in the act of not being exactly where he told Mother he would be. But Dick did not recognize the man, and the man showed no outward signs of knowing him.

"You know that name? Bizzy Holt?" The man asked. "No?"

Dick said nothing, certain he was being put on.

"She lives just outside of town in Montchanin with her... well, it's what they call a Boston marriage, we'll just leave it at that. Lucy Conrad. Allard Chemical heiress. But surely you know *that* name if you grew up around here." Still, Dick remained silent. "You see them together all over town in the summer. Matching haircuts, even." Dick realized he had never thought twice about how similarly his mother and Lucy styled themselves. Not just their bobbed hair but matching tennis whites and bare feet whenever socially acceptable, and sometimes when not.

"Bizzy was a Broadway star, you see, just like Mona up there." On the screen, Harlow and her costumed chorines were performing for the sole benefit of a champagne-swilling playboy who had rented out an entire theater all for himself. Dick's neighbor pointed to the tuxedoed millionaire in the movie. "And that's Bob Harrison, son of an oil tycoon. Only he ain't really Bob Harrison. He's based on the man Bizzy married in real life, heir to the Taxi cigarette fortune -"

"R. Wright Williams." Dick could not remember the last time he had heard his father's full name spoken aloud, much less by himself.

"Ah, see? You do know."

"No... no, just the names."

"And do you know what happened to young Mr. Williams?"

Dick hesitated and then offered, "I know he died before I was born."

The man appraised Dick. "Fifteen, you said?" Dick had not given the man his age but did not correct him. "This would have been 1932 so, yeah, before your time. There was a party down in Winston-Salem. That's where they make the Taxis. Fourth of July weekend. Big party at Wright's mansion. All of them drunk on illegal liquor. It was still Prohibition, you see. Afterward, with only the Williamses and Wright's best friend, a Mr. Buck Moore, left in the house, Bizzy told Wright she was pregnant. There was a big argument and Wright -" Again the man took a moment to examine Dick. "You sure you want to hear this, son?"

Dick nodded, no longer paying attention to what

was happening on the flickering screen.

"Well, Wright was shot in the head. That much is fact. And maybe the only fact to come out of that night. Bizzy and Buck Moore both told the sheriff's deputy that Wright had shot himself. But they had both been drinking, you see, and despite the two of them sequestering themselves in a room at the hospital for an hour to get their stories straight, their statements to the sheriff still contradicted each other."

The man took a moment to watch the original Blonde Bombshell do her thing, then said, "Williams died early the next morning. Without even doing an autopsy, the county coroner called it a suicide. The sheriff, though, knew something was rotten in Denmark and ordered an inquest. They exhumed Williams' body and did an autopsy. And this time the coroner ruled it a murder. Holt and Moore were both indicted by a grand jury in the first degree."

Dick closed his eyes to keep the darkened theater from spinning. The man went on. "It was front page news, even here. The only thing bigger that year was Baby Lindbergh. Lucy Conrad went down South and paid Bizzy's twenty-five thousand dollars bail, dressed in clothes so mannish that bystanders and reporters thought she *was* one. Hell, I've made that same mistake more than once myself." He cleared his throat. "Lucy brought Bizzy back here to hide her away on her daddy's yacht until a trial was scheduled. By the time she had to go back to North Carolina for the grand jury testimony, Bizzy and Buck had both developed some well-timed lapses of memory. Moore was telling his friends he had a secret he would take to the grave. During the inquest, he even denied things he had said to the sheriff earlier. Bizzy eventually claimed to have no memory of that night whatsoever." The man laughed, loud enough to turn a few heads in the theater. "Funny how amnesia works, ain't it?"

Dick opened his eyes and immediately felt as if the bright movie screen was pitching and yawing on a gimbal. He pressed his eyelids tightly together again and braced himself against his armrest.

"Was it murder? I don't think so. Suicide? I suppose it could have been. But I think it was probably just a terrible, tragic accident. One thing's for sure: only Bizzy and Buck know the truth. And they ain't talking. The Williams family - the richest and most powerful in the state, mind you - the Williams family, wary of a nationwide scandal like the Lindberghs had gone through, convinced the prosecutor to drop the charges." The man chuckled. "I tell you what, you couldn't get away with that now. But the truth, if you ask me, is that they didn't want a Williams heir born in prison, had Bizzy been convicted. And down there, with how they feel about Northerners and Jews, she would have been, believe me. Things like illegal hooch, wild parties, impotence, infidelity, those are things you sweep under the rug if you've got the money to buy the broom, if you know what I mean."

Dick was not completely sure he knew what those two *I* words meant, but he knew they were not good. Jean Harlow was now dancing a flamenco with a drunken Mexican cowboy and the man next to Dick fell silent for the duration. When the Bob Harrison character reappeared, the man said, "Six months later, Bizzy gave birth prematurely to a three-and-a-half-pound baby boy. Richard."

"Dick."

"Yeah, that's right." The man regarded his listener for a moment. "That's what they called him. Dick. Poor bastard had Williams family lawyers waiting outside the delivery room to see if he looked more like Wright or Buck. It took them two years to sort it all out but when the dust settled, Holt got seven hundred and fifty thousand dollars and Dick got a little over six million. 'Richest baby in America,' they called him. Poor bastard." He laughed and shook his head. "Hell, there was even fifty thousand dollars in Wright's will for his old pal Moore. Buck, for his part, did his best to stay out of the public eye after that, but story goes that when the news came out about Bizzy giving birth, Buck's buddies came to the Shell service station where he was a pump attendant - just down the road from the Williams mansion, actually – and congratulated him on being a new father. They set his hat on fire, story goes. Some old Southern tradition."

Dick thought he might vomit. The man said, "And they all lived happily ever after. At least Bizzy and Lucy did, I suppose. If you can ever really be happy in Delaware, that is. If you ask me, they'd be better off up in New York. There's a lot more…"

The man's voice was subsumed by the rat-a-tat-tat dialogue of Harlow and Powell as Dick rose and stumbled into the aisle. Stooping as he went, making sure to keep the shadow of his head from encroaching upon the lower border of the movie screen, he walked out of the theater.

Across the hall in the other theater, he found an unoccupied seat and dropped into it, his brain scrambled as if he had been zapped with Doctor Vulcan's Sonic Decimator. With a great deal of determination, he forced the derring-do of Rocket Man and his atomic-powered jetpack to displace the thoughts of murder trials and burning hats. Dick had heard his mother say, on more than one occasion, that only Hollywood and Washington, D.C. were home to more liars than Broadway. The man watching *Reckless* had been just that, Dick told himself. A liar.

*****

Later, after Rocket Man had saved the day, Dick waited on the bus outside the Arcadia, watching the sun go down. Always good at arithmetic, he figured in his head that you only get about twenty-four thousand sunsets, if your life is average. He had read, somewhere, that the average life expectancy of the American male was sixty-six and a half years. Most of those sunsets brought to a close an uneventful day and led into an uneventful evening. But once in a while, Dick knew, you had another kind of evening: electric with anticipation, alive with potential, and you watched the sun go down thinking maybe tonight would be unforgettable.

Dick sat on the curb by the bus stop and, with the help of a stick to write in the sandy soil, calculated his father's time on Earth. November 5, 1911 to July 6, 1932. Only seven thousand, five hundred and forty-nine sunsets. It didn't seem fair. But Wright Williams' life was not average. And, Dick told himself, his father had more of those alive, electric sunsets in his twenty years than most men do in their sixty-six and a half.

Dick did some more math in the dirt. If he had done it right, he figured he would live to see the year 2000. It sounded like science fiction. Maybe there would be real Rocket Men by then. Maybe he would be one of them. Maybe he'd be the first.

About The Author

Wade Beauchamp is from Winston-Salem, North Carolina. Over 30 of his short stories have been published in various journals and anthologies by such editors as Ryan North, Violet Blue, Lori Perkins, and Cecilia Tan. His work has twice been selected for inclusion in Susie Bright's *Best American Erotica* series (2005 and 2007). *It Rhymes With Luck*, a collection of his most popular shorts, was published in 2010. His debut novel, *Scream If You Wanna Go Faster*, was a 2013 Kindle Book Review Best Indie Book Awards Finalist. Follow the author at www.wadebeauchamp.com and www.facebook.com/AuthorWadeBeauchamp

More From Wade

More From Gold Dust Publishing

- <u>The House on Dead Man's Curve</u>
      By Jason Roach

- <u>Until Death: An Eric Kent Investigation</u>
      By Rey Nichols

- <u>Reflections</u> – Our charity book featuring over 40 authors contributing.